Gavin Goode

David B. Seaburn

Black Rose Writing | Texas

ISBN: 978-1-68433-298-4
PUBLISHED BY BLACK ROSE WRITING
www.blackrosewriting.com

Printed in the United States of America
Suggested Retail Price (SRP) $19.95

Gavin Goode is printed in Book Antiqua

To all the individuals, couples and families
I have worked with over the years.
Thank you for all you have taught me.

GAVIN GOODE

PART ONE

CHAPTER 1
Gavin Goode

"I don't know why and I don't know how, but I think I died today."

Gavin is a perceptive guy. He looks at this problem from every angle. Where is his body, for instance? Why doesn't he see anything or feel anything? Hear? Smell? Where has the world gone? He doesn't have a clue what happened. He doesn't remember anything. Surely there would have been a warning sign, something that cried out, "Mayday, mayday! Brace yourself!" But there was nothing.

He traces his final hours as best he can. Last night he watched some TV; then sat on his deck for a while, hoping to see a deer that had been roaming the neighborhood. Drank a Rohrbach's Scotch Ale. When the grandfather clock struck nine, he went upstairs, took a bath and was in bed by ten. Read until he couldn't see the words anymore. Was asleep by 11, 11:15 at the latest. Woke up at 3 to take a leak. Stood at the bathroom window for several minutes watching the full moon appear and disappear behind thin clouds. Slipped back into bed without disturbing Frankie. He listened for a while to her raspy breathing, her mouth open a crease, her hair mussed around her face. Smiled and went back to sleep.

His iPhone alarm went off at 6; he woke up alert, refreshed and ready for the day. He stood in front of the mirror assessing his face, his rounded cheeks and small chin, his narrowly set eyes and high forehead, thinning brown hair. Each morning he hoped he would see something different, but alas. He shaved, got dressed in tan Dockers, a checked shirt and work casual shoes.

As he reviews the previous twelve hours, he tries to remember if there was anything odd that he might be overlooking. Unexpected indigestion or dizziness or breathlessness that had come and gone? But there wasn't anything. For breakfast, he had an English muffin, dry, and then a cup of coffee, black. By then Frankie was up, sitting at her makeup table putting her face on. She was humming something. What was it? He leaned over and kissed the nape of her neck; she shivered.

"Goodbye, Gavin."

"Goodbye, sweetheart."

He drove the Infiniti this morning. He turned on *Morning Edition* and eased onto the expressway heading east to the city. Traffic was traffic, but it didn't bother him, even when a Mini-Cooper almost nudged him off the road. He was busy whistling, nothing in particular, just practicing how high he could go. He got off at the usual exit and took the usual shortcut through Highland Park, enjoying the proud elms. Stopped for another coffee at the corner café ("What the heck?"). He was feeling good because the barista, maybe twenty years old, complimented his shirt. "You just made my...well, month." He got to the lot forty minutes early.

He plunked down in his cubicle before anyone else arrived. Placed his coffee on the blotter. Pulled up the blinds to get a full dose of the rising sun. Booted his computer, took a few files from the cabinet beside his desk and dove into some insurance claims.

He shrugs, or imagines he shrugs, as he considers his morning. Ordinary is the one word he can think to describe it. Something must have gone terribly wrong, because he isn't in his office. He isn't even in his body. He isn't anywhere at all. By the same token, he isn't gone either. He's bewildered. "Where the heck am I? What's going on?"

He thinks back a little further, searching for clues. Last Tuesday he saw Dr. Nguyen for his annual. Blood test, prostate exam (not a fan), ticker check, everything was normal. "You are in good shape for your age, Mr. Goode," said the doctor. "What does that mean?" thought Gavin. "Someone my age? I'm fifty-two, which isn't young, I'll grant you that, but it's not old, not these days. Maybe in my old man's time, but not today. Fifty has to be 'the new'...something younger."

Dr. Nguyen's comments worried him more than he wanted to admit. When he got home, he told Frankie. "What if she had said that to you? 'Hey, Frankie, you're in good shape for your age?'"

Frankie brushed hair back from her face as her temple creased. "I wouldn't have thought anything of it. People see their doctors all the time and are told they're in good shape for their age and they drop dead almost the next minute. Other times, doctors warn patients that if they don't do whatever, then they may not live to see their grandkids. And those people eventually change doctors because they've outlived the one that told them the clock was running out." She closed with a tilted head and a matter-of-fact "No one knows when they're going to go; so why worry." Then she added: "Of course, I don't have issues; you've got issues."

She was right. He'd been afraid of death for as long as he could remember. Every lump or bump was cancer. And every odd looking crap was also cancer. He always assumed the Big C was sneaking around his insides, like ISIS metastasizing, calling up reinforcements, slinking around in his cracks and crevices, waiting for the right time to attack. It happens. Let's say you feel great but you're due for your flu shot, so you go to the doctor's and just as you are leaving, you say, "By the way, doc, before I go, could you take a look at this thing on my leg?" And your doctor's eyes narrow as she studies the tiny black bruise. She excuses herself and returns with a senior colleague who takes his glasses off the top of his head so he can get a better look, only to remove them again and shake his head. Your doctor shakes her head, too, and says, "Should have come in months ago." You know the rest.

Yep, Frankie is right. Gavin has issues. It all started with his grandfather, his Papa, who lived with them when he was a boy. He was close to Papa, who played catch with him, explored the woods near their house with him, read books with him, made bird houses with him, did just about everything with the young Gavin. As Gavin grew up and Papa got older, things changed. They didn't hang together as much. Papa stayed home watching TV most of the time.

One day Gavin comes home from school and Papa is sitting in his recliner, *Days of Our Lives* blaring on the TV. Gavin calls to him, "Hey Papa, how's it going?" When he doesn't answer, Gavin figures he can't hear, so he cranks it up, "PAPA, HOW'S IT GOING?" Nothing. So he walks over to Papa's chair and taps him on the shoulder, at which point, Papa slumps over to one side. Totally scares the shit out of young Gavin. He thinks of doing CPR, but he can't bring himself to get that involved with his grandfather's mouth. The creepiness factor is too high. Anyway, as far as Gavin can tell Papa is long gone.

So he calls his mother who totally freaks at the news. She drops the phone and dashes home as fast as she can. But no matter what she does, it still takes at least twenty minutes for her to get there. Twenty minutes alone with dead Papa. What to do, right? Watch the show with him? Talk to him? Close his mouth? Prop him up and comb his hair so he looks more like himself when Gavin's mother gets home? In the end, Gavin can't touch his grandfather.

It had been a long day at school. Gavin missed lunch because of a meeting with his school counselor and he's starving. So he goes to the kitchen to make himself a sandwich. He thinks of going back into the living room, but it seems disrespectful to eat in front of Papa, considering the condition he's in, so Gavin stays in the kitchen.

That's where he is when his mother gets home. Let's just say she isn't pleased and she doesn't understand Gavin's reasoning. "He's your last grandparent! At least sit with him! God knows he sat with you often enough!" Gavin wants to say, "Hey, I'm, like, I came home and there's Papa sitting in front of the TV, all dead, and no one's around and it totally scared the crap out of me. At least I stayed in the house. I didn't run out into the street screaming like a crazy person, which is what I wanted to do. Shouldn't I get points for that? It may not have been 'A' work on my part, but it wasn't an 'F' either; it was at least a 'C' or 'C-'." But in a moment of rare wisdom he doesn't say anything. He realizes that basically she is right, though he still feels that eating a peanut butter and sweet pickle sandwich in front of his dead grandfather would not have been in good taste.

Anyway, after this debacle, he can't get his grandfather out of his mind. Adding to that, everyone died over the next few years, aunts, uncles, a young cousin, a close neighbor, a friend even. What was going on? He ignored it as best he could. He didn't look at the deceased when he went to the funeral home. He hummed quietly to himself during the eulogies. He didn't talk about it with friends or his parents. He found that denial was an amazing gift. It was denial that enabled him to get up every day, ignoring the fact that death was waiting for him around every corner. If it weren't for denial, how could he do anything? How could he eat a pizza or brush his teeth or, when he was older, go to work, pay the bills, wash his car?

In recent years (probably even yesterday morning), Gavin read the obits every day.

He always celebrated the fact that his name wasn't there. Then he'd check the ages of everyone who had died to see what the over/under was, how many people were older than him and how many were younger. If there were more 'overs' than 'unders', he breathed a sigh of relief. If there were more 'unders' than 'overs' he figured there was something unusually wrong with those people, something (of course) that wasn't wrong with him. But this didn't always work. In many an unguarded moment, like when he was sitting on the toilet or mowing the lawn, he'd be chilled by the realization that Death could sneak up on him at any time, sickle in hand.

When Gavin looked at the pictures accompanying the obits, he could see denial in their eyes. They were smiling and sometimes laughing, maybe hugging a dog, or sitting beside a super-hot car, or holding up a great big fish they caught once, like they were saying, "Yep, I died, but look at this giant carp!" Gavin thought horror would be a more appropriate expression. When he died, he wanted his picture to look like that Edvard Munch painting, "The Scream"; he'd be standing on a bridge, holding the sides of his head with both hands, mouth open in a menacingly fearful 'O.' That would tell the real story.

But he is beyond denial now. He's been taken without warning. Despite his confusion, there's no denying *what's* happened, only *why* it's happened.

"Has Frankie picked a photo for the paper yet?" he wonders. He hates to think of her scrolling through a gazillion pictures on her phone to find the right one. He thinks of her going to Walmart to print out a picture of her dead husband. Her standing at the kiosk, people pushing their carts past her, announcements blaring— "Good morning Walmart shoprs! This is a sad day for Frankie Goode..." The cashiers always comment on the photos. "Someone had a special birthday!" or "What beautiful clouds!" Just being friendly. What will they say to Frankie? What will she say to them? Gavin hates to think of her standing at the checkout with pictures of him in her hands.

He should have gotten their printer fixed.

CHAPTER 2
Frankie Goode

Since Gavin left for the office early, she is home alone on a workday morning for the first time in memory. For weeks, Frankie has looked forward to this day. The house is so quiet that she can hear herself breathe and feel herself think. What a gift. She doesn't have to be anywhere at any particular time. She doesn't have to go into the store; her associates will be in charge. If there is a problem, they know how to reach her. But she warned them that the only matters of consequence are "the place is freaking burning to the ground" or "we are being held hostage by a disgruntled customer." They laugh, but more importantly, they understand— "Don't call the boss."

So, Frankie's Dress Shop is off limits today. It's Frankie-time. Gavin is thrilled by her decision to take a day for herself. He has been hassling her about it for months: "For goodness sake, take a day off. The place will still be standing when you get back. Nothing's going to go wrong. It's only one day." Frankie agrees with him, but she never acts. It isn't Gavin who owns a business. He works hard, that's for sure, but he doesn't have the same kinds of responsibilities. Employees depending on her. Stiff competition from malls and nearby boutiques. She isn't the CEO of a mega-corporation, but things can still go south in a hurry if she isn't careful, sometimes even if she is. One year she ordered yellow, yellow, and yellow; everything was some shade of yellow, even the prints and florals. That was the fashion forecast for the spring season, so she went for it. Then *Vogue* showed green, green and green; every shade of green you could imagine— artichoke, forest, mantis, asparagus, teal, olive, myrtle, even Army green.

She thought she'd die; as things worsened, she wished she would. She took out a major loan to cover her losses and keep the doors open.

She let one girl go, though thankfully, she was able to hire her back once the death spiral ended. It made her realize that anything can happen at any time and if you aren't on top of it, the results can be disastrous. That's why she likes being at the store all the time. Just easier that way.

She is different from Gavin, whose worries aggregate around other things. He might study a mole on his leg for several months until he is convinced it has changed color or that it is getting crusty or whatever WebMD says to watch for, then he'll worry like you wouldn't believe. As far as she is concerned, he doesn't worry about real things. He only worries about things that exist in his head. For example, when he lost his social work job in cardiology at the hospital due to a cut back, she was a nervous wreck, but Gavin was totally chill. In fact for weeks he acted like he was on vacation, growing a beard, watching old movies, eating far too much popcorn. She was befuddled (and frustrated...angry is the right word) by his lack of concern about what was, for once, a real problem.

Then one day she came home from work, a get-up-and-get-going speech memorized and rehearsed in the car, only to find Gavin neatly dressed in Farrah slacks and a blue oxford shirt. He had shaved off his patchy beard, and he looked good again. He leaned casually against the kitchen counter, a mysterious smile on his face, and told her he'd decided to leave social work altogether and go into insurance. Disappointed that she didn't get the chance to give her speech, Frankie held her tongue about this ridiculous career left-turn and smiled, her eyes a little squinty, her jaws a little clenchy. He put his arms around her briefly and then left the room.

Much to Frankie's surprise, a week later, Gavin entered a training program at Farmers Insurance. Gavin told her that they thought his background in social work was perfect. In no time, he was on board to become a claims adjustor. Frankie cheered him every step of the way even though she wondered whether this was going to work out. Turns out Farmers was right. Once again Gavin was helping people face life's cataclysms — houses burning down, cars stolen, businesses robbed. And he was there to do what he had always done — guide them through it.

For months he was happy. Until he discovered another mole. This one on the back of his knee. Frankie wondered if that made him happy, too.

Today, though, Frankie doesn't have a care in the world. Not only is Gavin steady-as-she-goes, but she met with her accountant earlier in the week and the dress shop is comfortably in the black. Business is booming. The Miss Me and True Religion and Rock and Republic jeans are "killing it," as her associates say, bringing in kids who have more money than God. Frankie has to admit she doesn't have to be there all the time. Things will roll along smoothly on autopilot.

It is about 8:30am when Frankie picks up her friend, Rosemary. "Hey girl!" says Rosemary as she leaps into the passenger seat. Off they go to Jitters. She loves Rosemary, even though, at times, she feels like she doesn't know her that well. She is ten, twelve years younger than Frankie, maybe more. She has straight dirty blonde hair that hangs to her shoulders; warm brown eyes and a crooked smile. She hovers over Frankie, which from anyone else would drive Frankie mad, but for some reason she likes it from Rosemary. Maybe because she is fun and lively and daring. And flirty. "My husband doesn't care," she says. "Just so there's something for him when he comes to bed every night." Frankie laughs, but wonders if anything Rosemary says is true.

They met at the shop in the early years, when Frankie was still desperate for customers. She waited on Rosemary one whole afternoon and a friendship was formed, even though Rosemary walked away with only a hair clip. It is hard not to like Rosemary, although she does have a habit of asking for small cash loans from time to time. She bursts into tears whenever this happens, obviously wanting to avoid taking anything from Frankie. She explains that she is running short on her monthly budget—"Your husband has you on a budget?" Frankie asks, incredulous—and that she only needs a little to tide her over, typically fifty or a hundred dollars.

She is so pitiful looking that Frankie always gives in. It takes a while before she sees her money again, but it's always returned with a tasteful little plant for the store or a gift card to Starbuck's. In time the cycle becomes a normal part of their friendship.

They grab their latte macchiatos, don their Yankees ball caps, slip on their Ray-Bans, drop the top on Frankie's pink VW bug and head west to the Galleria in Buffalo, wind tossing their hair, sun burnishing their arms, and Frankie's cell tucked deep in her bag where it won't bother

her. They dial in the 70s channel on Sirius and wail with the Doobie Brothers and howl with Cher. A few truckers lean on their horns as they pass, thinking they are sweet young things out on a lark. Speed reverses the perception of age, thinks Frankie; at seventy-five mph, fifty-one looks like thirty-five. And that's exactly how she feels.

The trip to the mall is a blur of talk, talk, talk, music and laughter. Frankie is breathing deep and feeling good by the time she reaches the parking lot near Gina's Nails where they will begin their adventure with a mani-pedi. Rosemary hops out of the car, stretches her arms skyward and then wraps them around Frankie. "Okay, girl, let's rock this place," she says with a growling laugh. Frankie looks up at the azure sky. Buffalo, and no clouds no rain no snow, beautiful.

Frankie grabs her bag, throws it over her shoulder and pulls out her cell. When she scans her messages, she's surprised to see five from a number in Gavin's office and ten more from a number she doesn't recognize at all. She squints at the screen and shakes her head. What's going on? When she calls Gavin, it goes directly to his mailbox, where his voice chirps in her ear: "Hi, Gavin here; please leave me a message and I'll get back to you as soon as possible. Have a great day!" Frankie's face goes scrunchy as she stares at the phone; then she decides to leave a message: "Hi Gav, it's me; gimme a call as soon as you get this."

Rosemary grabs her hand and asks if something is wrong. Frankie studies the list of missed calls, puzzled. Her heart skips two beats when the phone rings. She lets go of Rosemary and nestles the cell in both hands, looking at it as if she doesn't know what to do next. "Hello?" she says, a question mark in her voice. It is some woman, but her words are garbled. Frankie cups her hand over her other ear and tries again. "Hello." This time she hears the words "doctor" and "hospital." She clenches the cell and bows her head. "What?" The wind whips across the parking lot and blows the woman's voice away. "What do you mean? I don't understand." Frankie drops the phone to the pavement.

"Frankie?" says Rosemary. "Is something wrong? Frankie?"

Frankie opens her mouth, her tongue moves aimlessly, as she struggles to form words. She looks in Rosemary's direction but not at her, "Better cancel the mani-pedi." She feels her legs shaking, her stomach knotting. She tries to breathe but can't. She thinks, What have I done?

CHAPTER 3
MIKHAIL
THE AK-47

A Few Weeks Earlier

Mikhail is an acquired taste. His family has been around since the 1940s and in many quarters is still treated like royalty. In other quarters, though, they are hated. "Phhht, their problem," he would say. "Me, nothing wrong." Some might disagree, but there is no doubt that Mikhail is a larger than life figure who sucks the oxygen out of every room he enters. That's what he loves most about himself. "This is very true. No apology. I am named after my creator, the great Mikhail Kalishnikova."

Mikhail's reputation in the world is immense. His family has played a part in every war, every critical battle, every quibbling skirmish in the past seventy years, often on both sides. "I am equal opportunity weapon," he likes to say. "I am your faithful doggy, always there to protect and defend, to bring your enemy to the knees. I will tear their throat out and lick your hand very nice when I am done." Like I said, an acquired taste.

But he is an impressive specimen no matter what you think of his personality. "I am hugely long." Here we go. "Like I say, I am hugely long—barrel alone, sixteen of your inches, if you can imagine. I can pound, pound, pound with my massive big piston. I can single pop you or multi-pop you, whatever it takes to crush you into submission. And I tell you, I'm not popping beebees; I'm popping 7.62X39mm—M67 to you—cartridge with beautiful copper plated steel jacket—My God!—that makes excellent and beautiful penetration through anything at all, anything; nothing can resist my beautiful penetration, I tell you for truth."

Mikhail can hold thirty cartridges in his stamped banana magazine; a magazine that he says is so tough that you can hammer nails into concrete with it. "America like hammer time, right?" And what a wonderful sense of humor to boot.

Nevertheless, his personal story is an exasperating one. Instead of fighting in a world war or guerilla conflict or terrorist attack or gang bang or domestic dispute or stand-your-ground squabble, he has been relegated to the gun show circuit, where today he is being purchased by a Mr. Ben Hillman, who shows up in his little boat shoes and yellow shirt with an alligator on the pocket and a white Nike ball cap on his fleshy head. Mr. Hillman explains to Gus, the guy behind the display table, that he wants to buy an AK-47 as an investment. He already has a small collection of Colt handguns, but he doesn't have any rifles. As he puts it, he wants to graduate to the "big leagues." This infuriates Mikhail: "Mr. Hillman is a teeny tiny American baby man who lives in the pasty white suburbs with his teeny tiny baby wife and his teeny tiny baby son."

Despite Mikhail's dismay, Gus tells Hillman that he is in the right place. All Gus needs from him is something green. Hillman laughs at this, and his face turns an eager shade of red. Then he plunks down $995 cash. When Mr. Hillman asks how long he has to wait to get the rifle, Gus grins. "Like I told you, mister, you've come to the right place." It is a private sale, after all, one buddy to another; no need for all the rigmarole, all the paper work and government brouhaha. "This is still America, my friend," says Gus. "Long may she wave." Mikhail smiles at this. Hillman chips in another fifty for one hundred eighty rounds of ammo. Mikhail is stunned: "What is that? Minimum 1,000! I am ashamed!" Hillman wraps Mikhail in a plaid blanket and dumps him in the back of his Prius.

Making things worse, when he takes Mikhail out of the car, there are no battlefields anywhere. Instead, there are colonial houses as far as the eye can see with white vinyl siding and black shutters and paved driveways and manicured lawns and matching mailboxes and broad patios with tiki lamps and above ground pools and two car garages and basketball hoops and goddam dogs. Mr. Hillman acts like a puffed up big shot, his Ray-Bans on, as he sneaks Mikhail from the car after making sure that Mrs. Hillman isn't home. "What a little chicken baby!" thinks Mikhail.

Mr. Hillman hides Mikhail behind his back and goes into the house looking for his son, Christopher. When Mr. Hillman sees that he is playing *Resident Evil 5*, he blows his top. "Doggonit!" he says to Christopher. "You're only eleven. What the heck do you think you're doing?" Christopher shrugs, his eyes glued to the screen. To steal his son's attention, Mr. Hillman tells him he has a surprise, but that he will only show it to him if Christopher stops playing the game. They go back and forth for almost ten minutes before Christopher grudgingly relents, even though he has just reached chapter five.

Christopher can't believe his eyes when he sees Mikhail. "Wow, Dad, this is awesome!" Mr. Hillman is so proud he almost pops the alligator off his shirt. He reaches out to his son, new rifle cradled in both arms, new bond being built.

"Can I hold it?" asks Christopher.

"Sure, son," says Mr. Hillman.

Christopher takes Mikhail in his hands. "Jesus, Dad, it's heavy."

Mr. Hillman purses his lips. "You know we're not supposed to say Jesus like that, son. The Lord, and your mother, would not approve."

Christopher's mouth is still hanging open. He licks his lips. "Sorry, Dad."

Mr. Hillman teaches Christopher how to work the safety. Then he detaches the magazine and shows Christopher the beautiful M67 cartridges. Christopher's eyes bug out of his head. "My God!" Mr. Hillman's face is serene, like he has just come back from a successful campaign on the battlefield instead of a tent sale in a mall parking lot. Mikhail smirks to himself.

He understands, even respects, Mr. Hillman's emphasis on safety. Good to take the magazine off, he thinks. He is surprised that Mr. Hillman doesn't know that there is usually a cartridge left in the chamber, even when the magazine is removed. Always a good idea. You never know when you might be surprised by a terrorist at your door or a hoodie-person walking down the sidewalk, or someone randomly ringing your door bell at dinner time. "Usually one bullet enough to take care of business," thinks Mikhail, "if it's not big business."

Mr. Hillman grabs Mikhail and motions Christopher to follow him down to the basement. There he struggles to open a step ladder that is folded in the corner. Father and son laugh. Then Mr. Hillman grabs an old quilt from under a pile of crushed boxes ready for recycling and wraps the rifle in it. "This is unacceptable," thinks Mikhail. "Do they not understand who I am?" Hillman, his son steadying the tiny ladder, climbs up three steps and hides the weapon, the magazine, and the pathetic little box of ammo behind some empty cans of white latex paint. Hillman insists he will find a better place, but for now it will do. Then he swears his son to secrecy about Mikhail.

"Pinky swear," says Christopher.

"We don't need your mother to know about this," says Mr. Hillman. "You know how she can be about things." Christopher blushes with excitement and guilt for having a secret from his mother.

Their pact sealed, father and son go back up the steps, turn off the basement light and close the door behind them. Alone in the dark, Mikhail is despondent. "So here I am behind damn paint cans while my brothers all over world are fighting and killing. Where is justice?"

CHAPTER 4
RYAN GOODE

Ryan sits behind the counter studying the wrought iron chairs and tables with their curlicue legs and glass tops. The floor is a checkerboard of fire engine red and gleaming white squares. Hovering above each table are ceiling fans with draw strings tipped with imitation pewter ice cream cones. There are sheets of paper and two boxes of crayons on top of each table, and a red ice cream cone shaped napkin dispenser. Ryan purchased some old Isaly's skyscraper scoops that form rocket shaped cones, different than any of the three other ice cream parlors in tiny Ogdensport along the Erie Canal. Beside the counter is a glass display case with cartons of ice cream, the flavors written on colorful tags stuck to the curved front window. He has vanilla and chocolate, of course, and mint chocolate chip and cookie dough and blueberry and strawberry and peanut butter cup. But so does everyone else.

When he decided to buy the business, his father told him, "Look Ryan, this is a good idea, but you have to remember there are five other ice cream joints within two miles of you, not to mention Tops Grocery Store and McDonald's. So, you've got to be smart about this; you gotta have something that will make people say, 'Hey, let's go there instead of Lugia's.'" Lugia's is the Big Dog on the ice cream block. They have at least fifty flavors and people wait patiently in the dead heat of July in a half dozen numbered lines that stretch the whole way to the road. And their servings, my God, their small is twice the size of anyone else's large. It looks like a baby's head.

Ryan's father sounds supportive, even though his face is blank and he keeps licking his lips and swallowing. But Ryan has already signed the lease and is determined to take on the challenge. His wife, Jenna, who is a branch manager of a bank, cries when he tells her. His mother is speechless. He decides to call the place Curly's. He tells everyone that the name has a friendly, welcoming sound. He doesn't dare tell anyone that he has named it after Curly from the Three Stooges, that loveable lug who could endure anything, but who had little more common sense than a meatball.

He chalks up his previous failed business endeavors, the mini-golf course and the hot dog cart, to poor timing or bad location or the weather. It was a rainy summer the year he opened Ryan's Miniature Golfland, although the indoor mini-golf course a half mile down the road did fine.

"Why in the world did I order fifty gallons of Buffalo Wing Ripple?" he wonders. The distributor told him that "it is a zesty combination of mild barbecue sauce and brown sugar with delectable ribbons of dark chocolate. Big, big hit in Buffalo," he says. Buffalo wings are as big a deal in Rochester as they are in Buffalo, reasons Ryan, so why not?

What he doesn't anticipate is that the ice cream has a distinct chickeny flavor. Not yummy barbecue sauce, but something rawer. Customers grimace. Nevertheless, Ryan thinks he can pair Buffalo Wing Ripple with Potato Surprise, which is supposed to taste like sweet potato French fries. Not so much. And Sauerkraut Delight, which is his very own concoction, doesn't fare much better. It seems like a good idea, western New York being a cabbage mecca, but he overlooks the fact that fresh cut cabbage smells like shit. Who wants three scoops of shit on a warm summer afternoon?

Still, he believes that by opening Curly's he has found his place in the world, his raison d'etre. He doesn't know anything about making ice cream, less about selling it, but he loves eating it. (His mother reminds him: "I love wearing clothes but that has nothing to do with being a successful dress shop owner.") He can't remember the last time he has eaten dinner without ice cream for dessert. In fact, ice cream *is* dessert. Who needs pie or cake or cookies when you have ice cream?

When Ryan graduated from high school, his dad encouraged him to go to Penn State to learn the ice cream business, but Ryan thought "Who studies ice cream in college?" He goes to Oswego State to study accounting instead, which makes sense until he attends his first accounting class and realizes numbers form insoluble puzzles that put him to sleep.

He met Jenna during his first and only semester, though, and was immediately smitten. She had short blonde hair, a broad smile and a sculpted happy face. More important, she liked him. So, despite his mother's contention, college had not been a waste of time. He found love.

■ ■ ■ ■ ■

Earlier the same morning, before he headed to Curly's, Ryan called his father. When no one answered, Ryan left a message. He knows his father will have some good ideas about the ice cream dilemma, which is driving him to distraction. Ryan sits at the counter staring at his cell phone for an hour or more as if the world might come to an end if it doesn't ring.

He could call his mother, who has much more business experience, but she is tough-assed when it comes to Ryan's new adventure. She listens and nods when he speaks, but her face says, "I can't believe this." Ryan decides that talking to her about fifty gallons of Buffalo Wing Ripple isn't a good idea.

It is 9:40. Surely his father is at work by now. Ryan calls again. Nothing. So he calls Schmenkman, his distributor, and the conversation quickly devolves into a screaming match, a match that he cannot win. "Funny thing, I have the order form right in front of me. And, yes, the contract, too. As far as I can tell, fifty gallons is what you ordered and that's what you got. Whether anyone eats it is your problem, not mine."

Ryan pulls the phone away from his ear and glares at it. Schmenkman is reading the order form aloud like a lawyer closing his argument when Ryan's mother buzzes in and then Jenna right afterwards. He hangs up on Schmenkman and calls Jenna who is heaving and crying. Ryan's face goes white-chocolate-mousey and he slumps back on his stool. "Did something happen?" he asks, whimpery. "Jenna?" She is gasping.

"Honey? Is everything okay...?"

"I'm..."

Ryan stops breathing.

"Jenna!"

She tries to speak again but the line is muffled, as if Jenna has covered the speaker with the palm of her hand.

"Jenna! Your hand's over the thing. I can't…"

She's back. "I'm sorry…it's just…"

"Did something happen?"

"Oh…it's…"

Ryan's arms go goose-flesh and a cantaloupe-sized ball congeals in his lower abdomen. "Jenna!" When she gets control of the phone, Ryan keeps repeating, "Is something wrong with the baby, honey? I mean, are you okay? Did you call the doctor? Do you want me to? I mean, is something happening?"

Then he stops cold.

Jenna is talking now, but nothing she says makes sense. "My dad what?" Each word follows from the one before, but strung together as a whole, they are jabberwocky-like nonsense. "My dad what?" Ryan is standing now, his palm sticking to the counter top. "Might be what? What do you mean he might not be what?" Jenna says that Ryan's mother called her when she couldn't reach him; she is racing to the hospital now.

"Ryan, she said your dad got hurt bad." Jenna pauses.

"Hurt? What do you mean 'hurt'?"

"I don't know exactly."

"What, she didn't tell you?"

"Look, honey, she was all kinds of upset, but she didn't actually know very much, so I don't know; she just seemed scared."

"Scared?" His mother doesn't scare. Jenna falls silent. "What's going on? I called him just a little while ago." He doesn't say that his father didn't answer. He doesn't say that he'd been sitting at the counter for an hour waiting for his father to call back. Maybe saying he had just called his father would convince Jenna that she had heard things wrong, and she might say something like, "Oh, okay then, if you just talked to him, your mom must have been mistaken. Have a great day, sweetie." But she isn't fooled at all.

"You better go to the hospital. Like, now. I'm so sorry, honey."

Ryan doesn't answer.

"Ryan? I love you." Then she's gone.

Ryan stands in front of the freezer staring at gallons of faceless ice cream cartons. The freezer clicks on, the hum a welcome interruption to the silence enveloping him. He glances out the window as a car pulls into the lot. He puts on his Curly's cap and reaches for a dipper. He checks the phone and wonders for a moment if he has talked to Jenna at all. He almost calls her back, but isn't sure he wants to know. He convinces himself it is a mistake. His father is fifty-two, for God's sake. Fifty-two or fifty-three; either way, he is too young for hospitals and people not knowing what's happening. He always thinks he's sick, but he's never actually been sick. He works every day; comes home every night; does stuff around the house; Ryan and his dad get together a couple times a week for a beer at Rohrbach's. Been doing this for years. Routines, important routines, don't just stop without some warning. Things don't just stop for no reason at all.

An older gentleman with a grey mustache, maybe seventy-five, comes into the shop and orders a medium cup of chocolate peanut butter. "Coming up," says Ryan. The man walks along the freezer display squinting down at the flavor labels on the glass. He takes out a white handkerchief and blows his nose. Then he carefully folds the hanky back up into a perfect square and returns it to his back pocket, ready to be used again when necessary. Only old guys carry handkerchiefs anymore, thinks Ryan. Everyone else has tissue. Use it and toss it. But not this guy. You can wash a hanky and it's good as new. Use it over and over again. This guy knows that if you take care of a thing, it can last forever.

Ryan scoops the ice cream and watches the man closely. His gait is good; his posture is straight; he is slender enough; his hands are broad and his wrists are thick; his expression seems alert. He doesn't have any of that vague, forlorn-ish look about him that old people get. This guy is a handkerchief in a Kleenex world. He'll be around for a good long time.

Ryan dips a little more than usual into a medium dish, sticks a spoon in it and adds two napkins. He slides it across the counter as the man pulls a five from his wallet.

"You're in great shape," he says to his customer. "What's your secret?"

The man smiles as he spoons the ice cream into his mouth. He shrugs with his bushy eyebrows. "Just livin', that's all." He bows and then leaves.

Ryan drops the scoop into some water and runs his fingers through his hair. Just livin', he thinks. Simple. He nods his head and figures, Sure, something might have happened to Dad, but there's no reason to think the worst. "He's a handkerchief," Ryan says to no one. Got to talk to him about the Buffalo Wing Ripple. Dad'll know what to do. He always does.

CHAPTER 5
FARMERS INSURANCE
AROUND 8:45AM

It's a morning like any other for Shondra. When she arrives at Farmers, there is one other car in the lot. She stands beside her Toyota and stretches, then squints into the eastern sun. She smiles. A cool breeze cuts the sun's early warmth. "This is going to be a good day," she says right out loud, and then laughs. That's the kind of person she is and always has been. As far as Shondra is concerned, the good Lord has personally put everything where it's supposed to be just so we can open our eyes and see how beautiful it is. The most important thing to do each day is to praise God and mean it.

She embraces this belief with her entire being, but she also knows there is a lot of nastiness in the world. Sometimes, as positive as she is, it is hard to believe that everything that comes your way is a gift. Sometimes when you unwrap what life gives you, it stinks to high heaven. No matter how much you want it to be otherwise, every sniff is as bad as the last. In spite of life's contrariness, Shondra believes that if you hoist all the good and all the bad onto a scale, it will tip to the good, if only by a hair. And that's all that's needed to make a difference.

But this morning, well, this morning feels like a smile inside a smile, just the way the clouds ease on by and the air smells a little like talcum. "Good day, comin'," she says, her insides humming.

Shondra's reverie is interrupted by a pop, like a firecracker, distant, but sharp enough to turn her around. She stands stark still, her eyes wide, waiting for another pop but then it doesn't come, and a grin crosses her face as she heads to the office door. "From the sublime to the ridiculous and back again," she says to no one at all.

She likes getting to work a little early so she can write her 'to do' list, put things in order and finish any hold overs from the day before. If there's time, she'll get another cup of coffee and hit Facebook and Instagram to catch up on the world. My God, she thinks. Why did Leticia post this skanky picture? She must have been out of her mind. Just trying to stir up her man, who, in Shondra's opinion, isn't worth a damn. She is for sure getting a call from Leticia later, all crying and everything. That girl. Not me, thinks Shondra, those days are over. She is too old for foolish games. Besides, she has a good man, a man she loves, and even better, trusts.

Even Momma likes Hector, such a sweetie. And his momma loves her. Been together for a year. Ten months longer than she's ever been with a man. She can't say he's a handsome man, what with his crooked teeth and beat-up nose, but he's so good to her. He listens; he talks; he never gets crazy-assed angry; he makes her laugh; and when they are in bed, he can make her toes curl up in a tight little ball. And he works in sanitation. How much steadier can he be?

Shondra is all dreamy smiles when who walks in but Hector himself. "Hi, darlin' girl." Since there isn't anybody in the office, she wraps her arms around him and gives him a big wet kiss. But he's stiff and isn't making eye contact. He backs away and sticks his hand in his back pocket. Shondra thinks, What's this? Is he gonna break up with me? I'll kill him. Then she sees that Hector's eyes are misty and she thinks, Oh no, what's wrong? His momma? I'll bet it's his momma, her diabetes. God! Lose some damn weight! But the closer she looks at Hector, the more confused she gets. His face doesn't look sad or worried or nothing like that. In fact, he looks kind of goofy-faced.

There they are right in the middle of an empty office, the cubicles all around them, like they are stranded in Lego land. He comes closer and clears his throat.

"What's going on, sugar? Aren't you supposed to be at work?" She tries to smile but her bottom lip goes all quivery. He doesn't speak. Hector pulls his hand from his back pocket and there in the middle of his palm is a tiny velvet box. He holds it up in front of her face.

"What is this?" says Shondra, then holding her breath.

"Whadaya think it is, sweetness?"

She grabs Hector and hugs him and kisses him. He puts the box on top of the partition behind him and then twirls her around and around. Shondra, dizzy with joy, wonders if she'll ever be able to breathe again.

"Is this really happening?"

"It truly is." He digs into his pocket again, then remembers he's put the box on the partition. When he grabs for it, though, it is gone. They laugh nervously. "Must be around here somewhere," says Hector. He holds Shondra and kisses her gently twice. Then they look for the ring behind the partition.

And there it is on Mr. Goode's desk. Right beside Mr.Goode's head which is resting on the blotter. One arm is stretched out long, his hand still clutching his coffee mug. The other is dangling at his side. His feet are turned in at the ankles, like he is trying to press their soles together. Shondra is confused. Why is he asleep? He's never done that before.

Hector cries, "Blessed Virgin, Mother of God!" which startles her more than the firecracker, startles her like an alarm going off in the dead of night, quaking her to the bone. What is she looking at? What? There's blood everywhere. Blood like she's never seen before. Mr. Goode's head is covered in it and his hair is matted and sticky looking and blood's drizzling down the side of his desk, like a mass of red ants, dripping onto the floor, slow, but steady. "Lord God Almighty!" she says. Hector's upper lip is beaded with sweat.

This can't be. Shondra hates herself for what comes to her mind next. Hector is about to ask her to marry him; he has the ring and everything; this is the Big Moment, what she has been waiting for all her life. And then, damn! Mr. Goode is lying in a pool of blood on his desk. It isn't like she doesn't feel awful for Mr. Goode; he is a good guy and all. But this is supposed to be her shining moment.

It reminds her of the time in high school when she came home with straight 'As' and just as she was about to make her big announcement, her sister Shireen blurted out that she was pregnant. Of course, this situation is worse. At least, Shireen ended up with a beautiful baby girl. But Mr. Goode, well. Just the same, from this day forward, every time she tells the story of Hector's proposal, it will be upstaged by the story of Mr. Goode being there all dead and everything. Of course, she wishes this had never happened to Mr. Goode, but if it was already fated, why couldn't it have happened tomorrow? Is that too much to ask?

"What should we do? Is he dead?" says Hector as he tiptoes around Mr. Goode trying to see if he is breathing. Shondra gapes as she leans against the partition. She wants to say, "Where's the ring?" but she can see that would be hard-hearted and she isn't a hard-hearted person.

"Should we check his pulse?" Hector, his face twisted knot-like, reaches for Mr. Goode's wrist. He closes his eyes and tries to feel for a pulse but he is clasping Mr. Goode's wrist bone and gets nothing. In the meantime, Shondra sees the ring box sitting right in the middle of all the mess, the purple velvet now blackened. She nods at Hector and points at the box.

"What?"

"This is an awful day for Mr. Goode, that's for sure, the awfulest day you could imagine. But it doesn't have to be a total loss for you and me, does it?"

Hector looks at her for a long time, his mouth open, his eyes dull, his cheeks all hang-dog. His eyebrows wrinkle. "I guess you're right." Shondra tries to put things into perspective, saying that she understands this is not the most important thing going on in the world, not even the most important thing going on in the room, but it is still important. It is the beginning of something very special, something beautiful, and they shouldn't let it slide.

Hector reaches for the box, respectfully apologizing to Mr. Goode. He wipes it off with a tissue from Mr. Goode's desk. Then Hector gets down on one knee and looks up into Shondra's eyes. He holds the box out to her and opens it. Shondra could have cried but the circumstances seemed to mitigate happy tears.

Shondra's smile droops into a passable grin as she looks at the modest ring. She can't admit that she is disappointed because that would be ungracious and she isn't an ungracious person. But she always imagined that her engagement ring would shine with such brilliance that people would joke that they had to shield their eyes when they looked at it. They won't need to shield anything to look at this ring. She dreamed that her engagement ring would take her breath away, and it did, but not in the way she hoped.

Lucky for Shondra, Hector isn't focused at all on the box or the ring or her. He glances at Mr. Goode and shakes his head. Then he looks back at her and says in a voice as vacant as a shadow, "This's for you, darling. Will you be my bride?" They both look at Mr. Goode, then Shondra begins to cry as does Hector. "Yes, my sweet man, I will be your bride." Hector gets off his bloodied knee and takes her in his arms. They kiss the longest kiss of their blossoming relationship.

Then they call 911.

CHAPTER 6
GAVIN GOODE

Except for the times Frankie has talked Gavin off the ledge regarding his neurotic fear of death, they have never talked about actual dying. Given his current circumstance, Gavin thinks this is a woeful oversight. He has no idea whether she is afraid of dying or whether she thinks about it late at night when he can feel her tossing and turning or if she lives in happy denial putting one foot in front of the other each day.

He knows what she thinks about a great many other things, including *Downton Abbey*, for which she has unbridled adoration, the critical importance of teeth flossing, why May with its fresh-scrubbed air of promise is the perfect month, the unspeakably despicable character flaws of a certain president, not to mention how to pack for vacation or where to buy the best wine.

He even knows about Conner, something she could easily have kept to herself. As he recalls it, Gavin came home from work early one day and found his wife in the kitchen, her face beet red, her eyes weary from weeping. When he asked her what was wrong, she hesitated at first and then threw herself into his arms and told him everything.

Conner was her partner in the dress shop back in the day. Having been a clothier, he had business and money experience, while she had fashion sense, so it worked. He was a little older in a greying, ruddy, square-chinned, charming way. She depended on him and he was always there to advise, comfort, guide.

Much to everyone's surprise, at the end of year one the dress shop made a modest profit. He came to the shop for a champagne toast with Frankie and her associates. Once the girls left, one toast lead to another and before she knew it, Conner was holding her in his arms and kissing her, first searchingly, and then passionately. "Tongues?" was Gavin's first question, indelicate though it was. Turns out that it was more than a little mutual. When she explained how Conner removed her blouse, he sang "la-la-la-la-la" in his head so he wouldn't hear any further details.

At the end of this confession, Frankie laid her head on Gavin's chest and insisted they didn't go any further, that they didn't have sex, that she came to her senses. Feeling her so settled, so comfortable, so perfect in his arms, Gavin believed her. In the end, he decided it was a momentary lapse fueled by too much champagne and excitement. But that didn't mean he wasn't pissed or that someone didn't puncture the tires on Conner's BMW a week later or that someone didn't leave feces on Conner's front porch several times, or…let's just say Gavin stayed pissed. Several months later, Conner sold out and moved away "to pursue other opportunities." Gavin knew that Frankie ran into him from time to time at fashion shows and conventions but, unlike his cancer obsession, he never brought Conner up again, despite nagging worries.

So Gavin knows a lot about his wife, but he doesn't know anything about where she is on the matter of death. He remembers how awful it was for Frankie when her mother died. Gavin's mother-in-law was driving home early one morning after her night shift at Delco and fell asleep. Her car found a maple tree in someone's front yard, just two blocks from home. The owners heard a crunching thud and went to their bedroom window to see what had happened. It was deadly quiet outside. The car was wrapped snuggly around the tree.

When Gavin got the call and told Frankie what had happened, she stared through him. When he tried to hug her, she pulled away. When he spoke to her—"Honey, are you okay?"— she didn't answer. Instead she continued getting ready for work. She was putting on her coat when Gavin yelled, "Frankie!" and it was like she woke up from a dream. She said "What?" and started crying. But, just as quickly, she wiped the tears away like she was swatting flies, and began to make a list of everything that had to be done, who had to be contacted, and what should be included in the obituary. She went to be with her father and gathered her brothers and sister together and then organized everything—casket, burial plot, clothes for her mother, photo collage, funeral, post-funeral luncheon, everything.

She returned to work the day after the funeral, looking like she had been sleeping on a bed of nails. Gavin could tell that she was sad, even crushed. He could see it in how hunkered down she was emotionally. He could see new lines on her face that would never go away, but she kept going, like she saw something in her rearview mirror and didn't want it to catch her. Nothing could make her stop long enough to sit with what had happened. They never talked about it. They went forward. What else could you do?

"I wish I had asked more questions," thinks Gavin. "How did she feel? Was she afraid? When she got quiet, what was she thinking? What was it like to lose her mother? Did she ever wonder what it would be like to lose me?" It's a lot easier to talk about these things when you're dead, but much less helpful.

"I wonder how she's handling this mess." She'd been looking forward to having a day off in, like, forever. Do some shopping in Buffalo, go out for dinner with Rosemary, the whole deal. He wonders who called her with the news. He hopes she wasn't on the thruway when they reached her. He hopes she didn't have to drive another twenty miles before she could get off and turn around. Dammit. Has she called Ryan? Is she home yet? Has she gone to see Gavin, wherever he is? Jesus, maybe she doesn't even know yet. The thought of her not knowing, of her laughing and feeling carefree, trying on this outfit and that, all the while unaware her husband might be dead, makes him ache, the first real feeling he's had since his untimely demise.

And the ache remains. More than remains, it grows, it intensifies, as if tiny aches from everywhere have hardened into a single throbbing fist of pain; as if every dispersed molecule of his being is suddenly and inexplicably recalled; and obeying the summons, they have mustered for a reunion of sorts; packed, crashed and mashed together into the once familiar bundle of odd-fitting pieces that was his body. Is he coming back? Is he done dying? Whatever is going on, at the center of it is a torturous throbbing where his head once was. He doesn't try to move, fearful that there is something worse to come.

"What the hell is going on? Where am I?" Beeps and whirring and click-whoosh-bumping. Bright lights fill the space around him. Pitchy tones and rumbling vibrations. Voices?

"Hello! Hello! Is someone there?" he cries to himself. But no one hears.

CHAPTER 7
FROM THE ER TO THE OR

Dr. Buck Stevenson stands over Gavin Goode as he lies in the trauma bay, lifeless. He shakes his head and washes his hands. He lifts his patient's lids and looks in his eyes. Gavin exhales a breathy gasp. Takes his pulse. Examines the wound. Crouches over him, listening to his heart. It is clear to Buck that his new patient is in extremis. He summarizes the patient's status to a group of gawky medical students and interns who follow him like ducklings imprinted to his white coat: "Listen up. The patient has a penetrating wound caused by a projectile that has breached his cranium. Left side. Temporal lobe. We don't know what type of projectile is in there, but we can guess. It's clear he has intracranial hemorrhaging, but do we know if he has an intercerebral hematoma?"

When no one answers, Buck says, "Shake your head back and forth like this." Everyone shakes their head 'no'. "Excellent diagnostic work people." He glances at Gavin. "Despite successful resuscitation, our Mr...."—he looks at the chart—"...Goode, isn't so good. He's got a Glasgow of six; unaffected by any illicit substances or alcohol; eyes're closed and unresponsive. A little moaning could mean there's still something going on, or it could mean nothing. His posture is decerebrate." He pauses, jaw muscles rippling. "Any of you doctor do-goods know what that means?" Several interns wag their pens and bury their heads in imaginary notes.

One young doc, a woman with hair in a long braid, pushes her horn-rimmed glasses up her nose and answers in a falsely confident, medical monotone: "Decerebrate posture involves arms and legs being held straight out and toes pointing downward, rigid." She smiles inadvertently. Buck doesn't. "So, why should Mr..."—he checks the chart again—"…Goode care about this? Could it be just a flu? Or bad fish in his gut? Or maybe he's malingering? Why should we give a good bowel movement about his ridiculous posturing?"

The intern blanches, then clears her throat and speaks softly: "Because it's an indication of severe brain damage."

"Bingo," says Buck. He sticks a pen behind his ear and swipes his buzz cut with his other hand. He puts both hands on his hips, flexing his triceps. His goslings wait, breathless, to see what he will say next.

No one loves the ED more than Dr. Buck Stevenson. Every day he feels like he is suiting up for the Super Bowl. "It is absolutely, unequivocally, win or lose," he is fond of saying to fellowship recruits. "No ties. No rain delays. It's always fourth and one on the one-yard line with one second left on the clock. You do it or you don't." He loves the adrenalin rush of pulling a patient back from the abyss or digging into chest goo and coming out clean. "It's better than sex."

But Mr. Goode falls into Buck's 'other' category. He's arrived far too late for Buck to do a goddam thing. Gavin, totally crumped, is circling life's drain. In that sense, he's not a cooperative patient. It pisses Buck off. This guy is taking up space and time in my ED and I don't like it one bit, he thinks. His heart pounds and icy sweat runs down his spine. A dozen eyes watch and wait.

"Here's the deal, kids, we can describe what ails Mr…whatever his name is." Buck looks at his Nikes and then back at his residents. "But knowing what the problem is and solving it are two very different and sometimes mutually exclusive matters. There is nothing more for us to do here. We will send him off to CT land and, depending on what they find, he will either be turned over to our knife-wielding colleagues upstairs. Or to a funeral director." He tries to grin but the corners of his mouth can only sneer. One medical student yawns; another answers a page; the rest huddle.

Buck slips through the group and down the hall to the men's room where he leans over the toilet and vomits. Afterwards he scoops cold water with his hands and drenches the frustration from his eyes. He studies the face in the mirror for a minute and then heads back to the trauma bay, more patients waiting.

Dr. Ahmad Azziz unlocks his office door, turns on the fluorescent ceiling light, which starts to buzz. He takes a seat and rifles through his inbox before he heads back to the OR. There is a group picture of new surgical residents with personal profiles, a memo about an upcoming Grand Rounds, the monthly departmental newsletter and a single white envelope with his name printed on the front in pencil. He opens it. "Dear Dr. Raghead, Why don't you and your terrorist friends go the fuck back to wherever you came from..." He sighs and puts the letter back in the envelope.

Dr. Azziz had intended to return to his native Syria after medical school. He wanted to give back to his own country where healthcare needed every skilled hand possible. But then life in his country got worse and worse until he thought it would be too dangerous to go back with his wife, who, thankfully, had joined him when he began his surgical training years ago. The rest of his family, though, is in Syria. He stays in contact with them through social media, but it is often impossible to get through. He hopes that his brothers and his parents will one day come to the US, but with the changing atmosphere in his adoptive country, he doubts that day will ever come.

Life is worry. He tears the letter up and tosses it into the trash can. It is worry of a different kind in the US. He thought that because of his lighter skin, he might blend in more easily. He dresses in western garb, the finest suits and alligator shoes, and his English is nearly perfect. Being a doctor helps. But a handful of patients who are referred to him decline his services and go elsewhere when they meet him, even though going elsewhere may put their health at risk. Nothing is ever stated directly, but he knows what the issue is.

His wife, Haya, is outraged by these indignities. "What kind of country is this? What makes it so 'exceptional' when it treats us so shabby, when the hate is so open?" Of course, this is always said in Arabic, which sounds like fire crackling and shooting from her mouth. "Come now," Ahmad says, always in English. Then a plate will fly or a glass.

Haya wears the hijab and the abayah; she prays five times a day, a ritual she rarely observed in Syria. But underneath the hijab she is all western, wearing Macy's and Bonwit Teller and even Victoria's Secret. "Why this charade?" he asks. "I will not bend! I will not conform to something that is wrong. I will not deny who I am!" she answers. For this reason she holds onto as much tradition as possible, even though some clerks at the mall say bad things about her (until she takes out her Chase Sapphire card). She smiles at them but under her abayah she gives them the finger.

On the night that Gavin Goode comes to his OR, Dr. Azziz is returning just four hours after having completed a fourteen-hour shift. The OR reminds him of home where he often saw people shot with handguns and rifles, shredded with knives or torn apart by shrapnel from fireworks or homemade bombs. Women and children, too much. Suffering is suffering, no matter where you are on earth. The most he can do is use his scalpel to heal whoever he can, as often as he can.

In the OR, faced with 'to be or not to be' on a routine basis, Ahmad flows cool and still as a gentle stream. But when he gowns and puts on his gloves and mask, he feels like he is preparing to fight an evil that must be defeated by whatever means possible.

"So, Mr. Goode, you have come to me" he says, while bending over the CT pictures on his computer screen. There is a massive intracranial hematoma, a blood clot, like a blackened shroud enveloping a portion of his brain. For there to be any reason for hope, the clot must be removed. "Well," says Dr. Azziz, a sigh wheezing through his windpipe.

Despite the high tech wizardry of the OR and the aura surrounding surgeons and the magic they perform, Ahmad recognizes the primitive, almost cruel nature of what he is about to do. Gavin's head is shaved and stabilized with screws so it won't move during the procedure. Ahmad slices and pulls back Gavin's scalp, then clips it into place. Whirring drill in hand, Ahmad bores three holes into Gavin's skull and then cuts a triangular shaped bone flap away with a saw. Ahmad scours the open skull for debris and blood, like an oceanic explorer might scan the dark, cluttered bottom of the sea. He picks and sucks bits and pieces away from the grey, swollen tissue, removing the clot as well as the disfigured metal intruder that has crash landed there. Is it enough?

Hours pass. He pauses before beginning to close. He looks at the brain, its damp, cauliflower folds. He looks at the residents and nurses assisting him, his eyes scanning them. "There he is," says Dr. Azziz.

"That is Mr. Goode, his whole world; his memories of being a little boy; his laughter and sight, his walking and talking; his imagining and hoping and dreaming. Everything that makes him a person is right there, good people." He smiles under his mask. It is a vast universe in little more than three pounds of grey matter encased in bone.

Dr. Azziz knows there is no way to predict Mr. Goode's outcome. Having a bullet in one's skull is never good, but Gavin is lucky that this wasn't a curious bullet. It didn't meander and wander like an invader about to colonize someone else's homeland. It entered on one side and it stayed put in one lobe.

When he later examines the cartridge, he recognizes it as an assault rifle shell, perhaps from an AK-47. Many in his family have been visited by this weapon, this shell. He blinks and wipes perspiration from his upper lip as he studies the bullet, now lying in the metal tray, itself dead.

Dr. Azziz descends the back stairs to the first floor and makes the long walk to the Family Waiting Room. He's still wearing his blue surgical booties, scrubs, mask loosened around his neck and head cap that makes him look vaguely like an imam readying himself for evening prayers. The hostess volunteer points to a woman slumped in a chair, her eyes dark with uncertainty, her hair dull. Beside her are another woman and a young man, her son he assumes, because of their matching jaws.

"Mrs. Goode? I am Dr. Azziz. We just completed the surgery on your husband." A thin smile crosses his face as he unfolds his arms and lets them fall to his side. Mrs. Goode rises haltingly, then the others. "We have stopped the bleeding and removed the clot that was causing so much pressure." He pauses, letting her take in the words. "We also removed the bullet." He says this in soft tones, like he is telling her a secret that no one else should know. With this, all the color leaves Mrs. Goode's face, as if a plug has been pulled at the bottom of her heart. He waits again, this time placing one hand on her arm. The young man beside her steps back, covers his face and begins to weep. Her friend wraps an arm around her.

"A bullet," she says, her face collapsing as if sucked into a black hole. "I don't understand..."

"Yes, I'm afraid it was..." He squeezes her arm. Her gaze goes through him. He shuffles with discomfort. "Is there anything..."

"Is he dead? Is he going to live?" says Ryan.

The first question is much easier to answer than the second. "No, he is not dead. He is alive and has been taken to recovery. Soon he will go to the ICU where you can see him for yourself." He hopes the young man has forgotten his second question.

"And?"

"And?"

"Is he going to live?"

Dr. Azziz caresses his chin as he holds Mrs. Goode's arm with his right hand. A skin bubble forms as he bites his lower lip and considers how to answer. Will he live? If he means 'Will he live through the night?' again the answer is simple. If he means 'Will he live for a week or a month?' he can only offer equivocating statistics. He hopes he doesn't mean 'Will he go back to his same old self? Will he come home, go to work, be there for me as he always has, laugh and joke and enjoy life again?' That answer is also simple.

"What matters is that he is alive right now. And he is resting. And we have given his brain a chance. And the next forty-eight to seventy-two hours will give us much more to go on." Keeping one hand on Mrs. Goode's arm, Dr. Azziz reaches out with his other hand and places it on her son's shoulder. He takes a deep breath as if he is about to say something more, perhaps some words of comfort, but then he lets the breath out slowly, hoping no one will notice. One more squeeze and he turns to walk away. He hears Mrs. Goode's faint and puzzled voice. "A bullet."

When Dr. Azziz returns to his office, he locks the door behind him. From the metal file cabinet in the corner he takes his maroon and black floral and polka dot prayer rug, unfolds it and carefully places it on the floor. He removes his shoes and stands quietly facing the east. He thinks about Mr. Goode and his frightened and confused wife and son. He tries to clear his mind. He begins afternoon prayers, the 'Asr, raising his open palms to shoulder level and proclaiming, "Allahu Akbar," God is great.

CHAPTER 8
MIKHAIL
THE AK-47

Mikhail resents how puffed up Mr. Hillman gets when he goes to the gun club. "He shoot at terrorist targets, intruder targets, zombie targets, polar bear targets, little diamond shape targets, every kind of target. When he is done, he take off his cap and goggles and he wipe his brow and breathe deep, like he fights in big war. His friends, also suburban baby-men, smile and applaud and buy him Genny lite. It is a disgrace that I am misused in this way!" Mikhail longs to be in combat where it matters when someone pulls his trigger. "I am not a pop gun, a toy; I am manly weapon; I miss the smell of manly fighting."

Today he lies in the trunk of the car wrapped in his quilt while Mr. Hillman drives to Christopher's school to pick him up. From there Hillman takes Brick Landing to River Rd. and after a short while turns off on a grassy lane that leads to a grove of young birch trees. There Mikhail, leaning against a tree, watches as Christopher and his father balance pop cans and milk cartons and baked bean cans on a split rail fence. "Can I shoot this time?" begs Christopher. "That's why we're here," says Mr. Hillman. At first when Christopher pulls the trigger, Mikhail knocks him back on his butt. "Ow, Dad, that totally killed my shoulder." But Christopher sets his jaw and shoots again and then again until he can hold his new friend confidently, taking steady aim at his targets and even hitting them sometimes. "Atta boy!" Mr. Hillman shouts and pounds Christopher on the back. Christopher stands tall, stretching his back, arching his shoulders and pulling in his soft belly. Mikhail is impressed with the boy: "He clench his jaw like Rambo and make his shoulders go so far back that his chest might explode."

After each of these outings, Mr. Hillman reminds Christopher not to tell his mother anything. He kneels in front of the boy, plucked eyebrows raised, manicured finger in his son's face, and says one word, "Remember." Christopher rolls his eyes and heads for the car, tossing an "I know, I know" over his shoulder. "She's not a gun person!" Mr. Hillman calls. "She's afraid of them!"

Christopher soon realizes he has a marked advantage over his father when it comes to keeping this secret, an advantage that he is willing to use. Mikhail admires this, as well.

"Dad, I don't like lying to Mom. It makes me feel all crappy inside." He says this when his mother is in the kitchen, twenty feet from where he and his father are sitting. There is a crinkle across his nose, something he has practiced in the bathroom mirror, a look that makes him seem like a little boy, a worried little boy.

"Trust me it's better this way." His father snaps the newspaper and pulls it up in front of his face. Christopher is undeterred.

"I don't know. It doesn't feel right to me, y'know what I mean? Maybe we should tell her what we're doin'. Maybe that'd be better. I don't think it's good for a son to keep secrets from his mother. It's, like, I'm lying to my mom."

Hillman folds the paper and tosses it onto the coffee table. "You're not lying; you're just not telling her something that would…that would make her feel bad, that would upset her. You don't want to do that, do you, son?"

Christopher is unmoved by this argument, one he has anticipated.

"You know, Dad…you know what the church says about lying. It's never a good thing, is it? I mean, the Bible doesn't tell people—'Hey, you Israelites, go ahead and lie'— does it? Jesus wasn't a liar, was he?" His father swallows and looks at him, not sure what to say.

"Look, Christopher, I think this is better kept between us; mano a mano. This isn't a church thing. This is a family thing; a keep the peace thing." Then he opens his wallet and gives Christopher some cash. To date, this gambit has yielded young Christopher forty dollars in hush money.

Extortion is very American thing, is not? American as, what is it, apple pie, thinks Mikhail, admiring the boy's Yankee ingenuity.

Mikhail resents that Mr. Hillman keeps Christopher away from him when he isn't around. Hillman lectures his son about safety and badgers him with ridiculous fake news about the dangers of having a weapon in the house. He always takes the magazine and hides it where Christopher can't find it. "Such a dumb dope," thinks Mikhail. "Like I say, there is always a cartridge in the chamber, ready to go."

Today is teacher conference day and Christopher doesn't have school. He is old enough now that his parents trust him to stay home alone without getting into any trouble. He lies in bed playing games on his tablet for hours, finally getting hungry and wandering downstairs for a bagel, some Lucky Charms, and a bowl of ice cream. He is not a shy eater. He calls two friends but one isn't home and Magee, his neighbor friend, is at the zoo with his parents. Boredom sets in. He flips through the TV, checking Netflix, Hulu, Amazon, but he can't find anything remotely pornographic. His parents block everything. He knows he can find something on his tablet. Even Google Images. But then he has a better idea.

Down the basement stairs he goes, the dank smell making his face pucker a little, the darkness and quiet creeping him out. The basement has always been a scary place for Christopher, with its boxes stacked in every corner and its naked pipes and wires and torn insulation. People die in basements; worse, they get killed there. But he is a big boy and this is well worth the risk. Mikhail hears him, feels him coming closer. Christopher struggles with the ladder, banging an empty light fixture, dropping it once—"Geez!"—and with a mighty huff leans it against the wall near Mikhail's hiding place. Up the steps he goes, murmuring to himself. He rummages around some boxes, moving them this way and that, until he touches something familiar. It is the blanket where Mikhail is hidden. Christopher's face, red from exertion, beams. He backs down the ladder, Mikhail pressed against his chest, and steps onto the basement floor.

He giggles and hoots and pumps his fist in jubilation as he holds Mikhail in his pudgy fists. For Mikhail it is as if the two of them are one, the little boy's blood coursing through him. He understands— there is nothing like being alone with a weapon in your hands for the first time. Christopher aims Mikhail this way and that. He makes shooting noises—"Blam, blam!"— and wheels suddenly as if defending himself from an imaginary bad guy, someone about to kill his mother and father. He grits his teeth and juts his chin. He head bobs and struts around the basement, no longer afraid.

Christopher looks down Mikhail's barrel and studies his trigger. He tears the basement apart, checking every corner, every box, for the magazine. "Doggonit." He rushes upstairs to the garage, assuming that is the only other safe place his father could have hidden it. Paint cans, more boxes, oil cans, lawn mower, snow blower, firewood, wheelbarrow, bicycles, lawn furniture hanging on nails. Nothing shaped like a banana; no magazine. He gives up.

Christopher takes Mikhail in his hands again. Mikhail feels safe in the cradle of Christopher's palms; he is calm as Christopher raises and points him through the garage window, just the tip of his barrel, just enough for Christopher to feel like he is guarding a fort against marauding foreigners. Mikhail feels at peace as Christopher presses his cheek to the barrel and squints down the sight and then pulls the trigger clean. Christopher's heart stops beating.

The sound Mikhail makes is not a little boy's 'Blam!' It is like a fire-tipped hornet has exploded into the suburban air. Mikhail winces as Christopher drops him to the floor and steps back, his mouth wide and his chest sunken and breathless. He kneels, his face red, then white, then cold with sweat. Mikhail feels Christopher's eyes on him, as if he has no idea what he is looking at anymore.

He wishes he could explain to Christopher that there is nothing for him to do now. It is out of his hands. Once the sizzling M67 cartridge screams into the air, it is hell-bent for its destination, whatever it may be; nothing can stop it, not at twenty-three hundred feet per second, so fast that it isn't even a blur, it is invisibility itself. "Can you imagine what a thrilling ride that would be?" Mikhail is smiling.

He watches Christopher as he sits on the floor for the longest time listening, waiting, wondering if anything will happen. Will someone scream? Will police sirens blare? Will a nosey neighbor stick her head through the garage window and yell at him? 'Christopher, what in the world did you do? Where's your mother and father?' But nothing happens. Nothing at all.

Mikhail is still lying on the floor as Christopher gets up and tiptoes to the window to look around. Everything is normal. There are cars on the street; a young mother pushing a stroller; a lady bent over in her garden picking weeds; the sun breaking through light clouds; a breeze caressing nearby trees.

Christopher begins to cry. Do not worry, little man, thinks Mikhail. No one noticed a thing. And if they did, they did not think nothing of it. Life, it goes on. He knows that Christopher can't possibly understand what he has done. The M67 doesn't care where its journey ends or what havoc it may wreak. It is without conscience, without thought or reason, without care. It will hit anyone or anything in its path. It doesn't discriminate. It doesn't matter what it is aimed at. Oh, the beauty, the elegance of such randomness, thinks Mikhail.

CHAPTER 9
Frankie Goode

When Frankie starts screaming, emergency room nurses fly at her from every angle, trying to calm her, trying to keep her quiet.

"Gavin!"

"That's okay, that's okay."

But it isn't okay. "Gavin! Gavin! Gavin!"

"Please Mrs. Goode," says one nurse, her face grey and hard.

"Gavin!"

"Mrs. Goode, you must…" But Frankie can't hear the nurses. She feels her own throat vibrating; there is tautness in her neck, but she can't even hear her own cries. She cranes her body to look behind the trauma bay curtain just as they are whisking Gavin away to the OR. She sees his hand dangling. He doesn't move. He doesn't flinch. She wants to touch him. She watches and watches as he rolls away, hoping that he will sit up, confused about where he is, and say "What the hell is going on here?" She'd call his name — "Gavin!" — and he would run to her, apologizing for the inconvenience — "Tell me you didn't rush home for this" — and she would laugh and say it didn't matter.

But he is gone. Frankie looks in every direction, not knowing what to do. Rosemary approaches a woman bent over a computer at a nearby desk; the woman suggests they go to the family waiting room "up on surgery." Then she turns back to the screen, her face a dull glow.

Rosemary finds comfortable-ish chairs in a corner of the family waiting room and suggests Frankie take her shoes off, settle back and rest her eyes, because it's going to be a while. Frankie knows she should call Ryan back, but her lids are heavy and soon she is gone, too. She wakes up confused and disoriented, her eyes still closed. She hears Ryan's voice.

"I told Jenna to stay home," he's saying to Rosemary. "You know, with the pregnancy, she's nervous and, well, I don't want anything to mess up the pregnancy, you know what I mean?"

"Sure."

"Anyway, this'll probably be a big nothing, right?" A nervous laugh lifts his voice an octave.

Frankie keeps her eyes closed for several minutes more, not wanting to look at her son, not wanting to look at all the sad people in the room staring at their magazines and gazing pointlessly at the clock, not wanting to face the green and orange striped accent wall, not wanting to feel the thinning indoor/outdoor carpeting under her feet. But when her son abruptly stops talking, she opens her eyes. The surgeon is standing over her. He looks at Rosemary and then at Frankie.

"Mrs. Goode?"

Frankie stands.

"Dr. Azziz." He shakes their hands, formal but friendly. They stand in a circle, other families pretending they aren't listening to every word. What are they betting? Will there be good news? Will there be bad? Do some of them cross their fingers for good news, so they can feel more hopeful? Do others secretly wish for bad news, assuming that it's unlikely that bad news would come twice in a row?

Dr. Azziz points to the chairs and then pulls one up for himself.

"We have finished the surgery. There was a large clot causing extreme pressure on your husband's brain." Then he says bullet, bullet, bullet and bullet, bullet. She doesn't know why he keeps saying that word. It offends her; makes her feel violated. Ryan asks question after question, but all she hears is bullet, bullet, bullet. Why does he keep talking about this? Why is he holding her arm like she's a little girl about to be escorted somewhere she doesn't want to go? She decides not to listen, not to hear anything more even though he keeps saying things. How can someone with such a kind face talk about something so vile? His eyes are dark and warm. His teeth, white. His mustache, groomed. She likes the sound of his voice, resonant, yet soft, even melodic. How can he spew such lies? What is he up to? Dr. Azziz lets go of her arm and stands. He smiles down at her and his mouth moves again. Then he walks away. She watches him until he disappears around a corner. She mutters, "Bullet."

Soon they make their way to the ICU on the sixth floor. They push a shimmering silver button on the wall that's the size of a small Frisbee; there's a moment's pause before some invisible someone buzzes them in; they enter tentatively, like they are crossing the threshold of an exclusive club where happy people drink themselves nightly into comas. The rooms are organized like spokes on a wheel, the hub being where the doctors and nurses and orderlies and others sit and talk and study computer screens and grab folders from moveable carts.

"Excuse me," says Rosemary. "We're looking for Gavin."

"Last name?" says the woman behind the desk.

"Goode," says Frankie.

The woman looks at Frankie and then starts to laugh. "Oh my, you mean that's his last name, Goode; for a second I thought you were just saying 'good' for some reason." She shakes her head. "This day's getting longer and longer." She studies her screen again. "Okay, Mr. Goode is in 6-9012; it'll just say 12 over the door." She points behind her. "If you need anything, someone's always here."

Frankie stands at the door to Gavin's room, unsure whether she should enter, unsure whether the person lying in the bed is even Gavin. He looks like an art installation, like something Warhol would have dreamed up. Everything is white, white sheets and pale white walls and thick white gauze encasing his head, tufts of hair sticking out at odd angles; what she can see of his face is angry, red and swollen. Clear tubes run everywhere. Machines, like robots standing at attention, speak to each other in digital dialects.

Gavin's nurse doesn't explain what the machines are doing, but he does say, "Mr. Goode seems to be stable," his voice almost jaunty. Frankie is sure he rehearsed this line long before they arrived; wanting to greet them with something good, good but noncommittal. It's the same as saying, 'He's not dead yet.'

"Okay. Thank you," says Frankie.

"There are always reasons to stay positive," the nurse says, his words, like pieces of nothing, fall from his mouth.

Ryan stands on one side of the bed, his face long, his eyes damp. Rosemary comes to Frankie's side and folds an arm around her. The day started with such promise. But along the way, the world flipped; it rolled over on its back and gave up.

■　　■　　■　　■　　■

Earlier in the day, when she got the call about Gavin, Frankie insisted she drive home from the Buffalo mall, but by the time they reached exit 50, her hands were Parkinsonian. The steering wheel shimmied and the car shuddered. A state cop pulled them over and when he asked for her license and registration, she leaned forward and put her head on the wheel.

"My friend's husband is in a hospital in Rochester. We just found out and we don't know anything about what's going on and we're trying to get back as fast as we can," said Rosemary. The officer studied her with a chiseled stare. "He might not make it, we don't know."

Frankie glared at Rosemary. What was she trying to do? Why did she have to say that? As if that kind of talk has any place in any conversation with anybody about anyone, especially her husband. She laid her head on the steering wheel again.

The officer's lips were pursed as he took a deep breath. He stood tall, scanning the traffic, then leaned back inside the window, one palm resting on the handle of his gun. He stretched his neck to examine the inside of the car. "I'm so sorry, ma'am," he said and then returned to his patrol car, lights still blinking.

The traffic slowed to a crawl, each driver spying at them, either angry that their commute was being hijacked or curious about what crimes two women in a VW bug might have committed. Rosemary took over driving once the officer lets them go. Frankie rested her head against the passenger side window.

"Could I have done something...?" she said to the glove box.

"What was that, honey?"

Did she miss something? She knew he worried about his health. She knew he worried about dying. She tried to separate the wheat from the chaff of his anxiety. She tried to pay attention, to respond with care. But sometimes it was hard to take Gavin's complaints seriously. Sometimes she shook her head sympathetically, pretending to listen. Had something been going on all along? Was it a heart attack or stroke or something equally devastating? Something she might have foreseen had she been watching more closely? Was it possible to watch him more closely than he watched himself?

Her feelings begin to twist, warp, buckle inside her. Or could it have been her? Could she have put him in danger somehow? Is she responsible?

"I knew this was a mistake. I should've been there."

"Been where?"

"Wherever I needed to be."

■   ■   ■   ■   ■

Hours later, sitting in the ICU beside her unresponsive husband, Frankie reviews the last minutes she had with Gavin that morning. They were together in the bathroom. She reminded him she'd be staying in Buffalo for dinner, so he'd be on his own. He said that sounded fine; maybe he'd stop at Grandpa Sam's for dinner. Frankie was sitting in front of the mirror doing her makeup when he leaned in and kissed her on the neck. "Don't want to ruin the canvas," he says. She nudged him in the ribs with her elbow. "Got to go." She didn't turn to look. She couldn't remember if she had even said goodbye. Then he was gone and the house was quiet.

If she had looked at him would she have known that something was going to happen? Would she have felt the world quaking? "Remember not to die today; remember to live; remember not to get shot."

Rosemary sits beside Ryan opposite Frankie, Gavin between them, his bed like a dining room table set with fresh linen. When Dr. Azziz returns, he is wearing a tweed jacket and brown pants, a loosened tan and yellow striped tie at his neck. He pulls up a chair, sits and leans on his elbows, then smiles as if to steady himself. "There has been no change in Mr. Goode's, in your husband's condition. That is probably good news." He gazes at each of them, but no one speaks. "But I have to tell you that the injury to his brain is severe."

"Severe, how?" says Ryan.

Frankie's face shrivels.

Dr. Azziz shifts his weight in the chair and leans back before leaning forward again. "Your father's brain has suffered significant trauma. He may look like he's asleep, but he's in a coma at this point. This is not unusual. The bullet entered his temporal lobe," he says, pointing to the side of his own head. "While it stayed there and didn't veer anywhere else, which would have been worse, it is still, well, not good. You see there," he says, nodding at the tubing that disappears into Gavin's mouth. "We have him on a ventilator at this point. It will take some time before we see how he will respond."

"Respond?" says Ryan.

"Yes. Whether he will open his eyes, show that he is aware of things, breathe on his own…"

Frankie's back and shoulders lock. She slides forward in her chair and tilts her head so it is directly in front of Dr. Azziz's face. "Bullet. You said bullet before. Is that what you meant to say? Like a bullet from a gun that someone shot? At my husband?"

"Yes." Azziz licks his lips and pulls at his moustache. "It was a bullet from a rifle, we think."

Dr. Azziz could just as easily have said that Gavin had been struck by lightning or that aliens had dropped him on his head after a failed abduction. That's how much sense 'bullet' makes to Frankie. Gavin doesn't own a gun. As far as Frankie knows, the only time he has ever shot one was at a carnival where he failed ten times to hit the bull's eye in an effort to win her a dank, oversized stuffed grizzly bear.

"A bullet. From a gun, a rifle. How is that possible? Who would do such a thing?"

Ryan stops smiling and Rosemary gets up and stands behind Frankie. Dr. Azziz holds Frankie's arm. He shakes his head in response to her questions, but says nothing. Frankie's hand is turning white. Dr. Azziz let's go and stands. He pats both Frankie and Rosemary on the shoulder and then walks away.

For a moment no one moves. Then Rosemary wraps her arms around Frankie, hugging her stiffened body. Ryan comes to his mother's side and bows his head. He mumbles but she can't tell what he is saying. He stumbles to a nearby chair, sits down and starts texting. When he is done, he stands. He goes to Frankie and Rosemary and touches their backs. His eyes fill with tears. Then he walks away and leans against the wall, alone.

"Do you understand what the doctor said?" Rosemary whispers in Frankie's ear. Frankie looks blankly at Rosemary. Frankie stares at Ryan. He looks like a little boy in rumpled corduroys.

"Frankie?" She takes Frankie's cheeks in her hands and looks squarely into her eyes. "Frankie?"

Rosemary's face is so close that it is a blur to Frankie. She pulls away from her and tries to focus. "Of all things, this."

CHaPTeR 10
GaVIN GOODe

On Sunday morning, the day before all of this happened, Gavin Goode wakes up early, maybe 6:00AM. Usually he'd roll over and go back to sleep, but he is wide awake, so instead of lollygagging in bed, he gets right up, doesn't even bother to wash his face or brush his teeth, and goes downstairs in his plaid jammies. He pops a pod into the Keurig, pushes 'dark' and stands over the sink admiring the morning sunlight shimmering on the grey granite counter top. He listens as the Keurig dry heaves Eight O'clock into his cup. He waits obediently for the all-clear message to come up and then grabs the mug, the one with the thumbs-up fist on the side, and holds it to his nose. He adds Splenda, then some half-and-half and sticks the mug in the microwave for thirty seconds so it will be almost too hot to drink. Mug in hand, Gavin goes to the front door and picks up the morning paper from the front stoop. He heads back through the kitchen and onto their three season porch where he settles into the platform rocker. He slides the window open beside him so he can feel the morning air on his face.

It is uncharacteristically quiet. He notices the empty bird feeder on the pole. So he returns to the kitchen pantry and fills a plastic cup full of birdseed and then goes outside to fill the feeder. He stands in the yard, bare feet dampened by the dewy grass. The air feels moist on his face and he can smell the grass and dirt beyond the split rail fence along the back of his yard where ash trees sway. Back to his rocker he goes and soon goldfinches, wrens, sparrows and a nuthatch are chittering and vying for every available perch.

Gavin sits on the porch for over an hour before Frankie joins him, her mug of coffee in hand. He looks at her and smiles. "Morning," she says, leaning over to give him a kiss. She reaches for the Arts section and, as she settles into the rocker beside him, they fall together into a trance of contentment. Gavin loves the Sunday paper, the crackle of it when he folds back the pages, the smell of the ink, even the stain it leaves on his fingertips. It doesn't matter that most of the news is old by the time he reads it; he loves the ritual of sitting with the Sunday paper on his lap and drinking a hot cup of coffee until it is cold, Frankie at his side.

Gavin leans on his chin and studies the back lawn, considering whether he needs to mow it today. He decides it can wait. Then he looks at his iPhone calendar to see when his haircut is scheduled. He's happy to find that his week is full of appointments. He likes being busy. He likes meeting with clients and solving problems. Friday afternoon looks light, though, so he figures he will come home early and take Frankie to Niagara Falls for an overnight at one of the casinos. They could use some reconnecting time. He Googles deals and finds a great one at the Marriott.

That is all Gavin can remember about that one hour. And that was just yesterday. So much has changed during the ensuing twenty-four hours that everything he recalls could just as easily have happened a thousand years ago. Sitting on the porch listening to the birds? Reading the morning paper? Drinking a cup of coffee? Planning his week? Looking forward to doing something with Frankie? Gone, all of it.

None of these things crossed his mind when he was floating weightless in the ether, when there didn't appear to be a past to remember or a future to anticipate. But now that he is back, the ache of knowing everything is lost is too much. What happened to him? And why?

If he could only go back to yesterday. Today he feels like he's in Plato's cave staring at shadows dancing on the back of his eyelids, trying to figure out what is real and what isn't. Yesterday, everything was so simple, so clear. The porch was real. The birds and the trees. The coffee. Frankie.

More sounds. More shadows. Something's changed. Gavin wonders if he might still be alive. Not completely alive, but alive-ish. At the same time, he also feels dead. Also, -ish. He feels zombie-like, suspended somewhere and nowhere at the same time. "Dead is better than this." The thought frightens him. He loves life. He is one of those guys you'd pass on the highway who always has a big smile on his face; makes you wonder 'Why is he so damn happy?'

Every day there is something to remind him that life is worth living. Take yesterday. After his morning interlude on the porch, he goes grocery shopping at Tops. When he turns down the dairy aisle, looking for yogurt and cheese, there is a little girl, maybe two or three, lying in the middle of the floor, refusing to get up. Her mommy is at the end of the aisle, hands on her hips, shaking her head, but also restraining a laugh. She looks at Gavin and says, "She's my toughy-tuna," a grin in her eyes. Here is this mom trying to get her Big Shopping done, and her little girl is refusing to get with the program; and instead of yanking the kid's arm and dragging her away screaming, she stops to take delight in her feistiness, her spirit, her protest. She seems to love her for it. For reasons he cannot explain, this little scene makes Gavin feel that life is good.

But the scene Gavin is in today is different by a magnitude of thousand. Definitely not proof that life is plainly and simply good. More that life is a mash-up, good and bad, or very bad and modestly good. Both twisted together so tightly that sometimes it's impossible to tell exactly what you've got yourself into no matter how close you look or how far away you stand. He worries about Frankie. How is she doing? She was amazing when her mother died. But her mother had died instantly. This, whatever 'this' is, isn't instant, isn't clean. When her mother died, Frankie wasn't left with any messy questions: What do I do next? Is she alive? Is she dead? How do we know the difference? Will she come back to us? Or go away? Or neither? How long do I wait? Is there a plug to pull? If there is, would I ever pull it? Gavin knows their wedding vows had said 'till death do us part,' but never thought this was the point behind the poetry.

More muttering, and mumbling, and occasional shouting. Someone has to be out there. How to reach them?

CHAPTER 11
Jenna Goode

Jenna stands in front of the full-length mirror, her jersey pulled up so she can examine her belly. For weeks she has witnessed her body changing in ways that make her feel fat. Her jeans and skirts no longer fit and maternity clothes are too big. Ryan and her co-workers at the bank assure her that she doesn't look fat at all. Ryan says, "There's just a little more of you, that's all," which depresses rather than comforts her. She turns sideways. There is no doubt what is going on. When customers meet with her at the bank, they always smile; some dare to ask her when she is due. Her belly hasn't yet become public property, there for any passer-by to touch. Everyone tells her she is glowing and then they glow with her.

Jenna goes straight to the produce section when she gets to the store. She passes the green beans and peppers and squash, looking for the avocados. She smiles when she finds the right bin and chooses what she thinks is the perfect specimen. At home she sits at the kitchen table, the fruit cupped in her hand, examining its deep green alligator skin, purple at each end. "Good morning, Baby Goode." The website says that Baby Goode is the size of this avocado, four and one half inches long, weighing three and a half ounces. And that the baby is yawning and sucking its thumb. "My God," she says when she reads that its little fingers and toes finally look like little fingers and toes. She wiggles her own in amazement. "Seventeen weeks ago you weren't anywhere." She pulls the avocado to her chest, so happy to be pregnant again.

This morning, Ryan left before she was awake. He didn't remember that today was sixteen weeks. Usually they have sparkling grape juice to celebrate each mini-milestone, but today is different. The news about his father, so stunning, is too upsetting to think of anything else. Jenna remembers how devastated she felt when her own father died. Everything that had been meaningful in her life was flushed away. He was more than a father, he was her daddy. Colon cancer may move slowly, but it is relentless. She took the call in the hall of her college dorm. Her mother's voice was sharp, cold, indifferent. Always. Why had they adopted her? Jenna wondered, when it was clear that her mother never wanted her. She did all the things that defined "mother," but she was never a mommy.

Yesterday, when Jenna found out from Rosemary that her father-in-law was in the hospital, something about an accident, she was afraid to call Ryan, worried about how he might react, worried that she would scare him. Ever since the ice cream parlor opened, he'd been even more tentative, more fragile than usual. She rehearsed everything she wanted to say: "Ryan, honey, it's your dad; there's been an accident of some kind and they've taken him to General Hospital; I'm sure everything will be okay, but I wanted you to know so you could go be with him. Love you." She said it out loud once, maintaining an upbeat, almost matter-of-fact tone. It sounded perfect.

But when he answered the phone, the words congealed in her throat and all she could do was choke and sputter them out one at a time, and not in any decipherable order. He kept saying, "Jenna! Jenna!" She was gasping by then. "Did the baby die?" His words were a quick, firm, sobering slap in the face. Her forehead burned and smoldering tears stained her cheek. She wiped them away. Her voice turned banker steady, much like her mother. She told him exactly what she had rehearsed, but he wasn't soothed.

Through his tears, Ryan said, "I'm so sorry, I know you love him, too."

"You should go to the hospital, honey; I love you."

Sitting at the table with her avocado in hand, Jenna thinks about her father-in-law. She *does* love him. He is always supportive of them, especially Ryan; he's always there; always ready to help in any way he can. She can't imagine him dying. But that isn't the reason she cried to Ryan. The news about her father-in-law, so earth shattering in its suddenness, awakens feelings that Jenna has kept safely hidden for more than two years.

A few months earlier, when she found out she was pregnant, she counted the hours, then the half days and then the days and then the weeks until the seventh week when she took to her bed, explaining to Ryan that she was exhausted from all the morning sickness. She felt a little better when they clinked their glasses together on the eighth week, and better still every week thereafter.

Each new week provides another layer of defense; each new week gives her greater strength, especially if everything else in her life stays in relative balance. But the turmoil with Ryan's father exposes the chinks in her emotional armor. Things begin to seep through, and everything is awakened again.

■   ■   ■   ■   ■

The first time she was pregnant, she understood that spotting early in any pregnancy was normal, but her spotting was as steady as menstrual flow. Her first thought was to ignore the darkness of it, the persistence of it, but as the cramping worsened and the blood thickened with clots, she knew that all was lost. She wanted to fight it, to do something that would stem the tide, but all she could do was suffer it. She hated her body for the stranger, the enemy it had become. And when it was over, she quietly went about her day, trying to erase her thoughts about the beautiful future that had just disappeared.

She wanted to tell Ryan. She wanted to feel his arms around her. But he didn't even know she was expecting. Her mother had miscarried several times so she had decided to wait until at least nine weeks before announcing to anyone. How foolish. Eight weeks, twelve weeks, twenty weeks. Was anything ever safe? What would she tell Ryan? How would she explain it? "I'm pregnant; I mean I was pregnant, but…" It seemed impossibly painful, a story she couldn't share, words she didn't want to speak, because they would make everything true.

All the books and articles and online talk said it wasn't her fault. Miscarriage was frightfully normal, often happening without the woman even knowing. Everything she read told her she was innocent. One writer joked that miscarriage in nature is so prevalent that it's surprising anything is ever born. So why did she feel so guilty? She opened her Merriam-Webster and looked up the word "carriage," and it said "a means of conveyance," like a way to transport something from one place to another; safely she assumed. She also looked up "mis-."

And it said things like "wrong" or "mistaken" or even worse, "negating."

As she sat at the table, one hand on a cup of cold coffee, her pregnancy over, it seemed clear to her that "miscarriage" suggested responsibility; that she had failed as the vessel or the container chosen to transport precious cargo into the world. In response, the world said, "Go on with your life." And that's what she did. She worked harder than ever before, which resulted in her becoming a bank branch manager at what everyone thought was the unnaturally young age of twenty-nine. By then, though, she felt a thousand years old and her shoulders were about to collapse under the weight she bore.

■　　■　　■　　■　　■

Now she is pregnant again, something both of them wanted desperately. She tells Ryan immediately. They start nesting, painting, stenciling, carpeting what will be the nursery. The cashiers at Buy Buy Baby know them by name. But beneath the palpable excitement she feels a rumbling fear. The past is still tromping around in her heart, making everything about tomorrow uncertain. This time, though, she is determined. "I'll be damned if I'm going to have another miscarriage," is her daily mantra, her daily promise.

■　　■　　■　　■　　■

When Ryan calls from the hospital, she can't understand what he's telling her.

"Shot. He's been, a gun, there was a gun."

"What? What're you talking about? He's been what?"

Ryan is gulping and breathing rapidly. He tries to explain what the doctors said. Jenna's legs buckle and she grabs the kitchen chair. She tries to sit but ends up on the floor. Her head is throbbing.

"I don't know what's gonna happen. They aren't telling us anything. He's just lying there. He can't...He can't...talk or move or...I'm trying to wake him up, I am, but he's not...It's... I don't know..." Ryan voice is high-pitched, strained, barely audible.

"My God, Ryan, I'm so sorry, I'm so sorry, I am, but you can't give up hope, I mean, he's...I'm sure they...he's in the best hands possible, honestly…I'm sure they'll figure things out…that's what they do…" Ryan is heaving, wailing. "Honey, honey…" She struggles for the right words, hoping to soothe him, but also to stop him; to stop the hysteria that is crashing over him in waves, hysteria that could just as easily wash her away, endangering her and the life she harbors, innocent and helpless.

"Honey, honey, he's alive, he's alive, your father is still alive. They got the bullet, right, they got it, they took it out and the bleeding, the bleeding has stopped, right? Now he has to heal, his body, it needs time, lots of time…that's the thing, that's what's important, right? He's still here. He's still with us. Let's focus on that, okay?" She says this calmly as if she is reciting talking points from a presentation. "He's in the ICU getting the best possible care; he's healthy and strong, right?"

To her surprise, Ryan settles down. "You're right."

"Yes, I am." Her voice is strong, resolute.

"You're right," he says, as if to himself. They speak for a few more minutes; Ryan even talks about what needs to be done at Curly's while he is gone. He is upbeat by the time he hangs up.

Jenna lies back on the floor and breathes deeply several times. She focuses on the ceiling light above her, its yellow glow, soft and warm. She closes her eyes, her head still splitting. She splays her fingers across her belly and massages it. "There, there," she says. She glances at the clock on the opposite wall and hopes Ryan doesn't call again.

CHAPTER 12
RYAN GOODE

Ryan leans over his father and whispers. "Dad, I need to talk to you about this ice cream thing. I do. I called you this morning, but you never answered. And you never got back to me. I needed to hear from you. I needed to hear your voice, you know what I mean? Just a little 'Hey, Ryan, what's up?'" He forces a breathy laugh.

Ryan stands, looking for signs of something, anything—a deeper breath, a finger movement, an eye twitch. When nothing happens, he kneels. "I hope you got my message. I hope you heard my voice before…" He reaches out with one finger and touches his father's face, relieved that it is warm. Something is still going on, blood is still coursing, life is still happening.

"Dad, do you hear me?" Lines crease his cheeks and his hands ball. His father's head is swollen; his eyelids are charcoal and his face is red. "Open your eyes, Dad." The closer he looks, the less he recognizes his father. He feels nauseous. Ryan hates hospitals; they smell like bug spray and pee and old air that's been recirculated to death. A lightening chill runs through him. "Don't pay any attention to me, Dad; I'm just, I don't know."

The nurse comes in, leans over Gavin, smooths his lines and makes sure nothing is pinched. Then he smiles and looks at Ryan. "How do you think your dad's doing today?"

"Okay…the same… I don't know."

"Yeah, I hear ya." The nurse clasps his hands together in front of his chest, like a would-be evangelist, and raises his eyebrows in a sympathetic pose. "Much too early to tell." And then he leaves.

Ryan leans over his father. "Dad, you're nurse is a guy. His name's Lester, I think. He's in here every ten minutes or so to check stuff. He looks you over, but mainly he's about the machinery, you know what I mean?" Ryan sits on the side of his father's bed. He pulls the top cover down over his feet and pats his leg. "Jenna sends her love. She'd be here with me, but with the pregnancy and all. Mom went home to change. Don't even ask me how she's doing. Who can tell. She let me pat her arm. That was good." Ryan looks out the window at the parking lot, a neighborhood of modest frame houses just beyond.

He takes his father's hand in his. He looks at the port in his father's arm, a tube running fluid from it. "Believe me, Dad, if I could switch places with you, I would." His father's face remains stone still. "I guess what they say about comas may not be true. You can't hear anything, can you?" He looks around to see if Lester is in ear shot. "CAN YOU HEAR ME, DAD? CAN YOU? SHAKE YOUR HEAD!"

Lester comes at full gallop. "Do I need to remind you that this is the Intensive Care Unit? Please."

"I know, I know. But my dad and I always talk, I mean always, and I thought maybe if my voice got through — "

"We don't want to alarm the other — "

"I know, I know, but something's gotta be done or, I don't know…"

Lester takes another step into the room.

"Look," says Ryan, "this is my father."

"I know. I know this is the only father you have. I get it." Lester walks over to Ryan's side. "Are you okay? Can I do something for you? Get you something to drink?"

"No." Ryan takes a deep breath and sits up straighter. "Thanks."

"Need anything, just call," says Lester as he leaves the room.

Ryan gets up and walks to the window. He sits briefly on the ledge, then paces the room, trying to think of something he can do. Did his yelling send the wrong kind of vibe to his father? Did he make things worse? Maybe if he talks in softer tones, or prays, or plays some Billy Joel, Dad loves Billy Joel, or maybe if he brings in some candles like the ones at Yankee Candle at the mall, or burns some incense, maybe there is a way to break through to his father, then he'd have a chance of coming back.

"What do you need, Dad?" He goes to the hall and watches other loved ones coming and going, each trying to figure out what to do, trying to figure out how to save the day. He turns around and looks again at his father, who, swaddled in linen and gauze, could be anyone. He bends over, gaping at his face.

"Dad…Dad…I don't know what to do. I'm scared." Ryan falls back into a recliner opposite his father's bed. "I know, I know, take a breath, that's what you'd say. 'Take a breath, Ryan' and then you'd laugh like you were trying to tell me 'I know what this is like and, believe me, it will all work out, you'll see.' And I'd believe you." Every day when Ryan awakens, he utters a simple prayer, "Dad says things will be okay. Amen." He'll never admit it, not even to Jenna, but sometimes that is the one thing that will get him up. Sometimes he is afraid to swing his legs out from under the covers and put his feet on the floor. What might happen? What might go wrong? And then he thinks of his father and he gets up, sometimes reluctantly, but he does it.

But that well-worn prayer isn't working now. His father lies flat on a hospital bed, unconscious and unaware, mummified in bedsheets, tubes in his nose and mouth, residue of a bullet in his head. He doesn't even know Ryan is there. How are things ever going to be okay again?

Ryan gets up from the chair and stands beside his father. He inhales and lets the air out in a rush, settling his chest and relaxing his shoulders. He reaches for his father's arm.

"I wish we could have talked this morning. I wish I could've heard…" Ryan takes his cell phone from his pocket and punches in a number. Then he puts the phone on speaker. After four rings: "Hi, Gavin here. Please leave me a message and I'll get back to you as soon possible. Have a great day!"

"Ok," says Ryan.

CHAPTER 13
LESTER
ICU NURSE

When Lester came out to his mother in high school, she looked at him and said, "You're telling me?" She said she'd never seen a boy with such a keen fashion sense. His father, though, was a different story. It was hard for Lester to tell whether his father was more disappointed that he was gay or that he was going into nursing. It soon became apparent that in the two most important expressions of identity — who you are and what you do — Lester had failed.

His father declined to talk about Lester's sexual orientation, except to urge Lester not to be "one of those swishy fags," advice that hardened Lester's resolve to march in his first pride parade as Barbra Streisand. The bigger issue, though, for his father was Lester's choice of professions. As a fourth generation surgeon, he expected his son to go into the family business. So when Lester graduated college and decided to go to Penn because of its great nursing school instead of its great medical school, he could just as easily have confessed to being a gay ax murderer.

"What is wrong with you?" his father said.

"You think I'm crazy, like mentally ill or something," Lester accused. His father didn't even blink. "My God, you do!"

Lester's mother, who had cheered him on at his first parade, was no less alarmed. "Do you want to clean bed pans for a living? Wrist deep in other peoples' feces and a hundred other kinds of waste matter oozing from every possible opening; is that what you want?" She was a CPA.

Neither of his parents came to his graduation from nursing school. The gulf between them was never bridged.

Never one for cutting and suturing, Lester was more interested in what it was like to be the person under the knife. When patients arrived in the ICU, how could he help them get from point A to point B in a reasonable amount of time with minimal pain and suffering? He'd been at it now for nine years and while it wasn't always rewarding and some days all he seemed to do was respond to Code Browns (poop detail), he was proud to say that a majority of his patients left the ICU alive, rather than dead, because of the care he gave them.

Currently he has two patients, Mrs. Hempel in 5. She has pancreatic cancer and is recovering from Whipple surgery (Big Surgery). Mr. Hempel, who visits for six, sometimes eight hours a day, is a sweetheart. They are somewhere in their upper seventies, but vibrant and quick-witted. Mr. Hempel was an engineer at Kodak for almost forty years before he retired. "Got out before the whole thing collapsed." What a shame, thinks Lester. George Eastman would kill himself all over again if he knew what had happened to his baby.

Mrs. Hempel is in much better shape now than when the pain was so bad she could barely breathe. No infections, no bleeding, thank you very much. She'll be going to another floor in just a couple of days. Chemo and radiation to follow and a twenty-five percent chance of living another five years. I'd take those odds in a New York minute, thinks Lester, happy to be adding months, maybe years, to Mrs. Hempel's calendar.

His other patient, Mr. Goode in 12, is one of those patients that Lester takes home with him every night, not because he is demanding, but because he isn't. Sometimes patients come in so close to death that they don't seem like people at all. They come to him in a pre-corpse state. It is almost impossible for him to connect with someone who is so close to being no one. There's little Lester can do.

Mr. Goode is on the other side of suffering, which Lester sees as a plus, but that means he is also immune to Lester's help. He comes and goes every ten minutes; he checks the monitors and eyeballs his patient, keeps him comfortable, and tries to imagine who he was. A random shooting, an innocent victim, a guy at his desk doing his mindless work—it is almost too much for Lester to bear. "This world!"

Lester likes Mrs. Goode, who, even though she is obviously middle-aged, is sleek and stylish, her hair in gorgeous Bohemian combs and her feet adorned in gorgeous Kenneth Cole sandals that make her look like a model. She always smiles and greets him by name.

"Good morning, Lester, how are you?"

He is embarrassed by her kindness and consideration, since he feels he is serving no purpose. "The question is how's *he* doing?" he says, nodding to Mr. Goode, a hopeful look on his face. "Nothing has changed, which is…a sign of stability. Sometimes we measure progress by how little things have worsened," he blithers. She nods. She seldom asks questions, which leads Lester to believe she understands everything. "Do you mind if I ask where you shop? I love the way you look." What the heck? he thinks; if nothing else, he could at least engage. She tells him about her dress shop, a little of its history, but as her gaze shifts to her husband, it is apparent that she's only being polite.

He checks on Mrs. Hempel, writes a note and consults with an attending before coming back to 12. He is surprised that Mrs. Goode is already gone. In her place is the son, Ryan, who seems a little Bambi-ish.

"Good morning!" says Lester.

Ryan almost leaps from his father's side where he appears to be conversing. "Oh," he says. Ryan has a pinched Britishy face, narrow shoulders; he is smallish despite being taller than Lester by several inches, and his hair is thin and always sweaty. Lester feels sorry for Ryan. He is a lost soul, if ever there was one. As much as Mrs. Goode knows what's going on, Ryan appears befuddled by everything, the room, the monitors, the gauze covering his father's head, and, most of all, the unresponsiveness of Mr. Goode. Lester often hears him calling, even yelling, "DAD!"

"Is my dad any better?"

"Well, he has not gotten any worse…" Blah, blah, blah. "The body has its own clock, if you know what I mean."

Ryan nods, the rings under his eyes casting shadows on his cheeks. "I hope he's able to go home soon. I think he'd do better there."

Lester's eyes widen. He wants to say, 'Ryan, for God's sake, you father is gone and he's not coming back'. Instead he says, "It's always important to hope. That's what keeps us going."

"I guess."

"How are you doing?" Lester takes one step closer. Ryan instinctively clutches his arms to his chest. "I know how hard this can be."

Ryan steps back, looks at his father and says, "We're having a baby, my wife and me."

"Congratulations!" says Lester, happy that they are talking about something else.

"Yeah. I think it's fifteen weeks. Or sixteen." He pulls his mouth to one side. "It's hard to…"

"Everything's a jumble," says Lester, nodding to encourage Ryan.

"My dad has to be there, you know what I mean. He has to be there when the baby is born."

"I'm sure he'd want to." Lester shuffles his feet. He wants to say, Ryan, look, your dad will not be there, he won't; we should be talking about saying goodbye to him.

"I keep telling him that the baby's on the way." He looks at his father, lying motionless on the bed. "I think he knows." They are quiet together and then Ryan excuses himself, saying he has to go to the men's room.

Lester stands at the end of Mr. Goode's bed. He is sure that Mrs. Goode and Ryan will eventually face a difficult decision. Shut things down and let him go or wait for a miracle. Never in his nursing career, has he seen a miracle, although he has heard other nurses insist they have. People who've been comatose for months, even years, completely gorked out, waking up, dazed but otherwise normal, and asking for a piece of pizza or the score of the latest Yankee's game. Who knows for sure about these things?

Lester tries to convince himself that there is enough uncertainty to make room for this kind of ridiculous hope. He is a baptized Catholic, though he hasn't gone to mass in years, but he understands how the faithful can believe such things. He even prays for his patients. He doesn't kneel at the bed or anything, but on the way home he lifts them up to whoever or whatever might be there, hoping that it means something, even though he doubts that it does. Simple prayers— "If possible, let him live."

Just as often, he prays the opposite; that the person will die, stat. Suffering can render hope, well, hopeless. For some patients, their circumstances are so awful that death is the better option. Lester flinches every time he thinks this, even though he knows it is true. He often thinks of Irma. This was when he worked briefly in extended care. Irma was fifty-five and had suffered a massive stroke. She was a beloved elementary school principal and one day she collapsed in the parking lot, no warning.

Unfortunately she lingered for months. Her daughter and grandson came every day and cried at her bedside. When no one was there, Lester sat with her, stroking her arm or brushing her hair as she stared blankly; he put lotion on her feet and cleaned sleep from the corner of her eyes. One night he was sitting in the dark with her, listening to her gasp, her breaths desperate and rapid. She moaned and twisted and her face contorted. He didn't know what to do. How long could this go on? Such lingering, so pointless. So he increased her morphine drip once, then twice and then several times more until she calmed down, and then he increased it again and again, and her breaths came intermittently, nine, ten, fifteen seconds apart, and then not at all. He looked at her face, relaxed and peaceful. "Good," he said. He called the family and when they came, they thanked him for the care he'd given her, even though they had no idea what form it had taken at the last. They looked relieved for the first time.

As he drove home, he thought, I know I'm not God, but, well… He slept soundly that night.

Staring at Mr. Goode, Lester thinks he falls into the same category as Irma. He isn't suffering in any obvious way, like Irma was, but there is no reason to think that he is ever going to make it back to the land of the living, and if, by some stroke of luck, he does, he won't be a person at all anymore. Worse, this could go on for a long, long time. He can already tell that Ryan won't be able to handle the long haul. As for Mrs. Goode, Lester likes her so much that he doesn't want her to go through something she doesn't have to face.

But the ICU is a different animal. Everyone is on high alert. There are always staff coming and going. It would be much more difficult to help a patient out like he had helped Irma. Even so, he finds that he can't *not* think about it. Thinking about it is what keeps him awake these days. And thinking about it doesn't help. Instead of clarifying things, it confuses him and makes it more difficult to follow his heart and do what he feels is best.

CHAPTER 14
ROSEMARY

Rosemary throws her car keys on the counter and leans against the stainless refrigerator, trying to catch her breath. She holds her palms out and watches her hands shake. She can feel cold sweat on her back. She shakes her hands and tries to ignore it all. The only thing that matters is Frankie. She doesn't want to let her down. Frankie is her best friend, her only friend. She feels like she's known her all her life, like they came from the same womb. Frankie is everything Rosemary wants to be. She is so together, so successful, so effortlessly beautiful and seasoned. When Frankie breathes in, Rosemary breathes in; when she breathes out, Rosemary breathes out.

She sits on the kitchen floor, head in hands, and closes her eyes, focusing on Frankie's face; clean, geometric, with pencil straight jaw lines and a sharp chin, deep eyes, and a natural expression of knowing, of understanding, of wisdom. She shuffles through the purse on the floor beside her and pulls out her compact. She opens it. When Rosemary looks in the mirror, she sees primer and concealer and foundation; she sees powder and blush and contour cream; she sees mascara and eyebrow pencil and lipstick. What she doesn't see is a face. She doesn't see herself. And she certainly doesn't see Frankie.

Rosemary's husband always tells her she's "gorgeous," that he loves the way she looks and he loves the way other men look at her, which always seems odd to Rosemary. "Why does that matter to you?" she asks him. "I don't know; it just does; it makes me feel like I have an advantage," he says, his back to her.

She throws her compact back into the open purse and sits quietly, legs akimbo on the floor, her hands still shaking, her stomach aching. Rosemary hates that Frankie is going through this mess with Gavin. And that's exactly what it is—a mess—something she doesn't deserve and yet has to endure. It could go on forever. She slams her hand on the oak floor, but it still quivers. She straightens her legs then pulls her knees up to her chest and hugs them close.

Where is Frankie when she needs her? She was there years ago after the fall; and had practically nursed her back to health single-handedly when no one else seemed to care, when her husband was too busy with all his dealerships—"What do you want me to do? Quit my job?" Frankie lifted her up, kept her going.

It was supposed to be a perfect day. Rosemary beamed when Frankie said, "I can't think of anyone I'd rather go on a shopping spree with than you." There they were out on the road, wind in their hair, nothing on their minds. Frankie was feeling free and easy and full of life. A perfect day just when she thought she would never see one again.

If only Frankie had never checked her phone messages. It was supposed to be a day away from everything. Would it have made any difference if she had not found out about Gavin until she got home that night? She was so happy and then she wasn't.

"Oh my God," Rosemary had said. "Why did this have to happen?"

Frankie didn't answer, her attention already turned away from Rosemary and toward the hospital.

As she sits on the floor, Rosemary closes her eyes and thinks of her own accident. She can still see Frankie, looking self-assured, reaching for a strand of Rosemary's hair, tucking it behind her ear. "You can make it," she said. Simple as that. "Yeah, right," Rosemary said, thinking Frankie was crazy. But Frankie was right. She gave her enough confidence to dangle her leg over the side of her bed, and then stand on her foot and then limp to the doorway and then down the hall; she made sure Rosemary took her pain meds and went to PT, inching forward day by day.

"Am I still limping?" she had asked her husband.

"Just a little." He wasn't being critical, just factual, which was important to him. "I wouldn't lie to you," he said whenever Rosemary questioned him about anything from whether he'd taken the garbage out to whether he loved her anymore.

When she asked Frankie how she looked, she'd said, "Perfect! Just perfect!" And Rosemary believed her, even if it wasn't true. It was the kind of lie that friends tell friends to give each other hope. It took months, but Rosemary got back to normal, not her old normal but close enough, despite chronic pain that made returning to her job at the dealership impossible.

Rosemary's stomach convulses. She clutches her legs more tightly. Was it too much to ask for the gods to give her a day away from everything? From dusting and vacuuming the damn floors and shopping for groceries and waiting for her son to come home from school and wondering if her husband would ever come home from work.

But the day blew up in her face. Now Gavin's life is hanging by a thread, Frankie's world is upside down and Rosemary is limping again, if not outwardly, inwardly. Her thinking is wobbly and her emotions are ragged and again she is in the relentless grip of pain and need. "Suck it up," she chides herself. "Frankie needs you." She goes to the hospital every day for as long as she can, sometimes leaving early because of her own distress, never wanting Frankie to see what is going on.

God forbid that she finds out. As far as Rosemary knows, there has only been one close call and it wasn't with Frankie; it was with Gavin. She stopped by the house one evening to pick up a blouse she had ordered through the shop. She was about to get out of the car when she stopped for a minute and opened her purse in the half-light of dusk, looking for a boost. She tried to steady herself, but when Gavin tapped on her window, the contents flew out across her lap and onto the floor. She grabbed what she could and dumped it back into her purse, which she then tossed on the passenger seat. She opened the window, laughing hysterically, like it was a big joke. "Wow, you totally freaked me out, Gavin!" But the smile on Gavin's face had caved. He paused just long enough before speaking that it made her wonder what he was thinking. He cleared his throat. "I'm sorry, I'm sorry, didn't mean to…" he said politely, the friendliness gone. Rosemary hurriedly opened the door and gave Gavin a warm embrace, a rarity between them. "I scare too easily!" she said. She asked how he was doing, whether he had plans for the weekend, had he noticed how beautiful the sunset was, all the while holding his arm and guiding him toward the house.

She saw Gavin infrequently, but for weeks thereafter, she watched Frankie closely. Did she lean away when Rosemary came near? Did she make eye contact or look away when they talked? Did her laugh sound forced? Did she wait longer than an hour or two before returning

Rosemary's calls? She didn't notice a thing. Soon she felt comfortable around Frankie again, although she did her best to avoid contact with Gavin.

Looking at him in the ICU, so still, so unresponsive, so close to death, she realized she didn't have anything to worry about. She was relieved. "I am an awful person."

Rosemary looks at the wall clock. It is time for her to go back to the hospital. She gets up, goes into the powder room near the back door, splashes water on her face, draws deep breath after deep breath, trying to settle herself. Her face looks like a wrinkled paper bag. She makes it up again and forces a smile into the mirror. "How are you doing, sweetie?" she says, trying to find an easy-going yet concerned tone for her friend. Then she goes into the garage, gets in the Equinox and backs out.

As she approaches the entrance to the hospital, her hands are still shaking. She can't control them. She is afraid that Frankie will ask if something is wrong. She couldn't bear drawing Frankie's attention, her exacting eye; she couldn't bear the embarrassment of her questions, or her sympathy. What to do? Maybe she could call and say she's going to be late.

On the other hand, maybe she's not going to be late; maybe she's not going to the hospital at all. With this thought, she feels uncharacteristically placid, her hands almost calm, the knot in her stomach untying. I'll call her later, or tomorrow. Frankie will understand. She always understands. There is a sheen of perspiration on her face as she looks at the on-ramp sign just beyond the entrance to the hospital. She turns on her signal and takes the ramp to the expressway, hoping to find relief at her destination.

PART II

Chapter 15
In the News

The Farmers Insurance office where Gavin Goode was found slumped over his desk by a co-worker became an active crime scene. The police cordoned off the entire building, wrapping it in swath after swath of police tape. Chief Rockaway announced to the community that they were using every available resource to investigate the shooting. He invited the public to call the Crime Stoppers Hotline if anyone had information that would lead to an arrest.

When asked if this might be a terrorist attack, the Chief said he doubted it, but "in this day and age..." He then shrugged. Twitter exploded with video of the Chief's shrug leading to broad speculation about what he was hiding. Experts in nonverbal communication couldn't agree whether the Chief's shrug was "raised," which would indicate fear, or "curved forward," which would suggest defensiveness and deception, or a "classic shrug," which projects lack of knowledge or even lying. Most experts agreed that a shrug by a public official in a time of crisis should never be shrugged off. When questioned about this at his follow-up news conference, Chief Rockaway said, "What?" and shrugged again.

Detectives interviewed their two witnesses, Shondra Williams and her fiancé, Hector Rodriguez. Shondra and Hector reiterated their story. No, they didn't hear a shot; didn't hear the bullet penetrate the glass. No, Mr. Goode was not conscious when they first observed him. Shondra twirled the ring on her finger nervously, though admiringly, as she spoke. "Beautiful ring," said Detective Lincoln.

Family members were also questioned but there was nothing to link them to the shooting.

No credible leads have emerged, though social media speculation has run high about a nearby rod and gun club that had recently come under scrutiny because of loud parties that were upsetting to encroaching suburbanites. "I hear gunshots all through the night. Who knows what the hell they're doing. I bet they're militia or something; whatever it is, they're up to no good," said one unnamed resident of the toney Brigham's Cove neighborhood.

Richard "Rocky" Wesson, owner of Rocky's Gun Retreat, was adamant in his defense. "You can all go fuck yourself!" he tweet-stormed. "Just like the left wing to grab the scissors and try to cut the second amendment out of our Constitution every time something like this happens. Bad! We know our rights! If Mr. Goode had had a weapon, he'd be alive today. Sad! Back the fuck off!"

There were several letters to the local paper supporting both sides; some decried the "decline of civility in public discourse" and others asked what "decline in the civility of public discourse" meant. A group of clergy, including a local imam, called for everyone to reach across their differences to find common ground. "We are all Americans!" Bloggers questioned why the imam was included: "I don't remember any imams being on the Mayflower." Many speculated that this could be a "homegrown terrorist attack."

After a few weeks, the hotline went cold and Chief Rockaway confided to colleagues that "We don't have a damn thing. It's like that bullet came from nowhere. I don't think we're ever going to find the guy who did this." The headline in the paper the next morning read— Chief: We're Never Gonna Find This Guy. The community flew into a rage over "public officials who are doing nothing to make this a safe place for our children to grow up." County Executive Greely, who had tried to stay above the fray, finally broke his silence and went on a local public radio call-in show to assuage everyone's fears. It went well until, thinking his mic was dead, he was overheard saying, "If we catch this sonofabitch, we should take him out and hang him in the town square, just like they used to."

This outraged the Rev. Horace Brickle, President of the local chapter of Lift Us Up, who reminded the Executive in no uncertain terms that "lynching" was an "evil stain on our nation's soul," and that his comments implied that the shooter must be a "young black brother." The Chief Executive replied, "C'mon, that's not what I meant and you know it? Do we always have to be PC about everything? I mean, really, did anyone think that's what I meant?"

The city's temperature rose for a week or more, but when the Buffalo Bills won their season opener against the hated New England Patriots, 34-10, the conversation about the shooting vanished under the spell of NFL mania.

CHAPTER 16
FRANKIE GOODE

Frankie doesn't hear Rev. Lorde enter the room. She is sitting in a straight back chair near Gavin, her eyes closed, wanting to pray but not knowing what to say. It's been weeks and while they celebrated Gavin opening his eyes days ago, nothing has come of it. In fact, his face seems more desolate, his searching eyes darker and emptier. Frankie sweeps her face of a random hair with her cold hands, then notices low, polite coughs behind her. She stands and turns. She reaches with her hand. "Gavin, we have company this morning. I think this is the chaplain, am I right?"

Rev. Lorde, a rumple of a man, steps forward and takes Frankie's hand. "You have guessed right." He looks like someone's uncle, welcoming, a glint in his eyes, his broad mouth in a natural smile, a flutter of hair around his ears. Her eyes are mere slits surrounded by red puffy pouches; her mouth too tired for even a polite smile. "Your nurse, Lester, said you had requested a visit."

"Yes, I guess that's true." Silence follows. She sits down again.

He stands for another moment and then slides a chair across the room and joins her. "How's your husband doing?"

"His eyes're open now." Her face is expressionless. Her voice, staccato.

"Good."

She shrugs. "I don't know."

He waits, but she doesn't say anything else. "It's very hard."

She turns, examining his blue suit and stained tie, his practical shoes, his grey-streaked ponytail. "You don't look like a priest."

He laughs at this, perhaps a little too loudly. "Yes, well, you are right about that. I'm not a priest. I'm a minister. Protestant, not Catholic. No collars. Presbyterian, actually. Are you Catholic?"

"No," she says, nodding her head. "I'm not anything."

"That's okay." They both are quiet again as they watch her husband doing nothing. Rev. Lorde leans forward. "May I ask what happened?" She tells him her story, everything that has transpired since the day she went shopping with Rosemary. How he emerged from his coma and then entered a "vegetative state." A sign of hope, everyone says. But after a few days, the word itself— vegetative— feels more like a pronouncement, a punishment, removing her husband from one list and putting him on another one that is labeled 'hopeless'.

She also explains that the police have no leads; it is as if the bullet had come from the firmament, a bit of metal materializing out of nothing, going nowhere; a manmade meteorite charting an arbitrary course toward any target, no matter how unsuspecting. She confesses that she tries not to think about this aspect of their tragedy; she can't bear it.

She speaks with the placidness of people who feel nothing, yet her fingernails, buried in her fists, belie cuts that are deep. "I Googled this— vegetative state—and I found a better term. 'Coma vigil'." She turns and studies his eyes. "Isn't that a religious kind of word, reverend? Vigil. Something about keeping watch? Praying while you wait?"

"Yes, I suppose you could think of it that way. Lots of people in this place pray while they wait. It makes sense." When Frankie doesn't follow up, Rev. Lorde seems unsure whether to pursue the topic of prayer any further. He pivots. "What is your doctor saying?"

She reaches for the Starbuck's travel mug on the floor. "I'm sorry I can't offer you any."

"That's fine."

"Okay, so what is the doctor saying? Well, I've seen Dr. Azziz a few times and each time he says the same thing: we have to wait; time will tell us what to expect, how your husband will be. That was a few weeks ago. He's away. Vacation or something, I don't know. Now it's like we have a different doctor every day."

"I know what you're talking about."

She takes a sip and sets it down. She leans back in her chair and folds her arms over her abdomen, her body limp with exhaustion.

"I don't imagine you've gotten much rest. Would it be better if I came back at another time?"

Her eyes, a childlike quiver in their corners, meet his again. She reaches out and grips his arm tightly but briefly. "No. Please stay," she says. "My husband was…is…" She takes another deep, halting breath. "I don't know what tense he is any longer…my husband *is* a good man, someone who doesn't deserve this." She hardly opens her mouth as she speaks, her lips titrating her words, then releasing them in small doses so there will be no danger of overdose, no danger of saying how she actually feels, at least not prematurely.

"No. He doesn't," says Rev. Lorde, his deep, muscular voice resounding with confidence. No one deserves tragedy. He understands this intimately, his brother having died by his side while they slept together as children. He was so still when they awoke in the morning. Rev. Lorde was nine. His brother was five. While this chased his parents from religion altogether, it somehow pulled him closer to God, not in blind, sheepish faith, but like a wasp drawn to a ripe, yet fallen, apple.

Her face opens. Her eyes, more alive. "My son insists that his father is coming back to us."

"What do you think, Mrs. Goode?"

Frankie sits up and reaches again for her coffee, then rests it in her lap. "What do I think. I don't know exactly what I think about it. Is that odd?"

"Not at all."

"I don't like it when the doctors come in and they don't have any answers. I don't like not knowing. It puts you at a disadvantage, don't you think?"

Rev. Lorde crosses his arms and opens his mouth, but then Frankie speaks again. "When I was pregnant with our son, Ryan, my husband didn't want to know the sex of the baby ahead of time. He thought it'd be more exciting. I never told him, but I asked my doctor what it was going to be. It's always better to know. The uncertainty would have been too much to carry for so many months."

"I'm sure."

Frankie sips her coffee. Her breathing becomes lighter as she talks. She gets up from her chair and stands at her husband's side. "How silly that was. I mean compared to this kind of uncertainty."

Rev. Lorde gets up, as well, and stands beside Frankie. "We never know what we'll have to face, do we?"

Gavin's eyes dart back and forth, then close and open again. His mouth, an oval, an expression of confusion on his face.

"I don't know what to think of this," she says, nodding at her husband's busy eyes. "Is there something going on? Or is this just a random...I don't know what."

"Something's definitely going on, but what it is isn't clear."

Frankie leans over her husband and kisses him. She whispers "I love you" in his ear and moves a hair from his forehead with her fingertip. She lays her arm across his chest. "Come out, come out, wherever you are."

Rev. Lorde smiles. "It's always important to maintain hope."

Frankie presses a moist sponge to her husband's lips. She looks up at Rev. Lorde, a sympathetic smile on her face. "Why?"

Rev. Lorde seems to stumble over her question. His dark brows shade his eyes.

"I'm sorry, reverend. I've put you on the spot unfairly." Frankie says this quickly, politely, dismissively. "My son, maybe you'll meet him, is very hopeful. He's that kind of person." She kisses her husband again and then sits in the chair. "Gavin and I are going to be grandparents. Ryan and his wife are expecting." She looks at Gavin and smiles. "It's awful that Jenna has to deal with all this. It should be a happy time for any new mother, you know. But this, well..."

"May I congratulate you? Your first?"

Frankie grins and her face becomes smooth, her cheeks faintly rose-colored. "Yes, this will be the very first one." For a moment she forgets everything else, her voice rising with anticipation.

"How wonderful. Is your son like your husband, I mean, does he want to be surprised."

"Oh no, not at all; they wanted to know. And they'll find out soon." She puckers her lips and closes one eye in thought. "This week, actually. She still has a ways to go."

Rev. Lorde can't seem to help himself. "A new baby. Such an optimistic sign; you know, beginnings."

"Yes, I suppose." Frankie reaches for her coffee again.

He speaks, almost whispers, "Mrs. Goode, is there anything that..."

"That you can do for me?"

"Yes, I suppose that's it. Can I help in any way?"

Frankie turns her chair to face Rev. Lorde. Her dewy eyes narrow, as if she is deciding something. Her bottom lip stretches up over her teeth.

"Do you believe that this sort of thing, this thing that's happened to my husband, do you believe that if he had leaned one way or the other he might not have been...it might have missed him? Do you believe it was just a freakish thing?" Frankie looks at the floor as she tries to fashion her thoughts into words. "Or do you believe it was meant to be? Like it was written somewhere, like there was a reason for it? Do you know what I mean, reverend?" She looks up at him again, her eyes searching.

"Well...yes...I do know what you mean. But I'm not sure there is a simple answer. I think that God has a plan for us, but also crosses his fingers for our fate; not everything is in his control. I think."

Frankie looks at the floor again, her lips curled in concentration.

"Many years ago, when I was starting my business, I had a partner who was also like a mentor. As these things sometimes go, we got closer than I had ever intended. I loved Gavin more than anything in life, and still do, don't get me wrong, but I couldn't resist, I mean the attraction was real, it was strong, and, well, we had this thing, this very brief thing. Then he moved away."

"Well, these things do happen in many marriages and—"

"Let me finish, please." Rev. Lorde stops mid-breath, holding it there as she continues. "I told Gavin what happened, but I didn't tell him, well, everything. I couldn't. You'd have to know my husband. I'd never want to hurt him. He was wonderful about it. And I thought it was over. But when we met, this man and me, at a convention a year later, it happened again."

"I see, well—"

"And it's happened at least a couple times a year ever since. Gavin doesn't know any of this." With this, her eyes fell and her cheeks sank, and her ears grew crimson. "I hated myself for it the first time. And I have hated myself for it every time since. Sometimes, though, you do things. You don't think about them, you just do them; and if no one knows, after a while, it's like you didn't do them at all. I don't know..."

The ventilator's gnawing, one-man-band rhythm and the stale air close in on them both. Rev. Lorde doesn't speak. The corners of his mouth recede into tiny folds.

"I have never told anyone this." She looks at Rev. Lorde, her face taut. "No one. I knew that if I told anyone, everyone would know. Eventually. " Frankie reaches for her bag and pulls tissue from an outer pocket. She dabs her eyes and balls the tissues in her fist. "I love Gavin too much for that. But I also haven't stopped. I've tried, but I haven't stopped. After each time when I got back home, I'd vow to end it, but then months would pass and it wouldn't seem necessary. We were happy enough, Gavin and me. Why ruin that, you know?" She looks at Lorde, but he doesn't speak. "The big cost was hating myself for it. Not every minute of every day, but it was always there under the surface. Sometimes, like when we were out for dinner, laughing and enjoying ourselves and I would look at him and, well, love him, I'd feel this deep panic, like a nerve being twisted into knots inside, and I'd want to tell him, just like that, blurt it out and get it over; and ask his forgiveness and be done with it, but then I couldn't. Because the risk of it was too great; the chance of losing the one person who has ever loved me, well, I couldn't. And so I'd hate myself a little more instead. Then, like a fever, it would pass. Months later a convention would come up and I'd get excited and afraid all over again, and I'd promise myself that I'd be good, but I'd know I wouldn't; and around it would go, over and over. And so I'd hate myself a little more each time and I'd put it somewhere inside where no one else could see. Except me. And I'd hope it wouldn't show. And I hoped he'd never know, that he'd never be affected by it. You know what I mean? I never wanted something I did to hurt him. Now I don't know."

Rev. Lorde reaches for Frankie's hand, then places his other hand over it, as if warming a child come in from the cold. "Mrs. Goode—"

"No, please, I'm not ready for your kindness." Rev. Lorde doesn't remove his hands and Frankie doesn't take hers back. "I don't know how these things work. I mean, supernatural or spiritual things, religious things, whatever you want to call it, I don't know if what we do, if the secrets, do they affect things? Is there payback? Reckoning? I mean, Gavin is a good man, he's just living his life, doing his best...I love him more than anything...He's innocent, you know what I mean?" Frankie's fingers fold over each other as Rev. Lorde squeezes her hand. "I need to know, did I set something in motion?"

Rev. Lorde cocks his head to one side and puckers his lips, not quite understanding her meaning. "I'm afraid, I don't—"

"Did my, did my behavior, did my refusal to give up what I was doing, did it make something happen that otherwise wouldn't have happened?"

CHAPTER 17
Jenna Goode

Jenna runs the palm of her hand over her half-moon belly as the dishwasher hums in the background and the sun turns the kitchen curtains orange. On the table in front of her is an heirloom tomato. She picks it up and feels its relative heft, its firm skin. "You're about eight ounces now, my sweet baby." She talks to Baby Goode all the time now, especially since reading that the baby might be able to hear her.

She watches Ryan as he searches the closet for his Curly's jacket and hat.

"Honey?"

"It's in there. I saw you hang it up last night."

"Are you sure...oh, okay, here it is."

There is something different about Ryan. His back seems straighter these days. His gait steadier. His face doesn't have that startled look that she loved when they first met, like a boy discovering something new every day. That boy is gone, leaving behind a man whose jaw is firmer, and whose face is no longer surprised, or frightened, by everything. As odd as it seems, he is calmer, even happier at times. Things are turning around for Ryan. The news of his father's shooting is bringing people to the ice cream parlor in droves. They buy his gag-worthy Buffalo Wing Ripple and then linger afterwards to ask about his father, to extend their best wishes. Even with the season coming to a close, Ryan extended his hours on weekends and hired two more teenagers part-time.

Jenna pulls her jersey up and smiles at her belly.

"How's our little bundle?" Ryan kisses Jenna's stomach. "How you doin' in there?" Jenna runs her finger tips across Ryan's temple and draws him close, kissing his forehead.

"Are you going to stop to see your dad before you open?"

"Absolutely."

Visiting the hospital has become as normal as stopping at the store for a half-gallon of milk at the end of the day or going to the dealership for an oil change on a Saturday morning. Seeing her father-in-law in the ICU, which used to take their breath away, has become routine, just the way of things. They no longer pay attention to the monitors, they no longer notice the smell, they no longer dread the elevator ride.

Gavin's face has healed, mostly. He looks like himself again. Almost. The gauze is off. His eyes are open. It's like he's back, except that he isn't. Worrisome as that is, part of the routine is to set it aside. Leave apprehension in the parking garage when they arrive at the hospital. It serves no purpose.

Ryan pulls his chair close and gives Jenna a long kiss. "Yes, I'm gonna see him as soon as I leave. I have some things to ask him."

Well, not everything is normal and routine. Ever since his father opened his eyes, Ryan insists that his dad can hear him. Not only that, but that he can respond, as well. Jenna's been to the hospital several times since her father-in-law opened his eyes and she hasn't seen any supporting evidence. When the doctors parade in, he doesn't notice; when they speak loudly into his ear, he doesn't jolt; when they prick his foot, he doesn't flinch; when the nurses turn him, wash him, tuck him roughly, he never veers from his rag doll demeanor.

But Ryan believes that his father is moving his left index finger — "No, I'm not crazy; I've seen it!" — and that he moves it intentionally, indicating agreement with two flicks and disagreement with no movement at all. He acknowledges that at other times this finger moves on its own, as well, reflexively, involuntarily, meaninglessly. But that's different — "Everyone twitches from time to time; I know that." The doctors listen, but are adamant that the EEGs are more accurate than Ryan's insistent hopefulness.

Jenna listens patiently to Ryan as he rails against the doctors — "They don't know nearly as much as they think they do!" — but eventually he accommodates their skepticism as one perspective among many, the price of being "all medical about these things." Jenna knows Ryan believes that down deep where no one and no machine can see, his father is alive and well; he's lost in this fake "vegetative state," but eventually he will break out, like a chick from his mother's egg, or a superhero overcoming his kryptonite. "I'm telling you, he's laughing in there. Just wait, when he comes out of this, he's going to have a story to tell that will blow our minds."

Jenna is not convinced. A colleague at work told her about a cousin who was in an automobile accident. She landed in the same ICU, came out of her coma, eyes wide open for everyone to admire, and five years later she died in a nursing home from complications of pneumonia. She never broke out. Jenna doesn't tell this to Ryan. Even though his unfounded convictions about his father worry her, she likes the change in him too much to burst his deluded bubble. He is confident for the first time in their married life. He knows where he's going. He's making decisions on his own (even though he believes his father is guiding him, two finger twitches at a time). The business is turning a modest profit. And they have a baby on the way.

Jenna looks at her reddened hands. They match the patches she noticed on her cheeks and forehead the morning before. At first she freaked. Thank God for Google. All of these changes are normal. "If these marks are concerning, you can try a little concealing makeup. It works wonders!" She's like a teenager on zit patrol. She loves how the baby websites turn every change into an amazing little moment of discovery. Ryan isn't happy with how her skin looks—"Is there something I can get you at Rite Aid?"—but she sees each new outbreak as a sign that her chemistry, her biology is working its magic, doing what it is designed to do. She loves being in this territory, territory she hasn't entered before.

"You're sure you can make it by 11?"

"Wouldn't miss it," says Ryan.

Jenna smiles as Ryan kisses her one more time before heading out the door.

"Are you nervous?"

Jenna thinks for a moment. "No, I'm just excited."

"Me, too," he says and then's gone.

They said it was still too early a month ago, so today will be the day. Jenna has resisted thinking of names. It makes it all too real. It would be too easy to bond with something that has a name. Even a pet or a car or anything. The first time she was pregnant, she started thinking about names from day one. She couldn't help herself; she called her fetus

Chris, so it wouldn't matter if it was a boy or a girl. But when she miscarried, it was "Chris" that she lost. It added to her feelings of failure, as if "Chris" might know what had happened and blame her. For weeks afterward, she imagined conversations in which she was confronted, called out, belittled by her never-to-be baby.

Jenna gets up from the table, pours the rest of her decaf in the sink, rinses out her cup and dumps it in the dishwasher. She stretches her arms and back and then heads upstairs to the bedroom. She draws back the lace curtains and squints into the bright sunlight. She pulls out a pair of jeans from her drawer, the only pair of regular jeans that still fit, sort of. She reaches for the plastic bag on the dresser that has "Frankie's" emblazoned in pink on the side and removes the jersey, a gift from her mother-in-law. She holds the green T in front of her and smiles. It reads "Miracle in Progress" with an arrow pointing down.

Jenna admires her mother-in-law, and she thinks Frankie respects her. At times she seems more like a mentor than anything else, someone who studies her and tries to guide her, if only with silent applause and nods of approval when she likes something Jenna says about work. But she never feels close, emotionally anyway, to Frankie. In fact, when they aren't talking about work, she feels uncomfortable around her mother-in-law, much as she does when Frankie frowns each time Ryan brings up a problem at the ice cream parlor. Then she wants to scream "Help him!" more than anything else.

The first time Jenna met Ryan's father, Gavin asked if he could give her a hug—"I'm a hugger!"—and she consented, immediately feeling an affinity with him that increased with time. She loves how he supports Ryan. But he doesn't know much at all about running a business. Ryan listens to everything he advises, even when it amounts to little more than cheerleading— "If you want this bad enough, it will work out!" Jenna can help Ryan with loan issues and some money questions, but when it comes to how you start a business, grow a business, manage a business, his mother is the expert.

But she won't step in, which frustrates Jenna, even though Ryan would likely reject any assistance she offered. "She lost confidence in me when I flunked out of college," is Ryan's simple explanation for his mother's reactions to every venture he tries. "She doesn't see me as a hard worker; like I'm not a nose-to-the-grindstone guy; like I don't know how to struggle or fight for something." He says this often and when he does, Jenna listens but says little, mostly because she is embarrassed by the truth of what Frankie thinks. She loves Ryan's playful, affectionate, earnest, warm and tender side, but, then again, some days Ryan would stay in bed all day if Jenna wasn't there to roust him out.

Jenna never openly agrees with her mother-in-law, even when she makes simple, straightforward, common sense suggestions — "Have an open house; give everyone a coupon for a free cone!" — because there's always a tone of "You should already know this" that pisses her off. In private, when she encourages Ryan to consider his mother's ideas, he explodes and accuses her of not having confidence in him. He storms out. She falls silent. And so it goes.

In the end, it seemed almost impossible for her to reach out to Frankie and form a fledgling friendship, because of what it might have suggested to Ryan. Jenna was on a high wire and the pole often felt too short for her to keep balance.

So when Frankie came to the house one day with this gift in hand, Jenna was so taken aback by her thoughtfulness, even her tenderness, she cried.

"Jenna, I am so happy for you," Frankie said, taking her hand. "I just wanted to give you a little something. Let you know that I love you like a daughter."

Things changed after this. Previously, she never called her mother-in-law by name. She didn't even call her "Mrs. Goode," which would have seemed odd, stiff, even offensive. She spoke when her mother-in-law looked at her or she piggy-backed on conversations that were already in progress. But now, she could speak to her mother-in-law by name — "Frankie, good to see you." "Frankie, how are you doing?" "Frankie, what do the doctors say?" She's not her gal-pal by any stretch, but they are closer than mothers-in-law and daughters-in-law might typically be.

"Of course, I'm happy about it," said Ryan, noticing the change. But he blinked rapidly as he spoke and his voice was sharp as broken glass. Jenna decided it was advisable to nurture the relationship with Frankie, but not to talk about it with Ryan. At least not until he figured things out with her.

■ ■ ■ ■ ■

Even though she is barely showing, she decides to premiere her new T today, the one that Frankie bought her. She studies the Miscarriage Probability Chart like other women study baby name sites. At nineteen weeks there is a 99.9% probability that she'll go to term, that her baby will be born. "One-tenth of one percent," she says with a smile of relief. Even in the banking world this is an insignificant number. The fear of another miscarriage has loosened its grip on her. She is ready to write her new status across the marquee for all the world to see.

Jenna puts on the t-shirt and smoothes it across her belly. She grins at the words that embellish the front and looks in the mirror, for once admiring her changing form, her thicker thighs, her broader hips, her swelling breasts. She pulls her blonde hair back into a pony-tail and secures it three times with a purple elastic. She sits on the bed and reaches for her jeans, then decides to go to the bathroom before engineering her way into her Levis.

She leans forward as she sits on the toilet and parts the ivory curtains. There are a few leaves on the front lawn, though the towering maple that shades the house is holding strong, its leaves still green. When she gets up and reaches for the handle to flush, she glances into the bowl, then snatches her hand away and stands up straight, stiff, not sure what she is seeing, not sure whether her eyes are playing tricks on her. She puts both hands on her stomach. She stands silently, eyes closed, feeling for something, anything that might explain what is happening. "Okay. Okay. Be still." She doesn't feel any pain. None. "Good, good." And yet. She opens her eyes and looks into the bowl again, thinking she was mistaken the first time, that she saw a mirage, residue from some lingering worry.

Her eyes lock, her mouth falls open. The water is reddish brown, as dark as fallen maple leaves in November.

CHAPTER 18
Gavin Goode

It was not a special day. It was a Sunday, probably in October, Gavin thinks. How many years ago? He isn't sure. Maybe fifteen. He and Frankie are going to the mall. Frankie wants to buy a new dress for an upcoming event. He suggests getting breakfast first, but Frankie says, "I'm trying on clothes today!" They laugh about this as they drive down 104. He finds the perfect parking place near Macy's. "Your lucky day," says Frankie. Her smile is crackling fresh; her eyes dancing. She looks as beautiful as the day they first met in college.

The wind is stiff when they get out of the car. And the grey sky is threatening rain. Nevertheless, they toss their jackets into the back seat, wanting to be comfortable on their rounds. He puts his hand on the small of her back as they walk to the Macy's entrance. Frankie's hair blows across her face. Gavin smiles when she doesn't touch it.

Frankie is looking for something simple, elegant, something she can wear again and again without it being too noticeable. A dress that has classic lines; that can be accessorized easily. Gavin picks out a few. "Remember, I'm not eighteen, honey." He puts them back and continues the hunt.

The scratchy ring of hangers sliding along the rack. The faint first-day-of-school smell of new clothes. The softness, the color, the texture. The helpful grin of the associate, her lips bright red. She flips her hair behind one ear. Gavin can feel it all even now. It is a memory that seems to come out of nowhere.

"What do you think of these?" says Frankie. She holds three dresses; one, a deep purple sheath with buttons up the back; another, a scoop-necked slip dress, emerald green; and the third, a black satin flared dress with a delicate lace hemline.

They wend their way through the circular racks, heading for the 'Changing Room' sign. There Frankie disappears, dresses trailing down her back. She draws the curtain as Gavin finds a folding chair nearby, stretches his legs out in front of him and crosses them at the ankles. He sighs deeply, appreciatively. He looks at the mirrored wall in front of him, noticing a smile on his face, there for no apparent reason. He folds his arms and watches other shoppers, some with wrinkled brows, others wide-eyed, some in practical shoes, others in sneakers. Husbands, too, faces drooping, arms loaded down with coats that should have been left in the car. Wives calling to them: "Get that dress on the other rack, the print one, you know." Husbands filled with panic, as if being asked to scale the face of a glacier in their wing tips. Gavin chuckles to himself as each miniature drama unfolds.

He sees Frankie's legs under the curtain. Her flats come off and her jeans fall to the floor and lay rumpled at her feet. She lifts them with one toe and deposits them on what he assumes is a nearby chair. Her feet are brown, pale on the bottom; her toenails are pink, polish peeling slightly. Her ankles are thin, like a doe, sinewy. And her calves, he loves her calves for the delicate, perfect arc they form, connecting ankle to knee.

Why her feet are so busy is a mystery to him. Is she dancing, moving rhythmically to music he can't hear? She rises on her tiptoes as she puts on the first dress. She sways from side to side; takes two steps back and then forward again. Up on her toes, then down on her heels. Then one step back again. Up goes her left knee and then her right as the dress cascades to the floor. A hand comes down snaring the dress with the tip of her pointer. On goes the next dress and the dance continues. Gavin watches intently, his face at ease. And then comes the third.

He takes a deep breath and lets his body settle into the chair. Another husband raises his eyebrows and shakes his head as his wife adds two more dresses to the armful she clutches to her side. Gavin winks. He looks at his own hands, the creases on his knuckles, the blunt ends that his father had called baby stogies.

"So," says Frankie, posing in front of him. "What do you think?" It's the black satin, delicate lace at her knees. She stands on her toes, approximating the heels she will need to make it work. She looks like a girl, her body willowy, her face expectant, then satisfied with how she looks.

Gavin tilts his head to one side. Then the other. He scratches his chin as if he is in a quandary. Then grins. "Wow. Honey, you look fabulous."

"You sure?" Frankie turns her head to examine the back of the dress, her neck bows like a swan's.

"Absolutely." She comes down off her heels, leans over, grabs his cheeks in her palms and kisses him on the lips. Then she disappears into the dressing room again.

Gavin folds his hands across his belly, like a grandfather considering the pluses and minuses of life. His breathing is so even, so quiet that he doesn't feel like he is breathing at all, like there is no necessity for it. The only necessity is to be here in this ordinary place, waiting for his wife to come out of the dressing room.

His father told him once: "Enjoy your days, boy, 'cause there aren't going to be as many of them as you think." His face was deadly serious, his eyes unblinking, cigarette smoke encircling his head. Gavin, just a kid, tisked and looked out the front door for his friends. His father was always giving him Important Advice, warning him about growing up too fast or not maturing fast enough, educating him about sex ("…there's a male end of a hose and a female end and the male end goes into…"), or how to buy a car, or how to handle your mortgage payments, or, depending on his mood, the meaning of life itself. "Look at me," his father enjoined. "I'm telling you, pay attention. Pay attention! Not just to me, but to…" and he waved his arms in a world engulfing gesture. His eyebrows met in the middle, a sign of urgency. "Treat each day like it's the one you'd want to have back after all the days are gone." By then Gavin was running out the door, pretending to hear his friends calling. "Gavin! Gavin, I'm glad we had this talk!" Gavin looked over his shoulder and called, "Okay!" as his father took another draw on his Camel's.

His father might say Gavin is foolish, that he is squandering a precious wish, but Gavin feels certain that if he could have one day back, this would be it. The day of sitting in the dressing room waiting area watching his wife's legs, feeling like every part of him is smiling for no better reason than he is alive. There are plenty of other flashier days he could choose. His first homerun in Little League. The first time he had sex ("Thank you, Veronica."). The day he first saw Frankie in his business administration class; her stumbling in late, then realizing it wasn't Psych 101; how she curtseyed to the class as she left, her face freckly red. Their first date; she wore shorts and wedges that made her legs look ten feet tall. Or their wedding day, dancing all night, making love, making love, making love. The day Ryan was born, him taking Gavin's finger in his tiny hand. Their tenth anniversary trip to Paris.

There are many more obvious days than this one at the mall. It's a day devoid of glitter, or glitz or anything that might artificially jack it up. It is a plain old day, one of those days where you can get a true read on things, a clear sense of how you feel and what you appreciate, a normal day, for all intents and purposes.

He never tells Frankie about this. She buys the dress and they go home. If he had told her, first she would have laughed, then she would have thought he was crazy for picking such a mundane day, a day that probably didn't deserve a spot on anyone's list of top ten thousand days. In fact, it was doubtful that she would have even remembered that day. He is sure the dress is long gone and the reason for buying it is gone, too. Who knows? Maybe no one in that store, no one in that mall remembers that day, or more to the point, remembers those few hours when it became apparent to Gavin that life didn't need any special toppings to make it the tastiest thing he could imagine.

■ ■ ■ ■ ■

Is anyone out there? he wonders. Shadows and light. And even touch. He feels pressure where his hand should be; out there on his perimeter; gentle at first, and then firm and steady. He remembers the sensation of being held, of having someone take him by the hand, his fingers wrapped around a palm, the warmth of it, the safety of it. "Is this real?" It isn't an illusion, is it? Is someone holding his hand; is someone out there? Frankie? Hello! If only he could grab that hand and squeeze it so whoever it is would know he's here, that he isn't dead and gone. It's me! It's Gavin! If he can't move his hand, could he move his finger? Could he wag it, wiggle it, wobble it, make it shimmy and shake? Could he scratch that other hand so whoever it was would shout, so they would exclaim, "I think he's in there!" Skin to skin, they are so close.

Gavin thinks of that day, Frankie in her black dress, her bare feet, toes curled with satisfaction. He sees her face, her lips plumped, one corner of her mouth raised higher as she smiles; she looks at him sideways, as if hesitant, shy. He holds her there in his mind, a snapshot, a reference point. He holds her there while he marshals whatever is left of him to scream towards his hand, howling at it to move, to flinch, to do something, anything.

CHAPTER 19
LESTER

Lester stands over Mr. Goode, fluffing his pillow. He studies the dried sleep in his eyes, the cracks at the corners of his mouth, the pasty look of his skin. At first the family was encouraged when he opened his eyes. They were convinced that he could see, that in fact he was looking at them. But soon they realized his eye movements were as random as a bobblehead doll's. They still bend over him, searching those eyes, talking to him like he's a baby about to recognize them. They try to find encouragement in the fact that he isn't yet dead.

It's been like this for weeks. Lester knows that the laws of inertia are taking over. That the chances Gavin will stay the same, neither alive nor dead, are increasing with each passing day. He hates this aspect of medicine, that it can keep a person alive with no hope, that it can mislead families into counting on an improbable future. It's not only unfair, it is cruel. Better that Mr. Goode had died weeks ago, rather than becoming another cog in the vast hospital apparatus that manages, controls, governs him day in and day out.

"Morning!"

Lester shudders and turns. The bright shiny face of Ryan Goode grins back at him. A few steps behind him comes Frankie. And so the daily routine begins. Mr. Goode's son comes each morning and stays for a few hours before going back to check on his wife and then on to the ice cream parlor. He talks to his father, sometimes nonstop, and waits to hear what his father has to say, sometimes reacting with raised eyebrows, as if his father has communicated with him in ways that no one but Ryan can discern. Not so with Frankie who sits and watches and gets up occasionally to lean over her husband, her eyes grey and disappointed, kissing his forehead, then sitting again. She stays until lunch, then goes to her store for a few hours before returning for the evening shift. No one stays all night anymore.

Today is no different, as Ryan, his father's cheerleader, fans the flames for what has been a winless team. "C'mon, Dad, you can do this. I know you can. Look, Mom, look at his eyes. I can tell he's looking at me. I can see it. Look at his hands, will you? Did you see that? He's saying something, I know he is." He focuses on his father's fingers, insisting that the twenty-four hours a day random jerking is intentional, that his father is trying to reach them, to tell them that behind his death mask, he is a vibrant living being.

Frankie shakes her head, showing neither encouragement nor discouragement, much as a parent might equivocate with a child who is on the fence about believing in Santa Claus. When he beckons her again, she stands over her husband looking for supportive evidence of her son's claims. She raises her eyebrows and says, "Hm," then sits down again.

When she holds her husband's hands, it is less to interpret their movements, than to quash them. Lester notices that she is wearing jet black sweats, a pink T (wrinkled) and sneakers; her hair, usually coiffed, is pulled back in a tiny ponytail, her face unmade, like someone who doesn't expect to be seen, least of all by the man she loves.

"Can I get you some tea, Frankie? One of the nurses brought in the most scrumptious Darjeeling this morning."

"Maybe later, Lester, but thank you," she says, her eyes dimmed by a mournful smile.

Lester rolls Mr. Goode over on one side so he can start changing the sheets. Ryan pulls up a chair and sits beside his mother. At first they are silent, like two strangers waiting for the same bus.

"I gotta leave a little early this morning," says Ryan. "Jenna and I have an appointment."

Lester can hear Frankie shifting in her seat as if coming to attention. He tucks the sheet tight.

"Oh, of course, today's the day. How's Jenna doing?" Her voice, nearly melodic.

"Okay, I think. She's staying positive, you know."

"I'm sure she's worried." Lester sneaks a peek as Frankie places a hand on her son's arm. "I'm sorry you're going through this, Ryan. It's hard enough without..." She glances at Gavin, her son's eyes not far behind.

Ryan crosses his legs and folds his hands, his knuckles turning white. It seems to Lester that the ice has thawed a little between mother and son, not melted completely, but at least it's thinner.

"Look, honey, you don't have to come every day. I mean it. Nothing is going to change. Not immediately, anyway. You should be with Jenna. She needs you. It's not easy, what she's going through."

Lester glimpses Ryan studying his mother, his eyes blinking. He looks again at his father, the bed now made. "I know. But I'm afraid that if I don't show up..."

"What?"

"I don't know. Maybe he'll give up. Maybe he'll..."

Lester folds the sheets and side-glances Frankie. Her face softens as she leans toward her son. She rubs his back. "Ryan. Honey, there's nothing you can do. There's nothing any of us can do. Except wait."

Ryan backs away from his mother. "Don't say that too loud." His breathing becomes rapid. "Don't say that. Don't say anything that might..."

"Ryan, it's okay, really..."

"Anything can happen, I'm telling you. I've been reading things, all kinds of stuff about people like Dad. No one thinks there's anything going on. They just sit around waiting, talking like the person's not even there, but they are. They're, like, locked up or locked in, like they're behind a door and we can't open it but if we could we'd find them in there, waiting to come out. And they're aware of stuff, they know what's going on, they hear things, everything. That's why we gotta stay positive, talk positive, let him know we haven't given up, that we're pulling hard and that he's going to come back to us, he's going to wake up..." Sweat beads Ryan's upper lip.

"Ryan, please."

"I'm..."

"I love your father. I love him and I pray each day that something will happen. But I'm not..."

"What? You're not what?"

"I want to look into his eyes and see something, too." She gets up and stares out the window into a cloudy sky. "I want to hold his hand and feel something, just as much as you do."

Lester drops the sheets on the bed and looks at Frankie. For the first time, her face seems old, her hair thin and tired, her skin drawn. "Ryan, Frankie, I don't want either of you —"

"Mom, look, I'm sorry, I didn't mean..."

Lester watches as Frankie's chest draws in and her back straightens. "Ryan, honey, it's just...I don't believe what you believe. I want to. I do. But I don't. I've watched and I've watched, but I don't see your father doing anything. Nothing at all. I'm sorry. Your father was shot in the head and he's been in a coma for weeks and weeks with no sign of getting better. Ever. That's what I see when I look at him. He's right there, but I can't find him anywhere. It breaks my heart, but I can't ignore it. And I can't pretend."

"Frankie, I understand what..." Lester stops. It's as if he's no longer in the room. It's only Mrs. Goode and her son. Their faces have never looked so similar, their heads leaning, their eyes shadowy, their nostrils flaring with each breath, their hands helpless at their sides.

Ryan raises his arms, his fingers splayed, his shoulders arched. "I love him."

"I know you do, honey." Frankie presses her palms to her hips and takes one step toward her son. "I do, too."

Ryan shakes his head. He opens his mouth and then closes it and looks at his feet. He raises his head again and looks at her. "I don't know what else to do." He turns from his mother and reaches again for his father's hand. "Dad?"

Frankie goes to his side and puts one hand on his back, sliding it back and forth across his shoulders. "Dad, it's me and Mom." He squeezes his father's hand. "Can you feel us here, Dad?" Ryan's cheeks rise slightly into a half smile. "Let me know you're in there, Dad."

Lester watches from over Frankie's shoulders. Mr. Goode, unable to breathe on his own, unable to eat, unable to speak or move or control his own detritus, unable to be a person any longer, lies there, unaware. Ryan continues to encourage his father, while Frankie rubs his back and stares absently out the window, every muscle in her face slackened.

Lester's back aches, his fists clench. He's seen this a hundred times or more before. The loyal loved ones fatigued beyond words, their daily watch a ritual without direction, the fear of admitting the truth, the folly of hope, life languishing, death waiting confidently. He admires

Frankie's clear-eyed view of her husband's prospects, her toughness. He understands Ryan. There is always at least one family member who refuses to see, who refuses to recognize what is staring him dead in the eyes. They call it hope, but it's denial, pure and simple, denial dressed up like a unicorn riding on a rainbow. Silliness, thinks Lester. Worse, weakness.

Lester frowns and shakes his head, wondering what to do, how to help Ryan, how to support Frankie, how to prepare them for the inevitable. The only uncertainty is when it will come. And how.

He picks up the pile of sheets from the bed and dumps them in a bin by the door. He looks back at the mother and son, still as statues. He is about to turn away again when something catches his eye. But he sees nothing. He watches for another moment. What was that? Lester goes up on tiptoes so he can see Mr. Goode's hand more clearly. No, not the one buried in his son's weepy palms, but the other one, lying at his side, trembling. What's happening? Lester goes to the other side of the bed, unnoticed by the Goode's. He studies the busy hand, it is quivering and shaking. He sees something else. Something abnormal. Not in the hand itself, but one finger. The pointer to be exact. It isn't conforming to the whole; it's deviating, rebelling. He takes a little closer look. Yes, Mr. Goode's pointer is raised, raised and straight, like a mole peeking out of its hole, tentative at first, sniffing the air, searching its surroundings. It wags once, side to side, before resting again in Mr. Goode's hand. The finger goes up once more, this time wagging twice before giving up the ghost.

Lester gulps, but doesn't speak.

CHAPTER 20
ROSEMARY

Rosemary pulls into the parking lot beside the high school's football field; the Wolverines are scattered across the gridiron practicing. A smile crosses her lips as she thinks of her days as a skinny cheerleader on what was, for her at least, hallowed ground. She was a high-energy-do-everything-and-anything kid in those days with plans of becoming a writer. She was editor of the Echo, the school's newspaper, and president of Y-Teens. Popular with the boys as well as the girls. Voted most likely to do whatever she wanted to do and, more importantly, succeed. The future looked like a wide open playing field where she would shine.

She watches the boys, their pads balanced precariously on their narrow shoulders as they run through car tires and bounce off blocking dummies. Beyond the field is the back entrance to the high school, near the back corner of the parking lot, a place where she and Alex Calder used to make out. Rosemary feels a tingling sensation just below her navel as she thinks of his naïve searching hands. And those naïve searching years.

She went to community college after graduation with high hopes, but dropped out when she got a job as a receptionist in a car dealership. She was eighteen and she liked having her own money, her own car, her own apartment. She could write when she got older. Older came more hastily than she anticipated. She met her husband-to-be, the boss's son; they married and soon had a child and that was that. She never thought about being a missus or a mommy and suddenly they became her entire identity.

Rosemary spies a slender boy exiting the back entrance of the school. He walks toward the practice field, stopping to light up. She reaches for her purse. Another car pulls into the space beside her, a father, she assumes, there to watch and assess his son's workout. He looks her way and she nods. Then she starts the car and backs up three spaces so she is alone again.

The boy is taking his time, stopping to talk to friends. She can see him gesturing and arching his back in laughter. She strums the steering wheel with her fingers.

She was promoted twice at the dealership, eventually taking some classes in accounting so she could work on the books. In the meantime, her father-in-law retired and her husband took the reins. Life was not exciting but it was agreeable. They didn't want for anything and whenever the walls of her life started closing in, her husband would book a trip to New York or a cruise to the Caribbean. She'd return refreshed, not remembering how numbing things had been.

He is heading her way again, backpack slung over one shoulder, earbuds dangling.

She'd still be working at the dealership had it not been for the fall. "Fall" made it sound more dramatic, more horrifying, than it was. In fact, at first she didn't think anything of it. She was leaving the dealership when her right foot slipped off the curb. She fell like dead weight on her heel and then toppled to the ground. A couple of sales guys came to her rescue. More than anything else, she felt embarrassed. As she thinks back on it now, she can't remember if she felt any pain at that point. The next morning she couldn't get out of bed. In the ensuing weeks she wondered if her life was changing, perhaps irreparably. Ibuprofen and Tylenol first. But numbness and pain and difficulty walking led to an MRI which led to back surgery which was almost successful. Except for the pain. Her husband said, "You can walk, at least," whenever she complained.

The boy is standing by the fence, fingers hooked on the chain link, watching some friends on the field. All part of the process, she thinks. Keep it casual. Rosemary opens her purse and searches for her wallet. She checks her mirrors and checks the man in the car in front of her. His eyes are glued to the field.

Soon the boy starts walking again, slowly, as if directionless. He rounds the far end of the field and then crosses the lot. He scans the area as he pulls up his jeans and sweeps his fingers through his brown hair. She almost laughs at his posturing. He grins ear to ear and waves at her, like he might wave to his mother or the mother of a best friend. He quickens his pace. Rosemary lowers the passenger side window as he leans in on his elbows.

"How's it going, beautiful?"

"Fine, Jordy. How are you doing?" Rosemary turns sideways in her seat, her leg perched against the console, her arm resting on the wheel. Jordy gets in. "How are the college applications going?"

"Jesus," says Jordy. "If I have to write another fuckin' essay. I mean there's only so much you can make up, you know what I mean?"

Rosemary laughs and leans back against the door. There is a deliciousness to these rendezvous that is undeniable. "Don't drop the ball, young man."

"You're not gonna 'young man' me, are you? Not after all we've meant to each other." The man in the car is pulling away so Jordy opens the door and gets in. He has narrow set blue eyes, short sketchy hair, and a gapped tooth easy smile. She liked him from the moment she met him, a goofy ninth-grader at the time in need of some tutoring. "Who needs this shit," he said about math, which was why she started working with him.

"Look, Jordy, what have I always told you?"

"I know, I know, 'buckle down'." The wide-eyed little boy returns for a moment. She reaches for his hand.

"So, how's the senior project going? Submit your proposal?" He doesn't answer at first, instead looking out the window at the team. "Jordy?"

"I still got a week."

"Got an idea?" Rosemary says this with eager eyes and an expectant grin, like a kindergarten teacher.

"Don't do this, okay? I'm not your student anymore. Right? I mean, we dropped that, like, forever ago, once you, well, you know what I mean, right? So let's not do this teacher-student shit." Jordy's face goes hard, his eyes darkening.

"Okay." Rosemary removes her hand and sits up straight.

"You didn't need to take your hand away, y'know. You can put your hand wherever you want." Rosemary glares through the windshield. "Okay, Okay, I'm sorry. I know you don't like that, right?"

Rosemary turns, her face softer. "You're a kid, Jordy. Why are you doing this? It could completely mess up your future—"

"Jesus, don't preach to me. What am *I* doin'? What are *you* doing? You're the one who came to me, remember? First a little weed, then some oxy—"

"Okay. Stop."

"Whatever."

Rosemary closes her eyes and tries to breathe evenly. She places her forehead on the wheel.

Jordy taps her shoulder. "Are we doing business today or are we not doing business today?"

Rosemary doesn't move. "Okay, yeah, we're doing business." She feels waves of nausea as she raises her head and looks at the now empty football field. There aren't any other cars in the lot. No other mothers sitting with teenaged boys making deals. She can feel perspiration across her lower back.

Jordy drops his backpack onto the floor and unzips the top. He digs into a side pocket and comes out with a small Ziploc baggie with a half dozen blue ovals inside. He holds it out, but when she reaches, he pulls it back.

"Now, let me explain. I'm bringing you a mix and match bag, a bag of potpourri." He wiggles it in front of her eyes. Rosemary looks away. "They all look alike, don't they?" He holds it close to his face and sniffs. "Look at me now. I'm telling you, this is real. This is good. I should know. I never done you wrong, have I?" He waits until she shakes her head.

"These little azure footballs all look alike, don't they? But here's the beauty part. Some are oxy and some are H. And I know how much you like mixes. You can take these home and put them in a cute little gold pill box or an old prescription bottle, doesn't matter, no one will know. And I'm tellin' you, it kicks faster if you crush and snort or if you shoot."

Rosemary's shoulders are bent, her back slumped, her head hanging.

"Yeah, I know, you're not a fan. No tracks, no left over dust, I get it. Just take the damn pills then, and wait. It'll catch you. I guarantee."

Jordy tosses the bag into her lap as she rifles through her purse. "Ten percent off today." Rosemary thanks him but doesn't look up. This appointment is going like all the others. By the end, she doesn't look at him any longer. More to the point, she doesn't want to feel his eyes on her.

"About that senior project," says Jordy.

Rosemary reaches for the crumpled envelope buried at the bottom of her purse. She pulls it out and lays it on the passenger seat beside Jordy.

"Thanks," he says. "Okay, so the project. I'm not sure what to do. It's got to be some kind of community thing. Somethin' you do, like an event thing, and then write it up." He pauses, biting his lip as a glint shows in his eyes. "Don't laugh, but I was thinkin', like, of hooking up with that Sergeant Crawford guy; you know, the cop that runs the Dare Program. I loved him when he used to come to health class in middle school. Hilarious, imitating junkies and alcoholics, I mean he killed. Fuck, we made a float for the fireman's parade; good times."

Rosemary grabs the bag with one hand like it's gold at the end of the rainbow. She picks some hair that is stuck to her forehead. "Jordy —"

"I know, you gotta bounce."

"Jordy, be careful. You got your whole life —"

"Ahead of me. I know. Crawford pounded our heads with that all the time. Good man."

Rosemary looks at Jordy's hands. Not a wrinkle, not a mark. His face, as well. Same as his life. She was Jordy once.

"Y'know, Rosemary, since it feels like we're having a moment here, I wanna to tell you something I've kept to myself since the first time I met you at the library." He clears his throat and turns to face her. "You know what a MILF is, right?"

"I think I do —"

"Don't be all kinds of offended, but it means a 'mother I'd like to fuck'. That's how I've always thought about you." There is pride in his glowing face. "That's a compliment. I gave you a compliment." Rosemary's face is as blank as the empty scoreboard at the end of the field. "Aren't you gonna thank me? You're hot, y'know?"

Rosemary opens the bag and examines its contents, a half dozen blue tabs. This is part of the cost, she thinks. Her mouth opens a crack. "Thank you."

Jordy grabs her jaw and pulls her face to his. He presses his lips to her mouth, thrusting his tongue between her gritted teeth. Then again. Rosemary holds her breath and doesn't move.

"You got no idea how many times I've laid awake at night, like hard as a rock, thinking about my tongue in your mouth." His mouth hangs open like a child with a stuffy nose. "I guess I can cross that sucker off the bucket list. Thank you, Rosemary, I mean it. Maybe next time we can —"

"I have to go." Rosemary tries to smile, but her cheeks are too heavy. She presses the ignition and revs the engine. It's getting dark now and for a moment she is afraid. She nods at Jordy who finally opens the car door.

"Next time maybe we can get a little busy, y'know?"

"Bye, Jordan." She pulls away briskly as the passenger side door slams shut. She looks in the rear view mirror. Jordy already has his earbuds in. He tosses his backpack over one shoulder and walks away.

The rush hour traffic is dense. Rosemary steers with one hand, the other clutching her stomach, which now is as tight as a closed fist. Her face in the rearview mirror, devoid of makeup, looks homeless and raw, her hair like straw. The pain in her gut is taking over. She has to stop doing this. Has to. Just not today. Today she needs relief; today she needs to feel normal again. Then, once she is back to herself, she'll tackle this thing. She wipes her nose and eyes on the sleeve of her maize and blue striped cashmere pullover.

Horns blare as cars sweep by, angry drivers chomping at her. She looks at her speedometer, thirty-five. How to get across three lanes before the next exit. She drifts and drifts, turn signal flashing, apology on her face as drivers swerve to avoid her. Once at the exit, she turns onto Monroe Ave., and then into the Park Ave. neighborhood. On East she parks near the Frank Lloyd Wright house she so admires. She sits quietly, sheltered under a towering silver-leafed linden. Her cell squawks once, then twice but she declines both times.

Rosemary holds the bag in her lap. She looks ahead and behind; no one is on the darkened street. She shakes one tab into the palm of her hand. Her breathing steadies. She pops it into her mouth and swallows. She reclines her seat to let her body melt. She zips the baggie closed, but then thinks better of it. She reopens it and tilts it to her mouth, her tongue reaching for one more blue. She lays the baggie on the console beside her, leans back and closes her eyes.

Soon a deep, warm fog settles over her, swaddling her in chenille. Her eyelids hover and close. The world recedes like a tiny marble rolling into a yawning black hole. Every muscle, every nerve, every molecule falls into slumber. Nothing matters. How could it. All that's left is warmth and peace, perfection. She smiles. It's all good, she thinks. I'm fine. Couldn't be better.

Then she's gone. When she awakens, still in a haze, Rosemary thinks of Frankie. Poor Frankie with a half-dead husband. She hasn't seen her in days. That claustrophobic sterile room that smells of rot. Impossible. She's not going to make it to the hospital tonight either. No way. She calls. "Honey, I'm so sorry but I've been sick…yes, yes, that flu…I'm sure I'm contagious and you certainly don't need that…" Frankie understands. She always does.

Rosemary looks at the baggie again. Four left. She shouldn't have taken two. Was she too abrupt with Jordy? Did she make him angry? Hurt his feelings? Should she have played more? Will things be okay?

CHAPTER 21
RYAN GOODE

More than feeling hopeful, Ryan is committed to the *idea* of hope, like people are unquestioningly committed to their political parties no matter how foolhardy. Recently, he put a slip of paper on his nightstand that says, "Smile!" And that's what he does from morning til night, no matter how he actually feels. He can't expose his father to less than his complete and abiding optimism.

When the day ends and he is no longer on display, though, his thoughts race and then morph into a web of horrors; his father suffocating under the deadweight of medical technology; his baby unable to get out of the womb; the ice cream parlor tanking; everyone leaving him. Unable to change the channel on his thoughts, Ryan gets up each night and goes to the adjoining bedroom, turns on the light, watches TV and tries to sort through the clutter in his mind. And then put it to the curb.

Worse than these night time conjurings is his fear of what they suggest about him. That he is losing his confidence, that his certainty is fading, evaporating under the daily accumulation of contrary evidence. His eyes, so much clearer now than his heart, are creating doubt where staunch conviction had predominated.

Jenna is asleep when Ryan finally gets out of bed. He stands over her, watching her breathe. He is relieved that she is still, tranquil, that her face is placid, almost serene. She is free of her worries for now, *their* worries, about the baby. It is best that she sleep as long as possible, best that she stow away her anxieties. Ryan reaches for the quilt and pulls it over her shoulder.

He tries to compartmentalize his own fears about the baby and his father so that they don't merge and crush his spirit entirely. He commiserates with Jenna about the baby and what may lie ahead, but he keeps his own substantial anxieties at arm's length. His father needs his undivided attention; his father needs him to stay positive.

He kisses his palm and lays it on her hair.

Ryan dresses in the guest bathroom, revs up the Keurig, fills his travel mug and leaves. Instead of going to Curly's or the hospital, he heads to his parents' home.

Ryan, arms resting on the roof of his car, looks down the street, tar drizzled on its many cracks, great sycamore arms shading the sidewalks. He loves the house with its wood and stone exterior, the layered geometry of the front, the broad pillared porch, deep and protective. Ryan never understood why his father added a three season porch on the back, when the front provided the best possible view of life on the street.

Visitors often commented on how much larger the house seemed once they entered. Ryan agrees as he stands in the foyer. The ten-foot ceilings and milled beams, like railroad tracks stretching across an empty landscape, make the modest space seem expansive. The stone fireplace, charcoal-stained, deep as a cave, was the perfect place to hide when hiding was all he could think to do as a boy. The soft curve of the staircase, white spindles, like piano keys, leading to more open space. The kitchen, where they lived, checkerboard tile, granite counter tops, stainless refrigerator, double sink, oak table with four chairs.

"Mom!" Ryan calls, to make sure she isn't home. She told him she was going to her shop this morning and then to the hospital in the afternoon. She has inventory to deal with, pricing questions, spring fashion decisions.

Ryan goes into the living room and opens the grandfather clock. Its weights hang limp on the floor of the cabinet. He pulls the cranky chains, returning them to their proper places and nudges the pendulum into its rhythm. He watches the golden pendulum, its soothing arc, but then feels an anxious quickening in his chest at the thought of time moving on.

He breathes deep the smell of memories, his father's aftershave and his mother's perfume, coffee and toast and eggs, cinnamon and hot chocolate, leather and laundry, flowers picked from the garden. He noticed none of this when he was growing up, yet his senses stored them all and spritzed them into his memory when he most needed it.

As he thinks of his father lying, nearly lifeless, in the hospital, this warm nostalgia fades and the air turns chill as a mausoleum, stale and musty. He runs his fingers through his hair. There must be something, he thinks, something that will bring his father back, that will awaken him, that will shake him out of his deadly slumber. But what?

His father wasn't one to keep sports memorabilia or trinkets or vacation souvenirs. He never saw the point of clutter. Nevertheless, Ryan gravitates to his father's office in the basement, its knotty pine walls and threadbare carpeting, his steel desk and slumpy chair, both bought at a high school furniture auction; an easy chair and a soft, dusty sofa that frame the first coffee table his parents had ever purchased. Ryan runs his finger across the top of a filing cabinet, dust bunching under his nail. He never saw the point of furniture polish either. "Jesus, Dad."

Ryan plunks down at his father's desk and leans back in the chair. On the wall are pictures of their various trips to Disney World in which Mickey and Goofy figure prominently; there is also the obligatory photo of them plunging over the waterfall at Splash Mountain, their faces contorted in mock terror. Ryan rocks and smiles and thinks of the humungous turkey leg he ate and then threw up. There is a map of the U.S.A, a pin in every state they have visited, Alaska being the most distant. A couple of commendations from work. A pencil holder Ryan made in third grade. Desk lamp. Bust of Lincoln from their trip to Gettysburg. Pencil sharpener, paper clips in a tray, black Bic pens with no tops, and a stapler minus staples.

Nothing with the sentimental power to bring his father back from a coma. Ryan crosses his arms. He leans forward and pulls the handle on the side drawer of the desk. Under some paper and envelopes he finds a stuffed polar bear, about six inches tall sitting back on its haunches, a worn, twisted red ribbon around its neck. Ryan's eyebrows join and the corner of his mouth puckers. "What's this?" He holds the bear in front of his face, studying the button eyes. He balances it on the desktop and smiles. He must have been six, maybe seven. For Valentine's Day his father had bought him and his mother stuffed animals and candy. He remembers that he was so bereft over his father not getting anything that his mother took him to the pharmacy where he bought this polar bear. His father, rarely at a loss for words, was speechless. He hugged Ryan over and over.

"Why did you keep this?" Ryan wonders. He fondles it and smells it and rubs the coarsened fur to his face. "This may be just the thing."

Feeling confident, Ryan keeps searching for more, this time diving into the drawer on the opposite side. He shuffles through the papers and a few old phone books, piling them onto the floor. At the bottom he finds three leather-bound notebooks, brown and cracked. He rubs the first notebook with his thumbs and then unties the strap. He flips the lined pages. Nothing. "Hm." He opens it wider and flips through it again, then closes it and reties the strap. He does the same with notebook number two with the same results. "What were you doing with these?" Maybe he intended them as gifts, hid them away for some long ago Christmas and then forgot about them.

The third journal is tied shut with a knot, rather than a bow. He picks the knot and lays the book open on the desk. The pages are covered with his father's steady block printing. Sometimes in pen, just as often in pencil. Each dated, beginning in 1998. Ryan was in grade school. There were yearlong gaps when he didn't write a thing and then clusters of entries over short periods of time, a matter of weeks or months.

At first Ryan is hesitant to read his father's scribbling. Are there things he might have confessed in a heated moment that didn't represent his dad's true sentiments? Painful, yet fleeting grievances; long forgotten disappointments; pin prick injustices. Things that mattered then but eventually didn't matter at all.

But there is something magnetic about this find, making it impossible for Ryan to turn away. He opens to the first page.

Oct. 23, 1998 Cold today. Will rake leaves. Ryan to dentist.
Dec. 26 Christmas came and went. Ryan happy. New bike. Tree beautiful. No snow. Frankie returning gifts. Nap ahead.

Ryan reads several more scant notes, baffled. He skips ahead a few pages, now in the early 2000s.

May 12 Frankie's place opened. Yay.
June 30 Hot hot hot. Mowed the lawn. Drove to the lake. Had dinner.
August 16 Slept late. Cool on the porch. A deer. Coffee, two cups.

Ryan figures the polar bear will have to do. He leafs ahead to a page that is dog-eared.

April 13, 2008 Frankie going to Vegas soon. See C?

He notices that several other pages are folded, as well.

November 24, 2008 C. Again.
April 15, 2009 A day with C.
July 26, 2009 Time with C today?

Who is C? Ryan checks each entry for identifying information, a full name, a phone number, anything. No luck. Then he notices that each marked page is numbered in pencil under the dog-ear— 1, 2, 3... 8. There are eight entries about C. What was dad up to? He racked his brain for any Cs his father might know. There is Chester at the pharmacy; Chuck at the bake shop; Connie at Dad's work; Chris, the mail carrier; Chloe, a friend of Jenna's that Dad may have met at the wedding. That's about it.

Connie at Dad's work. What does he know about Connie-at-Dad's-work? Not much. Ryan met her years ago at a work function at Charlotte Beach. He must have been twelve, thirteen. Hot dogs and baked beans and volleyball on the beach. Couldn't swim because of algae plumes, but at least it didn't smell. He remembers getting so sunburned that he threw up three times later that night. Nevertheless, he recalls the day fondly. His memories of Connie, though, are vague at best.

He closes his eyes and tries to remember what she looked like. He could see a pair of Bermuda shorts and a shell, pink maybe, but no face, no hair, nothing to distinguish her. Just a female blob. Were she and his dad close? Hard to believe. Dad wasn't a flirt. At least not in Ryan's childhood memory. Maybe it's not Connie at all. But he can't shake her loose. Why did his father write 'C' instead of a name? What was he trying to hide? What was it about 'C' that he didn't want anyone else to know about?

Ryan leans back in his father's chair, literally shaking his head to rid it of these embarrassing thoughts. Nevertheless, it seems odd that his father would have these notebooks, since he wasn't one to write down anything. These notations were obviously important. Why else dog-ear the pages and number the entries? And then leave them at the bottom of his desk drawer? Ryan felt his stomach turning. Could there have been someone else? He hates himself for even thinking this.

In a panic, he Googles 'infidelity' on his smartphone. Trustify comes up. One-third of all marriages face infidelity, it says. What? That means that about sixty-seven percent don't. Much bigger number, for sure. He sighs. But then again, one in three. Mom and dad, he thinks, and me and Jenna. That's two out of three, the sixty-seven percent part. His nostrils flare as he thinks of a random grouping of three couples sitting around a table having dinner. One of those couples is up to their eyeballs in infidelity. He checks the stats again. Mainly men, those bastards.

Ryan impulsively calls his father's office:

"Yes, my name is Ry...Richard, and I've been in an accident...What?...No, a boat, I mean a motorcycle... yes... What?...Just a little banged up...Thank you...So, could I speak with Connie?" Tony Orlando and Dawn come on, tying a yellow ribbon round the old oak tree. He drums his fingers on the desk. "Yes, I'm here...What's that?...No one by that name...I thought...uh huh...fifteen years...okay, wow," and he hangs up.

He flips through his father's journal and several C-marked entries happened in the last fifteen years. It isn't Connie after all. Whoever she is. A relief. Ryan rocks back in the chair and tries to talk himself down from the cliff. "Stop being ridiculous." Even though he's been agitated about almost everything, this is just plain dumb. His parents have a strong marriage. They are still affectionate. He imagines that, every once in a while when the timing is right and they have the energy, they may still have sex. They are honest with each other, sometimes unsuccessfully, like the time his father told his mother that her legs were sturdy instead of shapely or when she told him he was an idiot for going into the insurance game. Is that enough to jump the marital ship and board a passing vessel? No, he thinks, calming himself, convincing himself that he is becoming overwrought for no reason. It's just the pressure of everything.

Ryan closes the notebook and throws it back into the drawer. He grabs the bear and stands, ready to head for the door as quickly as possible. He hits the first step and stops. He looks at the bear in his hand and then at his father's desk. He goes back to the desk, digs out the notebook and presses it under his arm. "There's got to be an explanation for this."

CHAPTER 22
Jenna Goode

The lackluster hospital corridor with its scuffed linoleum and dour portraits of physicians from long ago gives way to bright orange carpeting and dazzling murals of Big Bird and Doc McStuffin, unicorns and superheroes; kid music sung by kid choruses wafts through the air. The walls are green and yellow and red and every color one can think of, anything to grab a child's attention and make her think, "Gee, hospitals are great!"

Jenna no longer smiles when she reaches this inviting hall; she no longer notices the happy faces painted everywhere. Eyes forward, she hones in on the midwifery practice, opening the door and approaching the check-in. "Hi there!" Everyone is friendly, whether they feel friendly or not. It usually works. She forces a smile in return. "Hi." And finds that it stays, at least for a few minutes, while she sits staring at an article in *Parent Magazine*, entitled "Poop and Pee are Mommy's Friends."

The Big News broke at her last visit. They were glued to the monitor while the technician squirted goo on her abdomen and slid the probe across the mound of her belly, looking for genital specificity. They could hear the rapid popping of a new heart; they could see a film negative profile, a chin, a nose, a tiny fist, an arm reaching, a bum. Ryan and Jenna didn't speak; there weren't any words, just a tangible feeling of lightness in their hearts, their minds, their bodies.

"Look at that," said Mandy. "You're going to have a girl." She was carrying a little girl, something that Jenna, despite her protestations that it didn't matter so long as the baby had ten fingers and ten toes, had hoped for. But their excitement was short-lived.

"While we're here, might as well check everything out." The probe circled and circled and then focused. Mandy, their midwife, always grinning, eyes sparkling, was decidedly non-Mandy-like after the ultrasound revealed a "complication." Complication sounds less concerning than "problem." Complication suggests a hurdle or a hitch, a snag, something that can be overcome with a little thought and some good old elbow grease. Like untying a nasty knot. Problem puts a frown on your face; it confounds and befuddles; it makes you lie awake at night. They are knots tied in knots. Clearly, worse than complication. Unless you are the one bearing that complication, the one with the complication deep inside you. When that's the case, "problem" or "catastrophe" or "shit storm" could just as easily have been used. Because that's what Jenna and Ryan heard.

"You have what's called placenta previa," Mandy said, her smile back, but her brow furrowed. Jenna didn't hear much after that. When they left the office, she was clutching two fetal photos; she gazed at them trying to remember where everything was. At home, they searched Google for an explanation they were prepared to digest. Turns out the placenta, which was feeding their little girl, had slipped down in the uterus and was covering the cervix, which is to say, covering the one available opening for the baby to get out. No exit. A stone rolled over the entrance to the cave. Mandy made it clear that "this is not unusual; many women have it and they do well; the placenta has time to move back." Again, even though countless women have been diagnosed with this condition, getting the diagnosis yourself is unique; not unique as in special or exceptional, but unique as in "this is happening to me."

She wonders what today's visit will bring. "Mrs. Goode!" calls the nurse. Jenna still hesitates when they call her married name, expecting Frankie to appear. "Mrs. Goode!" Jenna follows the nurse into the hall where she is weighed and measured and then delivered to an exam room.

Mandy is a thick-waisted woman with glasses balancing on the end of her nose and greying, disheveled hair pulled into an off-kilter bun. When she enters the room, even the furniture pays attention. Rather than sitting behind the computer hanging from the wall, she pulls up a chair. She slides in close to Jenna, almost knee to knee.

"Well. The latest ultrasound doesn't show any change." She purses her lips and heaves a sigh. "There are two ways to look at this. Either, that's too bad." She tips her head abruptly forward to punctuate this option. "Or — it's good because your placenta hasn't moved any further across your cervix. That's the way we're looking at it." She reaches for Jenna's hand. "I think that's how you and your husband…"

"Ryan."

"…Ryan should look at it too." Mandy squeezes her hand, punctuation again. "Do you have questions for me, Jenna?" She gets up and goes to the chair near the computer, swinging the arm around so it is comfortably in front of her. She signs in.

"That doesn't seem like a good thing to me." Jenna measures Mandy's face and eyes. "I mean, wouldn't it be better if it had moved back or at least was heading that way."

Mandy takes her glasses off and lays them on the keyboard, her chin pointing at Jenna. "Yep, you're absolutely right. That would be the very best. And eventually I'm sure we will reach the 'very best'; I mean it, but right now we're satisfied with everything staying the same, stable; sometimes staying the same is progress; okay?"

"Okay. It's just, what I read, I mean I'm well into my second trimester and nothing is changing."

Mandy's eyebrows form teepees, crinkling her forehead. "That's why we've put you on pelvic rest. No sex, right? Gotta rest all that." Jenna feels like she is in the nurse's office in high school having a terribly awkward abstinence talk with someone who is in the Guinness Book of World Records for never having had you-know-what. "Okay? And no strenuous exercise, lifting, that sort of thing. And that's why we're not taking a hard look down there, no pelvics for the time being." Mandy's eyes stop blinking for emphasis. "No more bleeding, right?"

"Right."

"That's great." Mandy seems to wait for Jenna to echo her sentiment. She gets up from the computer. "Com'ere." Jenna stands as Mandy wraps her arms around her in a kind of bear hug that Jenna hopes won't disrupt her pelvic rest. "It's gonna be okay, honey." With the word 'honey' Jenna begins to cry. "Okay, okay, cry it out, that's good, too."

Jenna composes herself enough to check out, but once in the hallway, she crumbles onto a bench by the elevator, trying to catch her breath. She is sure that Mandy knows what she's talking about; she's seen this "thousands of times" over the years; and "trust me" it will be fine. For Jenna, though, this is not the thousandth time, not the hundredth time, not the tenth time; it is the first time, the very first time. But it is her second try at having a baby. Jenna presses her hand against her belly. "It's okay little girl." The elevator door opens; she enters and pushes the button for six.

When Jenna reaches Gavin's room, she thinks she's made a mistake. The man in the bed has hollow cheeks and a wasted face. His hair is sticky and his mouth is as dry as an old creek bed. She looks at him intently, as his eyes roam, and his hands, useless, twitch. Frankie sits beside the bed, her legs up on a stool, her head propped against the head rest, not asleep, perhaps staring out the window. Jenna's mouth feels parched. She takes a deep breath and knocks on the open door. "Hello?"

Frankie's legs go up as she twists to see who it is. She gives Jenna a half smile, then gets up and walks to her, arms open, and clutches her wordlessly. Jenna wraps her arms around her, and feels Frankie loosening her grip, though she stays in Jenna's arms. Frankie takes one small step back. This time her smile fills her face.

"You've just come from the midwife, right?" Jenna shakes her head. "How is everything going with our little girl?"

Jenna lets her arms slide from Frankie's back and both women sit.

"Jenna's here," she says matter-of-factly to Gavin. "You can talk to him if you want."

"Oh, yes, of course." She leans over the bed so she's in line with Gavin's eyes. "Hi...Dad, it's Jenna." Since her and Ryan's wedding, Gavin has jokingly, but persistently asked her to call him dad, something she feels uncomfortable doing. Nevertheless. "I'm glad...to see you, Dad. You look much...much better than you did...in the beginning of this, I mean." She looks at Frankie who nods her head as if to say, 'Good, keep going'. "You're healing up...Your head, your wound." She grits her teeth and feels her face flush. "I think that Ryan probably told you that we're having a little girl...you're going to have a granddaughter." She draws a breath suddenly as her heart skips. Jenna stands up, her hands still resting on the sidebars of the bed. She glances at Frankie, any evidence of a smile long gone. Jenna steps away from the bed and returns to her chair. She reaches for Frankie's arm.

"How are you doing?"

Frankie purses her lips and rubs one eye. "I'm okay," meaning I don't want to talk about it. She pats Jenna's arm and her demeanor changes. "So, you didn't answer me. What did the midwife say?" She smiles and her cheeks look like ripples on a pond..

Jenna explains what her midwife told her. As she does, Frankie's eyes are wide, unblinking, her attention seeming fierce, unsettling. Jenna shifts in her chair and clears her throat.

"Hm." Frankie's eyes defocus and her mouth screws up to one side briefly. "Well, I'm sure...I know many women have had this same thing...I mean it's not as rare as people think, which is good...You know?...What I'm saying is that it's not some random problem...they know what it is and what to watch for and what to do. Knowing what to do makes all the difference."

"Yes." Jenna leans away from Frankie, all her weight on one arm rest.

Frankie bows her head and then meets Jenna's eyes again. "I'm so sorry you've got to go through this, Jenna. I am. I wish I could take it away and make it smooth and easy so there's nothing to worry about except maybe what wallpaper to buy and what crib is best and...I'm sure things will turn out okay." She lays a hand on Jenna's forearm.

Jenna wants to believe this. She wants to feel confident about what is going to happen. But she doesn't.

There are two hard facts of life; one is that we enter the world; the other is that we leave it. As fate would have it, everyone succeeds at the latter, but not everyone succeeds at the former. Not everyone gets here. Entering is subject to contingencies, to vicissitudes, to exceptional circumstances, that aren't faced when we are dying. Death can be slowed, interrupted, postponed, but it moves relentlessly toward an outcome that is never in doubt. Birth is subject to failure. We can fail at birthing. I have failed at this, she thinks. And I may fail again.

On the pillow beside Gavin's head is the stuffed polar bear that Ryan found in his father's desk. He replaced the shredded ribbon with a bright red bow. From the looks of the bear, he may also have run it through the wash once, maybe twice.

"I was shocked when Ryan showed up with that bear. I didn't remember it at all." Frankie takes the bear in her hands and cradles it in the crook of one arm. "Very sweet." She looks at the bear quizzically. "You know, I think he thinks this'll bring his father back."

Jenna opens her mouth, but doesn't speak. Frankie touches the fur to Gavin's cheek and then to his forehead and then presses it into one of his hands.

"What do you think? Will it bring him back?" She sits the bear on Gavin's chest.

Jenna freezes, her eyes shifting back and forth, searching for the right words. "Well—"

"I'm sorry, honey, that's not a fair question." She leaves the bear perched on Gavin's chest and sits beside Jenna again. The late morning sun shines through the vertical blinds, leaving striped shadows on their faces. She reaches for the Starbuck's coffee on the floor and takes a sip.

"He loves his father."

"Yes. That is true." Frankie sighs and grins. "I guess things are going better at the ice cream parlor. At least that's what he told me." She says this with a question mark in her voice.

"Yes, they are."

"Good."

"He told me that you gave him some advice about marketing or coupons, or something. Anyway, he appreciated it. A lot. I think he just liked being able to talk to you without..."

"Without me criticizing him?"

Jenna swallows hard. "No, that's not what...I think...since he can't talk to his dad...I just think he appreciates the chance to talk with you, that's all."

Frankie's eyes settle on her husband again. Jenna's voice goes up a half octave, announcing a lighter topic. "I guess he's told you about the mystery he's trying to solve."

Frankie responds with puzzlement. "Mystery?"

"Oh." Feeling that she can't retreat, Jenna forces a laugh and folds her hands in her lap. "You know, the diary or journal, I guess." Nothing. "When he found the polar bear in the basement, he also found his dad's old journal. From I'm not sure how many years ago." Frankie's face is blank. "His daily diary?"

"A diary? Gavin? That seems so not-Gavin."

"Well, I guess it didn't have a lot of content, I mean, not much in the way of thoughts and feelings, mostly daily stuff, the weather, errands, that kind of thing."

"Huh, I didn't know he kept anything like that. I know he kept one of those week-at-a-glances, just for appointments. Is that what he found?"

Jenna doesn't like knowing something about Gavin that Frankie doesn't know; makes her feel like an interloper. "I don't think that's what it was. At least Ryan didn't describe it that way. Not a calendar; I don't know for sure."

"Oh. News to me." Frankie's head is cocked sideways but stays steady as she watches Jenna.

"It's probably nothing. You know Ryan, once he gets something in his head…" Frankie's face is granite still. Jenna is unsure whether to say more or let it go.

"And?" Frankie's face cracks into a smile, though her eyes don't.

"Well, Ryan found a bunch of dog-eared pages and on each page Gavin had written the letter 'c', capital 'C', I think, and Ryan is all 'What's this?' or 'What's it mean?'." She laughs without intending to and then crosses her legs and unfolds her hands. When Frankie doesn't say anything, she goes on. "He's, like, obsessed with it for some reason. 'What do you think it means? Who is 'C'? How can I find out?'" Frankie's face matches her pale white shell; she interlaces her fingers and then pulls them apart and rubs her hands on her jeans. "It's nothing, I'm sure. I think Ryan just needs distractions right now and finding his father's diary, or whatever you want to call it, with something in it that's, well, 'mysterious'," (she air-quotes this) "at least to him, I think it…I don't know, it makes him feel like he's accomplishing something by figuring this thing out."

"You're sure he said 'C'?"

CHAPTER 23
FRANKIE GOODE
A VISIT FROM THE CHIEF OF POLICE

"No problem," says Frankie. "Really, don't worry about it; things come up...yes...it's fine...okay...I'll talk to you later."

She stands alone in the living room, the grandfather clock in the corner striking ten. She goes into the kitchen and carefully takes her mother's antique coffee urn from the island and, returning to the living room, places it on the glass coffee table that is surrounded by two rockers and two easy chairs. She goes back to the kitchen for cups and saucers, cream and sweeteners and an assortment of Danish. What was she thinking? Far more than she needs, even if Rosemary hadn't canceled.

The front door opens and cool air sweeps into the foyer along with Ryan. He holds a plate covered in cellophane.

"Morning, Mom."

"Morning, Ryan." Her smile is too big, almost clownish. She pecks him on the cheek. "What's this?"

"Jenna sent along some snickerdoodles."

"Sweet of her." Frankie takes the plate and sets it on the table. "How is she feeling?"

Ryan shrugs. "It's hard to tell. She says she's okay, but she looks...worried, I guess."

Frankie looks around, then realizes there is nothing left for her to do. "I'm sure it will all be fine in the end." She pats Ryan's arm and leads him into the living room where they sit quietly, uncomfortably, waiting for the next guest.

"I hope he's got something for us. Anything. If they've been doing their work, they should have some answers by now."

Frankie nods but declines this invitation to speculate about the police investigation. It has been going on for weeks and weeks; they've spoken with the Chief multiple times, usually to answer his questions, seldom to share information; they watch the news conferences, initially held every few days, but seldom now. In the beginning they read the paper, but soon stopped, finding the articles gossipy at best. Will they ever be able to tell her who did this?

Shortly there's a knock at the door. Chief Rockaway stands at attention, his hat under one arm, his legs parted, one thumb hitched on his belt, his holstered weapon at his side. He wears tinted aviator glasses and has a butch cut, stiff greying moustache and a small scar under his nose, the result of surgery to repair a hair lip Frankie surmises. He grins politely at her; she nods politely at him; with a wave of one arm, she invites the Chief in.

Ryan greets him stiffly as the Chief steps into the living room. Frankie pours him coffee without asking if he wants any. Ryan lifts the cookie plate to the Chief but he declines. The initial pleasantness fades quickly, replaced by dreary silence. A fly lands on the lampshade beside the Chief, circles his head, makes a pass at the Danish and then flies off toward the kitchen. Frankie and Ryan watch as Chief Rockaway takes a sip of his coffee and returns the cup to its saucer.

"Well," he says, exhaling through his nose.

"Who did this to my father?"

He squints at Ryan as if blinded by the suddenness of his question. "That's the question, isn't it?" He slides forward on the lounger and leans on his knees, like a coach in a huddle. Frankie studies him closely, his hands now fidgeting with his hat, his mouth pinched.

"What can you tell us?" says Frankie. "What can you tell us about this…this thing that has been done to my husband…and to us?"

"First of all, ma'am, I want to tell you again how sorry we all are for this tragedy and for everything your husband and you two have had to endure. It's a terrible and senseless thing, that's for sure."

Frankie wants to move quickly past this canned official statement of empathy. "Thank you, I appreciate that."

"Chief Rockaway, please." Ryan is standing now.

Rockaway lays his hat on the coffee table and rubs his knees with his palms. He scratches his moustache with one finger and then smoothes it with his thumb and pointer. Frankie sees what is coming.

She can tell that Chief Rockaway is going to say many things but tell them nothing.

"Where to begin." The Chief raises his eyebrows to both of them. "Let me walk you through this. On the day of the shooting, we secured the area as a crime scene and began our examination of the evidence. We questioned those who were in the building, the witnesses, and those whose cars were parked nearby. Once the projectile was available to us, ballistics' testing showed that it was an M67, in all likelihood from an AK-47. The AK-47 has an effective range of about 400 to 700 yards. We determined from the angle of the entry wound that the bullet came from the west-southwest about a quarter to a half mile away. We canvassed the designated firing area and checked all the registered owners of AKs within a one mile radius. We also talked extensively to members of the gun club. We have opened a Crime Stoppers tip line exclusively dedicated to this action—"

"And?" Ryan is pacing, circling. The sun reflects off the glass table. Chief Rockaway shifts to avoid its glare. Frankie looks at the floor.

"Well, we've had over two hundred calls so far. But no leads. Nothing useful, to be honest. Some people just like to call things in. We didn't find anything suspicious among the AK owners or the gun club members. Our door-to-door efforts haven't..." He glances at Frankie. "I don't know what to tell you ma'am. I've never had something like this. I mean, there's always someone who knows something; but this time, it's like no one knows anything. We're a few months into the investigation and I've still got a team on it, but we don't know where to go next. We need someone to come forward."

"And if they don't?" says Ryan.

"They will; I'm sure of it. Someone will get twitchy about what they know or what someone told them and they'll come forward, if not because it's the right thing to do, at least to get the monkey off their back. The trouble is we don't know how long that will take."

"In the meantime, my father is lying in a hospital bed and he can't do a damn thing; he's just lying there, barely alive; and each day we go and we sit by his side and we watch and wait and we hope and we try to go on with our lives, which is total bullshit, and all you can tell us is that there's nothing, there's nothing to go on." The Chief's eyes are elsewhere. "You know, his first grandchild is on the way; his very first;

and he should be there to enjoy it like any proud grandfather, but chances are he won't be; and the person who's responsible for this is just out there, living life like nothing happened, sitting down to supper every night, going to work or whatever the hell he does all day, with no reason to be concerned, because you...you..."

Ryan kicks the coffee table; cups topple and saucers slide across the oak floor.

"Ryan, please!" Frankie is on her feet glaring at her son. "Sit." Ryan stares at her and then leaves the room. Frankie's mouth falls open. "Ryan, please come back." She watches for a moment, but when he doesn't return, she sits again. "I'm sorry; it's just—"

"No need to apologize. I get it. This's his father and he wants answers even more than I do and I want answers more than anything, I promise you." The Chief's military posture is gone as he slumps back into his chair. He shakes his head back and forth, like a faulty pendulum on a clock that is losing time. "It's like no one shot your husband. I mean, he was shot, but it's like the trigger was pulled and the bullet went out and it happened to find your husband, but it wasn't like it was pointed at him." Frankie stops breathing. "I'm sorry, I know that doesn't make sense, but I've never had a case like this. There's always chatter, there's always noise; and you just have to listen hard to find the right signal, the one that tells you what happened. But this, I mean, there's nothing but silence. I don't get it. The bullet went out, but from where? And it found your husband, but why?"

Frankie's lips part but she can't speak. Her eyes well, but she can't cry. She watches through a blur as Chief Rockaway struggles with his uncertainty and tries to make sense of what happened. Frankie puts a finger to one eye and then a finger to the other, skimming off the moisture. She takes slow deep breaths to recover her voice. "It's possible that you'll never be able to answer these questions, am I right? It's possible that no one will come forward? That this will just be something terrible that happened." The Chief's jowly face sags. "You hear about this all the time. A crime, a case, whatever you want to call it, goes cold and everyone who was involved gets old and retires or dies or something, and it just sits there in a cardboard box somewhere with a number and a name scrawled on it. On TV miracles happen and cold cases, that's what they're called, right, cold cases get solved. But that's why they do those shows— it's so rare that they're ever solved, that they're ever closed. So rare that sponsors will pay millions and people will watch, morbidly curious; I know, I've watched often enough. But that's not the way it is. Most of the time, when something goes cold, it stays cold. They never find the, the…" Frankie feels her insides wobble.

The Chief speaks in a tired monotone, as if reciting well-worn lines from a play. "Mrs. Goode, this is not a cold case; it's an active case and it will stay active as long as possible. We will do everything in our power to find the culprit and bring him to justice. You have my—"

"Perp. That's the word. They're always getting the 'perp' on those cop, those police shows. Right? Perp?"

"Perpetrator, that's correct. Not just on TV…"

"And most of the time the perp is a family member or friend, something like that; at least on TV; cops look everywhere but eventually all roads lead to the husband or wife, someone that was supposed to love them…" Frankie's face is in her hands. Then she gets up suddenly, her back straight. "I'm sorry, Chief, I am. I know you are doing the best that you can. I know that you care about what happens, that you want to catch whoever did this, the 'bad guy', I'm certain of it." She puts her hands on her hips and then lets them slide. "I don't think my husband cares at all; I don't think he has any idea what happened, let alone who did it. He can't possibly care about anything. You know, they have him on a machine that breathes for him. He doesn't even have to try." Chief Rockaway shifts in the easy chair, his weight forward, ready to stand, eager to go. "The technology is amazing, it truly is. Of course, it doesn't matter. It's going to end up a cold case."

The Chief gets up from his chair and reaches out to Frankie, his broad, calloused hand open. Frankie extends her arm, her wrist limp, her fingers half-closed. She doesn't expect his hand to feel warm.

Ryan is standing in the foyer by the open front door. It's raining now, a sideways, gusty, swirling rain that hits you from every possible angle. Chief Rockaway pulls his hat down tight and turns his collar up. Then he exits the door, half-running to his waiting squad car.

Frankie stands in the middle of the living room deciding whether to pick up the saucers or let them lie. She hears the floor creak as Ryan returns. "Mom, it does matter, everything matters. I'm sorry I got…angry…but don't get me wrong, I'm still hopeful about this, about Dad; I am."

Frankie bends over and picks up a saucer. She turns it several times in her hands. It was painted by her grandmother, delicate roses and baby's breath, a garden fence, sunflowers. She tries to remember her grandmother, but she can't. "Okay," she says absently.

CHAPTER 24
GAVIN GOODE

Hospital, this's got to be a hospital, thinks Gavin. People keep touching him in places where no one would touch me, not even Frankie. He can feel 'hospital'. He can smell it, like dead flowers stuck in his nasal cavities. On the other hand, sometimes it's sweet and delicious; anything but hospital; it's people coming and going, and leaving traces floating in the air. He knows he's inhaled Frankie, he's sure of it. When he does, he exhales as fast as he can, pushing the air out, so he can draw her in again, but sometimes she's gone and he's drawing in nothing. Frankie! No one can hear him.

His head bobs, eyes dart, hands thrash and flail like a nozzle-less hose gushing water. Frankie! He doesn't know if he has legs anymore. Something's there, but can he call them legs? Can he call his feet 'feet'? Do any of the names apply?

Sometimes he feels like a bird is pecking him or he's being pricked with a pin, like everything is pinching him. Sometimes he know he's rolling over, turning or being turned this way, then that, but who is out there? Who is doing this to him?

It's like his life's dangling from a wall socket and the power is ebbing and flowing and when it ebbs he says 'Goodbye, goodbye, goodbye', and when it flows he says 'Thank you, thank you, thank you'.

His finger is the only thing that hasn't betrayed him; it is the only thing that works. He's the man on the moon beeping faint signals through this tiny antenna to a universe that isn't paying attention, a universe that thinks there is nothing out there but deep space.

And so the days and nights go for Gavin.

It is 3AM and he is alone except for the hoses and monitors and other paraphernalia, his constant companions, ever working, doing what his body can no longer do. The lights are turned low. The shift is changing and there is talk in the hall, cases being reviewed and passed on.

Staff and family comment routinely now about how good he looks. His wound is healed, gone. His hair is back, covering the surgical scars. His face is still sallow, the color of whey, but that's his normal look now; his old look is gone forever. His son talks to him almost continuously, sometimes beseechingly, then tentatively, like a child not wanting to disturb a napping parent. When Frankie comes alone, after the initial "Good morning, honey, it's me; I love you," she is hushed, soundless for long periods of time, not reading, not surfing, just sitting, staring, sipping coffee, seldom eating. Others come and go nervously, never staying long, never knowing what to say.

When he thinks of that sweet smell, hoping it's Frankie, it's Lester instead. He wears the most delicious cologne, Pivoine Suzhou by Armani. He buys a bottle at Sephora every year, no matter the price; he worships its lingering freshness, its celebration of the Chinese peony, the flower of happiness and grace. A trace on each wrist and behind each ear. He is the angel that Gavin inhales, that Gavin hopes is the one who loves him most.

No one but Lester knows about Gavin's finger. His secret is the most important one of all, a secret that others would covet if they knew, a secret that would transform this vigil into a sacrament, a renewal of hope. Since the first time he saw Gavin pointing his finger, wagging it with purpose, Lester has seen it happen a half dozen times more. Most often at night when everything slows down and quiet descends and anything out of the ordinary stands out. Patients code at night. Fingers move at night. Gavin, like an infant child, is reaching out to the world, not knowing who or what is there, just hoping that someone will see him, that someone will notice his efforts. Lester is that someone. He is the one witnessing this awakening, this resurrection of sorts.

Gavin's finger is his declaration, his pronouncement that he is still a full-fledged member of this world, not the next. He assumes that if Frankie or Ryan or someone notices, they will sound the trumpets and pull him, all of him, back into the world where now only his finger exists. And so, he broadcasts his faint signal, he blinks his light, hoping the power will last, hoping for rescue.

Lester is that witness; he is the one who sees and recognizes. He is the one who is assessing this signal, its strength, its meaning. Is it a harbinger of return? Or is it the final flicker of departure?

He undresses the body. He cleans the body. He dresses it again. He talks with the family. He listens, not just to their words, but their sighs, their groans, their aches. He lingers when others have left. He wonders what is right and what is wrong. Does right and wrong matter? Is compassion a question of right or wrong? He considers. Should he act or should he wait? Is Frankie ready? Ryan is not ready and never will be, not in a year or ten or fifty. He would swoon and never get up again. Frankie, though, she will grieve and be done with it; she will go on and life will open up to her. She will be fine.

Gavin knows nothing of these deliberations, these machinations. He believes that the world wants him back if only it knew he was available. He trusts the world to struggle for him, to tug and pull and heave and hoist so that he can rise again. And so he howls and bellows and wails with one lone finger.

Lester, seeing it move again, reaches for Gavin's finger and holds it softly in his palm. He looks at Frankie, her head back, her eyes closed, and opens his mouth, but doesn't speak.

CHAPTER 25
Frankie Goode

The north corridor of the hospital is a quarter mile long or longer. There are few patients and families here. Mostly administrative and faculty offices, conference rooms and labs, all the bits and pieces that make an academic hospital. Those who walk this corridor seldom speak, seldom make eye contact; their faces are preoccupied and numbed by whatever deadlines and expectations they are facing.

Frankie likes walking down this corridor. She likes not having to speak to anyone; she likes not seeing bereft families holding each other or sleeping in straight-backed chairs; she likes the anonymity; not having to listen to Ryan or chat with Lester or commiserate with Rosemary, who is in the throes of God knows what; she likes not being with Gavin, not having to look at his wasted self, not having to watch him disappearing, not having to keep a stiff upper lip or pretend to be hopeful.

She reaches the intersection where a sign reading *Chapel* points left. Another seventy-five yards and she's standing in front of its unassuming doors. She enters the chapel from the back. There are five or six rows, forty chairs at the most, all of them empty. There are faux-stained glass windows along one wall, lighted from behind and casting a warm rainbow glow across the floor and up the opposite wall. The altar has a modest table draped in white cloth, a Bible on a stand in the middle. Behind it a mosaic of the twenty-third Psalm rises twenty-five feet above the altar, its words weaving down from ceiling to floor. Each time she comes, she reads the Psalm in a whisper to herself. "The Lord is my shepherd, I shall not want..." She has come so often that she can close her eyes and recite it by heart. "...yea though I walk through the valley of the shadow of death..." The feel of the words, more than the words themselves, is soothing, the rhythm calming, the cadence like the beat of an invisible heart.

It was Rev. Lorde's idea to come here. Their first conversation ended in silence, not uncomfortable silence, more a silence of recognition; what she had told him begged for answers that didn't exist. "For now I will think and pray. And what I'd suggest to you is that you visit our chapel, not because you're a religious person, but because it'll give you shelter when you need it." He said it might help her family, as well, but she hadn't told anyone about her visits to the chapel or her talks with Rev. Lorde, which occurred about once a week, sometimes more often. At first, she was afraid he would try to flip her, that he would try to convert her, so he could add another ring to his halo. Her guilt would have given him staggering leverage. But he didn't. He listened, shared his own thoughts, puzzled with her and gave her space.

The only unease she felt came when he prayed at the end of their get-togethers. He would take her hands in his, bow his head and offer his supplications, his thankfulness, sometimes wordlessly. Soon, though, she not only got used to this ritual, she looked forward to it, less because of what he said than the feel of his hands holding hers. She could let them go limp, confident that he would support them. It helped her feel less alone. It gave her legs the strength to walk back to the ICU. It helped her heart continue beating. It made it easier to breathe.

She didn't tell anyone about the chapel or her visits with Rev. Lorde because she didn't want them to misunderstand what she was doing. She didn't want them to think better of her than she deserved. She wasn't one of those people, after all, who read the Bible and went to church, who felt subsumed by a God who looked after her, who might even send a miracle her way in times of need. She was more broken than that. She felt more like a bag of fragments, remnants placed on an altar, not knowing why.

What she's been doing all these years is bad, even though she doesn't think of herself as a bad person. She believes there are two kinds of people, those who are good and do bad things from time to time and those who are bad and do good things from time to time. She is a good person doing something bad; although since she's been doing it for such a long time (and knows it's wrong), she worries that she's crossed a line and has become a bad person masquerading as a good one.

If that's the case, there is no hope for Gavin. She read somewhere that when two people are married for a long time, their bodies start to influence each other; their molecules comingle, like tall grasses and wild daisies in a field, or pushy commuters on a subway. However it takes place, couples shape each other invisibly and (mostly) unintentionally. So a husband and wife are married for sixty years; he dies and she dies a week later. Makes sense.

Can the same be true when someone is unfaithful? Can the lies, the broken trust infect a partner, weaken him in some way, making him more vulnerable, putting him at risk? Can the very darkness of the world seep through the cracks of infidelity, allowing the worst that the world can offer to enter there? All she wanted to do was protect him from a painful truth.

Frankie looks up at the mosaic and starts reading it again. Her face feels weighted and immovable. She closes her eyes. She hears a door swoosh shut behind her and senses someone coming near. He clears his voice and sits down beside her.

"How are you doing today, Mrs. Goode?" Rev. Lorde is wearing a navy blue suit and a pale blue tie. Frankie has never seen him in such formal attire. In fact, she wondered if he even owned a jacket, let alone a suit. Rev. Lorde laughs at the look on her face. "Surprise, I know. Meetings today. I have to look as close to professional as possible."

When someone else enters the chapel, Rev. Lorde suggests they go across the hall to his office. There are floor to ceiling bookshelves on one wall packed with volume after volume of thick musty tomes. Here and there are chalices and photographs of ruins or cathedrals or landscapes. His desk has the requisite pictures of wife, son, daughter, both kids in their teens, although their hairstyles suggest the pictures are dated. Papers, manila folders, and journals are stacked high on either side of a blotter covered with doodles. There is a plaqued photo of a baby in a high chair with a bowl of spaghetti spilled on her head. The caption reads: "This is the day which the Lord hath made; we will rejoice and be glad in it." His leather chair huffs and creeks as he sits.

"Please," he says, gesturing to another leather chair.

Frankie feels she has learned more about Rev. Lorde by looking around his office than she's learned in their many conversations. And yet, she feels she knows him. And trusts him.

She updates him about Gavin; that there has been no change; that Ryan still insists that his father is trying to reach them. She tells him about Jenna and the baby; that things are not going as they had hoped; the placenta is not budging and she is worried about her daughter-in-law. "This just can't happen," she says. "I'm sorry," he says. As for her business, "It seems to run itself," she says with a shrug. "That's good," says Lorde and she agrees, although secretly she wishes it didn't; she wishes she was needed, that there were problems to address, because then there would be something for her to solve. "And your friend, Rosemary is it? You were worried…" Frankie curls the corners of her mouth and raises her eyebrows. "I don't know what's going on with her. She's gotten so unpredictable. Not that she wasn't always a little, I don't know, erratic; maybe that's too strong a word…but it's the only one I can think of." Erratic is too kind a word. Rosemary has called several times with apologies about not visiting or excuses for not doing something she said she would do. Worse, she sounds odd, flaky, off-kilter, like she needs to go into the shop to get her head realigned.

"And you, how are you doing?" This is the pattern they have fallen into. She goes through a laundry list before they get to the real question.

How am I doing? she wonders. When she doesn't feel sad or afraid, she thinks she's doing okay; but then she realizes that it's not that she feels okay, it's more that she doesn't feel anything, that she's enclosed in bubble-wrap, padded against random feelings that might enter or exit. Sometimes she likes the buddle-wrap because feeling nothing is such a relief. Other times, she's surprised that no one hears her screaming inside at the top of her lungs, terrified by the never-ending nature of what's happening; that this will be her life: get up, go to the hospital, watch Gavin, watch Gavin, watch Gavin, stop by the dress shop for a few minutes, go home, go to bed but don't sleep, try to remember the last time you ate, get up, do it again. The days are no longer differentiated; they no longer need names.

Frankie takes a deep breath. Her shoulders ache. "I talked to him."

"To…"

"Conner." She called him to explain that she had to cancel plans for the next convention, that something unexpected had come up. That was weeks ago. But she didn't tell him about Gavin. He was his usual not-a-care-in-the-world Conner; didn't ask what was going on. "No problem.

Next time." Easy-peezy. He didn't attach, at least not in the beginning. He seemed to live in a worry-free zone, unlike Gavin. She never had to take care of him, or watch out for him. He was self-sufficient. A dreamer, wanting her to live his dreams. To her, it all felt like play, pure and simple.

Despite their long history, she never got to know Conner any better than she had known him when they were colleagues. The relationship, such as it was, never deepened, never broadened. Sometimes they talked about their lives, but usually they ordered in and then went to bed. It felt good. Very.

In the aftermath, though, it always hurt. She fought tears for days and struggled not to tell Gavin, which would have crushed him. And her. She fought just as hard to overcome the self-hatred that clung to her like a bacteria. After a few weeks she would regain her balance, put the whole thing on a shelf in her mind, and go on, as if it were over, as if she had put it behind her. And then it would happen again. It became life.

"You talked to him? May I ask what you told him?" Sometimes Rev. Lorde's face looked like a contour map, usually when all his feelings merged.

"I told him everything."

When she called him more recently, Conner seemed genuinely stunned to hear what had happened to Gavin. He stammered and coughed and his voice cracked several times. Hearing his sadness fertilized her own. Tears engulfed her throat and made it impossible to speak. She had to hang up. He called her back almost immediately, but she didn't answer. A half hour later, she called him.

"Was it as difficult as it sounds?"

When he answered, she could tell he knew what was coming next. Frankie was surprised that it was easy. Ending, that is. They spoke for little more than a moment. After she hung up the phone, she sat at the kitchen table for a long while. The refrigerator hummed and the sound of wrens at the birdfeeder outside fluttered into the room. She was disappointed that she didn't feel anything. Despite how physically vulnerable she had been with him, she realized that there had been little affection and even less intimacy between them. She struggled to find a good explanation for what had happened, what she had done. Failing that, she opened the refrigerator and uncorked a bottle of pinot grigio and filled a delicately stemmed glass.

"I think you did the right thing." Rev. Lorde's face looks relaxed; his eyes are steady and kind. "I do."

"Then why don't I feel any better?" Frankie looks past Rev. Lorde at a painting on the wall behind him. Her eyes fall on a single contorted face in the print of *Guernica*, head thrown back, mouth agape, eyes beseeching. She feels ashamed of her own pain.

"My son found some journals or notebooks that my husband kept."

She explained that Jenna had been the one to tell her about this first. A few weeks later Ryan broached the subject. And when he told her about the mysterious dog-eared pages and the suspicious C notations, her stomach knotted and then began to roll as if she were weightless, her insides floating with nausea. She showed puzzlement, but no curiosity, wanting her lack of interest to stem the tide of Ryan's obsession. "Who knows? It was so long ago that your father probably wouldn't even remember." When Ryan hinted that his father might have been, well, involved with someone, Frankie couldn't help herself. She burst with anger. "What are you saying? How dare you even suggest such a thing! Your father, goddammit, you'll never find another man as loyal, as faithful, as loving as your father! You should hope to be as good as your father! What are you thinking? You of all people, Ryan. We loved each other! We love each other!" Ryan was so taken aback that he almost fell over the chair behind him. He cowered, hands under his chin, shame dragging down the corners of his mouth.

In the ensuing weeks, they didn't mention it again. They tiptoed around each other, at first, being polite, respectful, Ryan earning his way back into her fold. She extended herself to him, not wanting him to suffer for her duplicity.

"There is a chance that Gavin knew or at least suspected." Frankie's head is bowed. She hears Rev. Lorde shifting in his chair. He settles but doesn't say anything. Now he must see what a terrible person I am, she thinks.

"Mrs. Goode, I'm not sure what to say. You're tied in so many knots. I don't know, they must be strangling you."

"Maybe that's okay. Maybe I should be strangling. Maybe I should be the one—"

"Stop. This doesn't accomplish anything. For you or your husband."

Frankie white-knuckles the arms of the chair, digging her nails into the leather. "Look, you don't seem to get it. I betrayed my husband, the one person who has loved me more than anything. There's no coming back from that."

"Sometimes a thing is done and it can't be undone; it's just there and it won't go away and you have to find some way to live with it.....you have to say, 'this was a piece of the whole...but it wasn't the whole'." Rev. Lorde turns his head, one hand on the side of his face, then turns back. "Look, you can't let your guilt get in the way of your love for Gavin. That would destroy everything."

Frankie shakes her head as if to loosen her thoughts. "I don't know what you're saying. Just forget it all?"

"No, that's not what I'm saying. There's no forgetting. But there is forgiving."

"Really? What am I supposed to tell my husband, 'Honey, I've been having an affair, but don't worry, God forgives me?' What good will that do?"

Rev. Lorde's chair creeks as he leans forward placing both palms on his table. "You're right, God's forgiveness isn't the issue. It's your own."

"Forgive myself."

"Yes."

"Well, I can't do that."

"Why?"

Frankie's can't feel her heart. "I respect Gavin too much to just forgive myself."

CHAPTER 26
RYAN GOODE

Ryan hand packs a pint of Bear Prints. He presses the hardened ice cream into the container with the back of his scoop, studies it and decides he can get one more scoop in. He bends over the cooler and digs deep, coming up with a skyscraper of vanilla ice cream filled with fudge swirls and mini-peanut butter cups, his father's favorite. He presses it into the rest of the ice cream, smooths the top and crams a lid onto the carton. He shakes out a bag, drops the ice cream in, adds two spoons and some Curly's napkins, then folds the top closed.

Ryan believes that his father is responding to the stuffed bear. He can't say exactly how, but there's a difference. It might be his father's head. It always seems to be turned toward the bear, like he senses it's there. Or his eyes. When Ryan holds the bear to his father's cheek, his eyes don't shuttle back and forth quite as much. Instead they quiver, like he's trying to hold them steady because he feels something nearby.

He's told Lester about these observations but Lester doesn't appear to take much stock in them. He doesn't disagree, at least not outwardly; it's more that he seems unmoved, unconcerned, as if he's listening to a child explaining that the only reason clouds move is because the earth is rotating.

Ryan is undeterred by skepticism. Even his own. There is no room for doubt, he tells himself each day. There is no room for doubt when life is in the balance. If there is any hint that his father may come back, may live, then conviction is the only appropriate attitude.

He remains confused by C and what it means. Jenna was befuddled by it and his mother became enraged that he hinted at his father being unfaithful. For days afterward they steered clear of each other even when they were in the same room. But, to his surprise, his mother's position mollified. She talked to him, asked his opinion about his father, seemed appreciative of what he thought, and expressed support for him and Jenna. He didn't understand this change but he liked it. Time also minimized the significance of C. Whatever it was, it was gone. And even if it had been *something*, how could it possibly matter now?

He is pleased when the one person he finds in his father's room is his father. He stands over him for a moment, watching his eyes. He takes his hand and moves close to his father's ear. "Hi, Dad, it's me."

When this ordeal began, he spoke to his father loudly and distinctly, like an amateur actor going on stage for the first time. He always identified himself — "This is your son, Ryan." Then he'd talk about the weather, something he noticed other loved ones doing. "Colder than usual today, Dad, but it's supposed to warm up tomorrow; the weekend should be beautiful." Or he'd express consolation and encouragement — "I'm so sorry that you're going through this, Dad, but you're kicking this thing's ass, I'm telling you; you look a little better every day; just hang in there." Also something he heard others saying.

Everyone was on the same Titanic, playing music as fast as they could, no matter how much the deck swayed. He developed nodding acquaintanceships with members of other families on the unit. They seldom talked about the problems of their loved ones. Instead they talked about the weather. In time they would disappear with their loved ones, transferred to other floors, nursing homes, rehab facilities, or to funeral homes and crematoria.

Ryan no longer feels awkward here. This is his home away from home, the place he goes to be near his dad, much like getting together at a coffee shop before the accident. As before, he comes to ask advice and just talk for talking sake. His father's responses are different than they were, more nuanced he liked to think, more subtle, more demanding of Ryan's capacity to listen and to decipher and to understand.

"Dad, I brought you something pretty cool today." Ryan takes the ice cream from the bag and pries the top off. He holds it under his father's nose. "Can you smell it, Dad? I think you can. Yeah, it's your favorite. We've eaten a lot of this stuff together, haven't we?" Ryan digs in with one of the spoons and closes his eyes as he savors the flavor. "Wow. The vanilla is like sweet cream, isn't it? And the dark chocolate, like bark off a tree." He presses the ice cream between his tongue and the roof of his mouth and closes his eyes again. "God, that's good." He takes another spoonful. "I know. The peanut butter bits are your favorite. Remember you use to add peanut butter cups when you thought they were missing." Ryan chuckles.

He watches for a response from his father. When he doesn't see anything, his face turns bleak, like it's 6AM on any Monday morning. "Here, let's try this." He pulls the other spoon from the bag and puts a little ice cream on the tip. Then he dabs his father's lips. "There you go." The ice cream melts over his lower lip and onto his chin. Ryan saves it with the spoon and puts it back on his father's lip, this time tipping some into his mouth.

"Is there any for me?" Lester stands at the door, a disapproving grin on his face. "Gotta be careful; your dad's not swallowing. He could choke." Lester's broad forehead is pink, his eyebrows teepee-ed.

Ryan drops the spoon onto his father's chest, removes it and wipes the linen with a napkin.

"No need, I'll be changing the bed anyway."

"I was just trying to...I think Dad needs different stimulation, you know what I mean. Things that are familiar to him. Stuff that might bring him back. Dr. Azziz seemed to think this might be a good idea." Ryan caps the ice cream carton, wipes his father's mouth and puts everything back into the bag. "I just think that if we don't do something, he's going to stay wherever he is; that's he's going..." Ryan waves the back of his hand at his father, unsure whether to say anything more for fear of hurting him.

"Well. I've said from the beginning that hope is our ally."

"Yes."

Lester strides to the bedside and turns Gavin on his side. He pulls the sheet away from the mattress. "If doing these things makes you hopeful, then I'm all for it." He slides by Ryan and rolls Gavin the other way.

Ryan steps back as Lester blankets the bed. "Can I help?"

"That's not necessary. Why don't you just sit and relax a minute."

Ryan doesn't sit. He goes to the window where he can observe Lester. Something is different. In the beginning, Lester would speak to his father, explaining everything he did. When he turned him, Lester would hold his father's arm and move him quietly, as if not wanting to awaken a baby. He would smooth the sheet under his father's chin and make sure his head was up on the pillow, not tilting to the side where his neck might knot up. He would cover his feet with a blanket. And his eyes, his eyes were always on his father, checking for reactions, not wanting to cause discomfort or pain.

Now he moved with the robotic swiftness and efficiency of a skilled assembly line worker. It could have been anyone in the bed. Or anything.

"You don't think he's alive, do you?" Ryan's voice is neither confrontational nor accusatory. It is plaintive.

"What?"

"My dad. You don't think he's alive."

"Of course, he's alive. His vitals are steady, heart rate, blood pressure —"

"No, I get that. The machines are still running. They're telling you things, whatever, but that's not the same as being alive."

"For now, it's the same thing as being alive; they're the only thing we have to go on." Lester turns back to Gavin. He adds a pillow as he checks a monitor and adjusts a drip.

Ryan, in his wrinkled denims, untucked plaid shirt and scuffed Nikes, looks like a little boy waiting for the bus, wondering if it will ever come. "You don't get it. All of this, this stuff, is only taking care of his shell, his outsides."

Lester stops what he's doing, sits on the edge of Gavin's bed and cocks his head in Ryan's direction.

"You know what I mean. Don't get me wrong, it's important, but it's not my dad. He's inside there." Ryan heads to his father's side and places his hand on his head. "Here's where he's at. And the machines can't see him in there. They can't. He's stuck."

Lester sighs. "Like I said, hope is —"

"No, I'm not talking about hope; I'm not talking about wishes or maybes or crossed fingers. I'm talking about what's for real. I know my father and he's more alive than any of these monitors can tell. This isn't about medicine; it isn't about stuff you can measure; things you can find in blood; this is bigger than that." Ryan skids to the end of his reasoning and in the quiet that follows he senses that what he is saying has all the gravity of smoke.

Lester stands and reaches out to Ryan, his hand on Ryan's arm. "Ryan, look, everything you just said is, well, it's hope. It's the stuff you can't see…"

He continues to talk, his voice steady and rhythmic and soothing, but Ryan isn't listening. He's staring at his father; actually not at his father but his father's left hand; and not at his whole hand but his finger, his pointer, to be exact, as it rises stiffly. It doesn't flop or wiggle or flick as if it was being hit by random jolts of electricity. Instead it rises intentionally, cautiously, purposefully. And it isn't rising on its own. It is rising because someone is making it rise.

Ryan catches Lester's eye and points at his father. "What's that?"

CHAPTER 27
MR. HILLMAN AND CHRISTOPHER

Mr. Hillman sits in the driver's seat, Christopher at his side. He struggles for the keys that are buried deep in his pocket. Ever since the police canvassed the neighborhood, Mr. Hillman has been on edge. He was embarrassed to have his son watch him lie to the officer who came to their door. "No, officer, we don't have any guns in our house; it's just too dangerous." He had put his arm around Christopher's shoulder as he said this. Christopher had pulled away and gone to his room.

Maybe the canal would work, Hillman thinks, but then he remembers that the state empties it every fall. It would be easy for workers to see an AK-47 in the muck along with the usual shopping carts and occasional cars. He thinks of the Genesee River gorge where the water spills over steep falls before rushing toward the lake. But with the ubiquity of surveillance cameras, there is no way to ensure privacy and anonymity. Earlier the same week, the police posted video of a bank robber from two dozen cameras in businesses, homes, ATMs and traffic lights across the urban landscape. The only thing you couldn't see was the guy going to the bathroom. It was like a reality show, except it was reality. It is almost impossible to go places and do things without someone seeing or hearing or knowing everything you do. Hillman is a fan of public safety, keeping an eye on anyone suspicious, anyone who sticks out like a sore thumb. But sometimes it's a problem. This is one of those times.

"Where are we going?" Christopher slumps in the passenger seat. "What are we doing?" He looks at his father with washed out eyes hidden behind lowered lids. He doesn't smile anymore. "I'm tired." He yawns and stretches but he seldom sleeps. And when he does, he wakes up in a cold sweat, mouth wide open, eyes unblinking.

■   ■   ■   ■   ■

Since what Mr. Hillman and Christopher call "the thing" happened, Christopher's teacher has called several times concerned that he has changed over the previous few months, that he is "different." Mr. Hillman fielded these calls and insisted that he and his wife were trying to figure out what was going on with their son. Hillman told his wife about the teacher's calls but minimized their importance. "A boy being a boy." Eventually they faced the unavoidable parent-teacher conference.

"He doesn't join in anymore. Everyone loves him and yet, I don't know, he seems preoccupied, worried, unable to concentrate." Ms. Kramer sat in a student chair at a table with Christopher's parents. Christopher was excused from the meeting so they could have "grown-up talk." "I've asked him if there's anything on his mind and he just shrugs his shoulders and says 'no'. But I can see it in his eyes." She paused to let this sink in. "I'm sure you've seen a difference, too."

Christopher's mother seemed confused, incredulous. "I don't know what, I mean… you're saying what?"

Mr. Hillman turned to his wife, trying to engage her. "You know, honey, we've noticed that he's a little moody at home sometimes. He doesn't like doing his chores sometimes, that sort of thing." Mrs. Hillman went silent, wrung her hands and appeared entranced by Ms. Kramer's shoes.

"I thought this might just be developmental, you know, emotional growing pains. It's pretty natural. But on Monday he burst into tears during math class and when I tried to speak to him, he left the room, as if he were afraid of something. That's when I called you." Ms. Kramer pointed at Mr. Hillman with her eyes. Mrs. Hillman seemed dazed, as if she were stumbling through a dream.

Mr. Hillman assured Ms. Kramer that he would talk to Christopher, that they had a close relationship, did things together, that his son confided in him. She gave him names of counselors the school had used. He thanked her and promptly threw the list away when they reached the parking lot. Mrs. Hillman headed to her own car without saying a word. "What in the hell is wrong with you?" called her husband. He sat in his car, watching his wife turn into traffic. He put the key in the ignition and then pulled it out again. He slid the window down to let in some air. He tossed his sunglasses onto the dash and pushed his seat back so he could stretch his legs. There were kids in the school yard playing soccer; others playing some kind of tag. Their boisterous laughter and shouting, their youthful symphony, brought tears to Mr. Hillman's eyes. What are we going to do? he thought.

■   ■   ■   ■   ■

He had been in his office at the dealership when a bulletin interrupted the morning talk radio show with news of a shooting. Everyone in the area near the shooting was asked to stay in their homes and to call 911 if they had heard or seen anything unusual. They went on to say the police thought it was a lone shooter, and that one person had been hit. No news about the person's condition. Hillman had leaned back in his chair, shaking his head, anger rising as he assumed some hooded punks were probably to blame. He commiserated with one his salespeople about the "state of the world today" and how this was "why everybody's angry all the time."

When there was nothing more to say, he went back to his monthly sales reports while his employee headed back to the show room. "Bag as many as you can!" he called. They were nearing the end of the month with a quota to meet. It was like this almost every month. Pressure, pressure, pressure as the month wore on and then a dramatic release when they made or exceeded their numbers. Usually some calls to loyal customers announcing special early leasing options or rock bottom prices on new cars did the trick.

When the half-hour news went into greater detail about the shooting, Mr. Hillman dropped his pen and pulled his radio closer. They reported there had been a single shot from what they thought was a semi-automatic rifle. The victim, still unidentified, worked at Farmers Insurance. He was found at his desk unconscious, a single hole in a nearby window. The Chief of Police tried to calm the community, saying there was no evidence to suggest this was a terrorist attack, despite the long distance precision it had taken to "hit the target." Nonetheless, he expressed relief to reporters that a nearby elementary school had been closed for the day "or who knows what might have happened."

He picked up his phone and called Christopher to make sure he was okay and to see if, well, everything was tucked away where it should be. His son didn't answer. He hung up and drummed his fingers and then called again. This time, Christopher answered. "Hi, buddy. Just checking to see how the day is going," he said, his voice edgy but cheerful. "I wondered if you heard about the thing that happened nearby, the accident, not *real* nearby, but anyway, I wondered if you had heard anything..." His voice trailed off when he realized Christopher wasn't speaking. "Christopher? Are you there?" All he heard on the other end was whimpering and short, raspy breaths, like Christopher was about to collapse from physical exertion, like he was faltering at the end of a lengthy race. "Christopher? You're scaring me. Can you say something?" Christopher exhaled a guttural moan and dropped the phone to the floor.

With that, Mr. Hillman understood exactly what had happened. "Okay," he said in a whisper. "You're okay, son," he said a little louder. "Can you pick up the phone? Christopher, please, can you pick it up? Daddy needs to hear your voice." The sound of Christopher weeping faded. "Christopher!"

∎　　∎　　∎　　∎　　∎

It wasn't until Christopher heard police sirens and saw patrol cars zooming through his neighborhood, that he understood that something had gone horribly wrong. Comforted by the silence that followed the shot, Christopher had put the AK back where it was supposed to be, then he had gone to the kitchen for a bowl of ice cream covered in Hershey's chocolate syrup and beer nuts. There were sweat stains under his armpits but basically he was feeling fine. No harm, no foul. He figured the bullet had found a tree or a vacant lot. He whistled his relief, patting himself on the back for how lucky he was. He dove back into his ice cream.

But with the sirens screaming and his insides going hollow, everything changed. He knew the police were after him. He knew they had figured the whole thing out. Maybe a neighbor had seen him but didn't say anything, calling the cops instead. He put the spoon down and went to his bedroom. He lay under the covers and held his eyes closed, as if the world might go away if he didn't look at it.

When it was quiet outside again, he breathed yet another sigh of relief, assuming they weren't after him. He even laughed at how silly he was being. No way they could guess what he'd done, he thought. Nothing pointed to him. He threw off the covers, reached for the remote and clicked on the TV only to see a crime scene shot from a helicopter, the announcer going on and on about "a shooter on the loose." "Shit," said Christopher, even though his father would have yelled at him for swearing.

He jumped off the bed when the phone rang and was completely undone by the sound of his father's voice. Later when his dad got home, Christopher confessed the whole thing. His father's mouth hung open like a dying fish. "Dad?" His eyes were glassy, wild-looking, like he'd stepped out of a Stephen King movie. "Dad!" When his father didn't answer the second time, Christopher began to panic. He couldn't breathe and his legs wobbled; his face turned red as a ripened strawberry. His legs collapsed like a folding chair and he found himself on the kitchen floor wondering what was going to happen.

By then his father had come to his senses. Mr. Hillman picked his son off the floor and made him stand up straight. "No time for this, Christopher. We've got to do something; we've got to...I don't know...do something." He paced the kitchen while Christopher sat on a kitchen chair, his head on the table, trying to catch his breath. "Okay, okay," said Mr. Hillman. "Here's what we're gonna do." Then he paced and circled the room some more. He stopped and started tapping his forehead. He pulled up another chair and got as close to Christopher as he could. "Look, son, this is...this is not your fault...it's not...I mean it just happened, an accident, that's all; this thing was a bad accident that could have happened to anyone. Right?" Christopher lifted his head from the table and shook it once before letting it drop to the surface again.

Hillman's mind was racing. He started tapping his forehead again and pacing the room, his eyes closed. "Okay, son...so, here's the deal. We are not going to tell anyone about this. No one, you got it?" Christopher didn't move. "No one would ever suspect a little boy. No one." He was breathing more evenly as his ideas sputtered on. "Accidents happen. They do." He turned his gaze to Christopher. "It shouldn't ruin someone's life. I'll figure this out. We just have to wait until things quiet down. We just have to act normal and go about our lives."

In the weeks that followed, Christopher missed ten days of school, got into a fight with a girl at recess, stopped doing his homework and, at times, didn't speak to anyone, except his father. Christopher's fear bore deep into his bones. "When is this going away?" he asked. "Soon, son, soon." But soon never seemed to come.

He wanted to talk to his mother but felt bound by the promise he'd made to his father. Anyway, she wasn't herself either. Some days she didn't get out of bed until noon. And when she did, she would stay in her pajamas until just before dinner. Then, instead of cooking, she would order out. His father and mother spent more time talking in their bedroom than usual, his father often leaving brusquely after slamming the door shut. When Christopher would ask what was wrong with his mother, his dad would say, "Nothing to worry about, son." And so he worried more. Sometimes he thought his head would explode.

■　　■　　■　　■　　■

"Are you okay, Christopher?" Mr. Hillman holds the steering wheel steady but his eyes are on his son, his thick bushy auburn hair, narrow set brown eyes, long face, baby cheeks, pudgy hands, his little boy-ness. My God, he's only eleven, Hillman thinks. "Christopher?" His son stares at his Nikes. "Are you okay?" Christopher doesn't seem to hear, doesn't respond at all. Mr. Hillman reaches for his son's arm and grabs it firmly. "Look, this is going to be okay, I'm telling you. Have I ever lied to you?" Christopher looks at his father and then back at his shoes.

Hillman's voice turns more upbeat. "Okay, so here's the plan. You remember going out Breakneck Rd. that time? You and Mom and me? We found this secluded spot to have a picnic. No one for miles. Remember?"

"Sort of."

"Well, the road's been closed for months. I guess part of it caved in, so it's done for. No one will drive there again."

"So."

"So, that's where we're going. We'll get rid of it there."

Christopher sniffs and wipes his nose on his forearm. "I don't like this."

"I know, I know, but we knew we'd have to get rid of it; we couldn't keep it around the house. Things have died down so now's the time."

"That's not what I mean." Christopher pushes himself into an upright position. "I can't stand not telling Mom. I can't. Every time I open my mouth it's right there, ready to come out. It's like I can't talk to her at all, just because of this thing." Christopher wipes his eyes again and tucks his hands into his pockets.

Mr. Hillman pulls a tissue from his pocket and gives it to Christopher. Hillman's lips are pursed as he studies his son's face. He tries to speak but then holds his breath, realizing his voice is shaky. He tries again. "Look, son...I'm so sorry about all this; you having to deal with this thing. No one your age...it's not right, not right at all." He sees the baby in his son's face and puts a hand on his shoulder. "About your mom, you know, she's not doing well herself right now. It doesn't seem like she can take much more herself. You know?" Christopher turns his head to face his father, his eyes lowered. "You don't want to make things worse for her right now, do you, Chris? I mean, if she knew what you did, it might, I don't know what it would do to her, but it wouldn't be good. You know what I mean?" Christopher's shoulders sink as he shakes his head. "Atta boy, you know I'm right on this one, don't you." Christopher shrugs and turns his head to the passenger side window, deep woods speeding by.

Breakneck Rd. comes to a sudden halt at a barricade held steady by multiple sandbags and a DOT sign saying "No Trespassing." Mr. Hillman gets out of the car and coaxes Christopher to join him. "Don't forget your jacket." Christopher gets on his knees and reaches for the blue windbreaker lying on the back seat. He wraps it around his waist and ties a knot. "Warm enough?" He doesn't answer.

Hillman opens the trunk, rolls back the mat, removes the quilt-shrouded AK and a box of ammunition. He tucks them under his arm and looks around. He reaches for the shovel and tosses it to Christopher. "Okay, that's everything." He closes the trunk, trying to avoid a slam. He scans the area again. No cars. No houses. Nobody. "Let's go."

Hillman slips through the brush on one side of the barricade, Christopher trudges along a few feet behind him, shovel over his shoulder. They head down the potholed road, grass and cornflowers growing through the cracks. Ash and maple and hickory trees are scattered across the hillside, a creek one hundred yards or more below. Oak trees, their leaves curling, line the road on the opposite side. There is color everywhere as cooler breezes and freezing nights have set the dying process of autumn into motion.

"Listen to that," says Mr. Hillman. The rapid ratta-tat-tat of a woodpecker echoes through the trees. Mr. Hillman smiles. "Sounds like a machine gun, doesn't it?"

Christopher isn't listening. He squints up at the sun shining through a fur tree. "Where are we going, Dad?" He plants the face of the shovel into the ground and leans on the handle. "I'm tired."

Hillman looks in every direction trying to decide where the burial should take place. He notices a notch in the hillside surrounded by bushes and tall grass. "Follow me." Christopher drags the shovel behind him. When they reach the spot, Hillman clears away the dead leaves and pine needles with his foot. "This is it." Christopher doesn't move. "C'mon Christopher, start digging."

"What?"

"You have to do some of this."

"Why?" Christopher's body slumps into an s-shape. He leans on the handle again and lets his head fall between his arms. "C'mon, Dad, really. I mean, I don't want—"

"You don't want what?" Mr. Hillman's voice is sharp as broken glass. Christopher straightens his posture. "Do I have to remind you why we're here? Didn't I tell you every day that you weren't supposed to touch that goddam rifle?" He's pointing now. Christopher falters, his legs buckle. Hillman catches his breath. "Look, like I said, you start and if the ground's too hard, I'll take over."

Christopher haphazardly presses the shovel to the dirt with his right foot, which slides off. He tries again. This time he digs a few inches into the cool earth and turns it over on a small mound.

"There you go," says his father. "You can do this."

Christopher puts his foot to the shovel again and this time leans with all his weight as the shovel cuts through the dirt. It is black with streaks of clay and worms wiggling in alarm. He goes down again and again, extending the hole out to the length of the AK.

"Do you need help now?"

But Christopher is intent on finishing the job. Perspiration covers his face and arms. He digs faster and tosses the dirt onto an ever growing pile.

"That's good."

Christopher doesn't listen. He keeps going, as if his life depended on it, as if he were digging a tunnel to another world.

After several more minutes, Mr. Hillman steps in front of his son just as he is about to dig again. "Chris, really, that's enough. It's plenty big enough. You did a great job." Christopher lets the shovel drop to the ground as he leans against a nearby maple.

Mr. Hillman places the AK into the hole and sprinkles bullets around it, like he's putting the finishing touches on a birthday cake. "Ok." He places his hands on his hips and looks down at the rifle. Christopher comes to his side. His father pulls him closer. "Well, that's the last we'll see of that thing."

"Good riddance."

Mr. Hillman pats his son's back. "Yeah, I suppose."

So long Mikhail.

Christopher reaches for the shovel, but his father takes it from his hand and starts covering the would-be corpse. Christopher gathers some leaves and scatters them over the freshly filled hole. He adds some sticks and then walks over the grave several times until it looks almost natural again.

"That should do it," says Mr. Hillman, but Christopher is already heading back to the car. "Chris?"

CHAPTER 28
ROSEMARY

Rosemary stands in the powder room just off the kitchen, her hands on the counter top as she leans close to the mirror. Her eyes are red and the lines bracketing her mouth are rutted. She touches her face with her fingertips, as if she is afraid the skin might peel or fall off. She runs both hands through her hair, now thin and lifeless as fishing twine. Her hands shake. She wipes tears from her eyes and bows her head.

The air is cool but the sun seems piercing. She squints as she unlocks the door to her car and slides in. She holds the steering wheel for a moment until she feels confident enough to start the ignition. Once into traffic, her shoulders press up around her ears as horns blare and cars zoom by her angrily. She wants someone to post a Rosemary Alert, telling everyone she's doing the best she can, so please give her a break.

The hospital parking garage is a torturous series of switch back curves, narrow lanes and cars jumping out randomly like ghosts in a haunted house. She has to park on the roof, where the shrill, eye-splitting sun awaits. She tight rope walks to the elevator, her heart pounding. She reaches the ground floor and emerges into the lobby, teeming as it is with worried faces and crying children, and walks stiff-legged down the corridor, cutting through the crowd like a ship through rough waters. Success. She leans against the back of the elevator and, thankfully, someone else pushes six and she can relax. When the elevator opens, the doors to the ICU are right in front of her. She sighs and leans into the final leg of her journey.

"Is something wrong?" There is alarm in Frankie's face.

They haven't seen each other in weeks. Rosemary called her often enough, though, to see how she was doing, how Gavin was doing. She told Frankie she had "that flu that's going around, the one they're talking about on the news, but it hasn't killed me yet." The black humor in her voice seemed to alarm Frankie. "Rosemary!" But Rosemary managed a laugh and moved on. "Any change in Gavin." No. "I am so sorry. How are you doing?" She barely heard anything that Frankie said, but mustered the appropriate nonverbals to appear engaged. "Uh huh...oh my..." These brief conversations became a weekly ritual. Frankie never questioned the flu diagnosis even though Rosemary was clueless about the symptoms. Rosemary appreciated her friend's decorum, but feared that her reticence to ask what was going on was a sign that she knew intuitively, that she could hear in Rosemary's voice that she was coming undone.

■　　　■　　　■　　　■　　　■

Rosemary has no idea how she ended up on life's back alley, how the suburban dream had slipped away. All she wants now is to be pain free. Her doctor referred her to a pain clinic. Useless. Therapy, equally useless. He even put limits on her medication, refusing to increase the dosage, refusing to refill when she ran out before the end of the month, refusing everything that might help her. No matter what—"I'm telling you Dr. Henrickson, I went away overnight and left the bottle there...Yes, I called, but they couldn't find it...I know I'm two weeks early...it's not my fault."

Nothing had been her fault. She slipped off a curb. People slip off curbs thousands of times each day. How many end up losing their lives, watching their dreams fade away? Since the doctors wouldn't help her, she had to take matters into her own hands. Do you think that's what she envisioned for her life? Do you think she wanted to spend her days sneaking around like a criminal, hiding in plain sight so no one would know what she was doing?

"What the hell is going on with you?" is her husband's most empathic comment. He's no help. He's not there for her, never was, never will be. And her son is in his own world most of the time. He doesn't seem to be aware of anything but the TV, his iPhone and his laptop. Kids. He seldom even looks at her, let alone asks how she is doing. At times, she wonders if his aloofness is a problem or just a phase. Who knows?

"Rosemary? Really? Are you okay?" Frankie pulls her closer, wrapping Rosemary in her arms, then looking her up and down. "What happened to you?" Rosemary sees worry, shock, incredulity, embarrassment in her friend's eyes.

"It, like, hit me; I mean hard," she says lamely. "It just took hold and wouldn't let go."

"But this has been like, two months." Frankie's eyebrows find each other and her lower lip disappears under her front teeth.

Rosemary glances at Gavin, who, by comparison, looks like the picture of health. She considers telling her friend what is going on, telling her that she is strung out, that she is as lost as a person can be. But the words turn dry as dust before they reach her lips.

"You should have seen me a month ago." She steps back from her friend and turns her attention to Gavin. "Compared to you, I haven't been through anything. I mean, this long…this is so long…this, I don't know what to call it…this whole process, I guess, it must be tearing you apart inside, I mean it, I don't know how you come every day…I mean, I know you love Gavin, that's why you come, but I don't know how you do it. How long do you think this will go one?" Her cheeks redden. "Oh shit, I didn't mean it that way, I mean, of course you'd do this forever if you had to, but…" She gains control of her mouth and closes it.

"Why don't you sit down, Rosemary, please." Frankie leads her to a chair near the window. "Let me get you some bottled water." She opens a soft pack and pulls out a crispy cool bottle, opens it and holds it out to her, as if water might be the solution.

"I mean, y'know, you don't have to do this for me. I'm fine, I am. I'm on the mend, as they say. I'm not contagious or anything." She tries to flip her hair with a turn of her head. Frankie's mouth falls open. "Please don't look at me like that. Look at me some other way. Look at me like it's the first day we met or it's that wonderful day we went to Buffalo." Rosemary swallows hard. "It was going to be such a wonderful day, remember? Just the two of us girls. The wind in our hair. Remember the men blowing their horns at us." Her head wags as she grimaces. "I'm so sorry it turned out like this. Gavin is so young. Isn't he? And you, you are younger than I could ever be."

"Rosemary."

"I know that's not exactly true, but it's just that you are—"

"Rosemary, are you on something?"

Rosemary tosses her head back and forces a laugh. "Am I on something? Is there anything I'm not on? That's the question. They have me on antibiotics and antihistamines and anti-inflammatories, all the anti's they could find. I'm a walking pharmacy!" Frankie leans away. Rosemary takes a deep breath. "I'm kidding, half-kidding. I think the medicine has thrown my whole system off, you know what I mean? I'm sorry, I shouldn't have come."

Frankie looks sideways at her. "No, no…I'm happy to see you. I am. I just had no idea…"

"Well, I didn't want to worry you." Her heart stops pounding although she can still feel the pulse in her neck.

Gavin groans in the background, the sound of him getting louder. He squirms from side to side and his arms shudder and wave. Rosemary sits frozen. Frankie looks at Gavin but doesn't get up. "You remember Rosemary, don't you, honey?" When Frankie turns back to her, Rosemary recognizes for the first time the toll that all of this has taken on her friend. Her eyes are sunken; they've lost their youthful patina; they are on life-supports, dull, blank. Rosemary begins to weep, her tears trickling down the creases in her cheeks.

"Honey, no, no, Gavin does this all the time. You just have never seen it. It's normal for him. We worry when he doesn't do this. The big news is that recently Ryan saw his father move one finger; moving it like he was doing it on purpose. I didn't believe it at first, but Gavin's nurse said he saw it too." Frankie gets up and goes to her husband's side. She bends over and speaks to Rosemary while examining Gavin's face. "He just hasn't moved it for me. Not yet, at least." When she turns back to Rosemary, she sniffs once and then clenches her jaw. "But I keep watching. You know, it's what we have."

Her matter-of-fact tone confuses Rosemary who sucks her tears back into her eyes, feeling it's inappropriate to weep, especially since the tears should be for Gavin, but aren't. They're for Frankie. Not just for her; for her and Rosemary together. Rosemary has had an invisible power cable plugged into Frankie's energy ever since the day they met in the dress shop. The further removed she was from her friend, the more rapidly she could feel the energy seeping, trickling, flowing out of her. She had always felt that in time she would develop her own energy source. She was getting close when everything happened.

"That's good then, right? I mean, his finger. It's a sign, maybe?"

"No one knows. The doctors listen and shake their heads but never commit, if you know what I mean. They never say, 'Terrific!' and they never say 'That's bullshit'. It's like we're all infants here and they assume it's not necessary to correct us because we'll eventually grow out of whatever infantile things we're holding onto." Frankie is sitting again, her legs crossed, newspaper and coffee on the floor beside her. "Ryan has decided it's a good sign, a promising sign."

"What about you?"

"I don't know."

Rosemary feels a shiver down her back and knuckles in her stomach. She wants to stay but her body is saying, 'Get out of here!' She forces herself to sit, fists in her lap. She is glad when the nurse comes in. Another person in the room seems to shift the balance, freshen the air, relieve the pressure to say anything. The nurse speaks in friendly tones to Frankie, who smiles and engages him about the weather, his weekend in New York, the musical that was "to die for."

Rosemary watches the slow transformation in Frankie, how she opens like the last crocus of winter. She stands and approaches Gavin, who has settled down and is staring at the ceiling. Or so it seems until she gets closer and realizes his eyes aren't looking at anything. They are deep in his sockets, at rest, purposeless. He is the only one who is not suffering, she thinks. He's been delivered from having to deal with this tragedy. He is free.

The nurse asks her to move to one side so he can examine Gavin. He talks continuously with Frankie, even chuckling and joking, as if nothing unusual is going on, as if Gavin isn't in the room, isn't lying there stuck in the world even though it's obvious he's no longer a part of it. Maybe it's better to act normal, to say and do the things you would say and do if a catastrophe weren't unfolding in the room. Maybe it's better to pretend your way through such things.

She's tried facing life head on and it doesn't work like the self-help books promise. The way to conquer your problems is to muscle through them, they say. Marshall your courage and discover your strength! Change your life in three, maybe four or even twelve, easy steps! What happens if after the second step, you fall off a cliff? If the cliff is right there in front of you, isn't it better to go back or go around or just call it a day and go home?

She's tried to stop and has learned that not stopping, even with its inevitable, what do they call it, downside is better than stopping and not knowing what will happen next. At least that is what she hopes.

But down deep where no one, sometimes not even Rosemary, can see, she fears she's wrong. She fears there is no escape and no way forward. She fears she's dancing on quicksand.

"You haven't seen it yet?" The nurse is talking about Gavin's miracle finger.

"Not yet. But I'm watching."

"It is a bit like hide and seek. And I'm not trying to be flip. It's just that it comes and goes and can't be found."

"My son has seen it several times."

"I know that's what he says. What he believes."

Rosemary watches as Frankie shifts in her chair as if surprised by a tack on the seat.

"Believes. What do you mean?"

"Don't get me wrong, I've seen the finger move. Ryan has seen the finger move. I know he believes his father is communicating. I guess I'm not sure. Maybe he's right, but there's so little activity, I mean, your husband's brain…" He fades as if not wanting to say 'your husband's brain is just mush now'.

Rosemary holds her breath, curls her toes and doesn't move. They are *all* perched on the edge of something. She is not alone. In fact, maybe there's always a cliff right in front of you or beside you or just around the corner. Maybe the easy-goingness of life is the lie. She shakes her head vigorously trying to lose her thoughts.

Frankie's eyes seem glued to Gavin now. She is like a guardian on a high wall. But instead of watching for danger, for enemies, she is watching for hope; she is watching for hints of light and for the movement of fingers.

"I'm sure it's real." Rosemary is surprised by the sound of her own voice. "I mean, it has to be real. He wouldn't still be here if it wasn't real." She looks at the nurse, his eyes seem ready to roll, but they don't. "It's like, I don't know."

"Maybe," he says. "This is why we do this work, you know. Because the unexpected can happen." Rosemary is unconvinced by the nurse's passive tone, his bland recitation. He doesn't believe anything he's saying, she thinks. Frankie doesn't seem to recognize this. She smiles at the nurse as if comforted by his empty words. Am I wrong? Rosemary wonders.

She stands abruptly, a wave of nausea passing through her. Her legs are restless. She walks to the window and places her hands on her hips. She is breathing rapidly.

"Rosemary? Are you okay?" Frankie is on her feet.

"Ma'am?" says the nurse. "You look flushed."

Rosemary feels the room shifting under her feet and her body losing its center. She no longer feels she is standing at all. She wobbles and Frankie rushes to her, grabs her just as her legs buckle. The nurse helps her sit down again and then leaves. "I'll get you some juice and you'll feel all better again. Don't be alarmed. This happens."

Don't be alarmed, thinks Rosemary. Don't be alarmed.

"Honey, really, you're not well, I can tell. You're just not yourself yet. I had no idea how sick you've been. I feel awful." Frankie is kneeling on the floor holding Rosemary's limp hand in both of hers. "You shouldn't have come. This is too much. I'm so sorry."

Frankie's face is so close that Rosemary can study every pore, every follicle, the dramatic line of her brows, the perfect angle of her nose, the tiny scar below one ear. She wants to fall into this intimate world, this beauty, this safety. Frankie leans forward and kisses her on the cheek. Rosemary caresses Frankie's cheeks with her hands and then kisses her long on the lips.

Frankie, startled, pulls away. "Honey, no." She wipes her lips with the back of her hand and then returns to her chair. "No." Her voice is soft; her eyes are steady; her jaw is set. "You are my friend, Rosemary. And I love you. You know that."

Rosemary laughs loudly. "Oh my! What was that? I'm so sorry. The medicine, it makes you lose your mind a little..." Rosemary checks her phone. "Look at the time. I had no idea. I have to get going." She is breathless as she stands. The nurse returns to the room, a container of orange juice in his hand. "I won't be needing that. I feel much better, thank you. Thank you for your kindness." She wipes perspiration from her lip.

"Rosemary, stay, please. Rest a few minutes."

"No, what can I say, I have to…" As Rosemary backs from the room, her eyes meet Frankie's, sadness to sadness. "I'll be back."

Once outside the ICU, she leans against a wall to steady herself. Then she stumbles toward the elevator. Soon she is back on the roof of the parking garage bent over an abutment trying to breathe. She looks at the vast tree-lined cemetery across from the hospital, the University library and city center beyond it.

She pulls her cell from her bag and checks the time. School's out. She is about to text Jordy but hesitates to push send. She looks down from her perch at people coming and going from the hospital, like bees to a hive. She knows that each one of them thinks they are the center of the universe, that their hopes and fears are unique, that the world is here to bend to their will. And so they flit, they skitter, they rush from here to there assured of their importance. She wants to scream so that for even briefly all eyes will turn toward her. She opens her mouth but nothing comes out. She looks at her phone, the message ready to go, and pushes send. In an instant, Jordy replies, "Okay."

Jordy, always slick, always ready with a quip, is dull-eyed as he approaches the car. He holds his backpack at his side. His hair is greasy and his shoulders are bowed. His face, always bursting with life, is vacant, deadpan.

"Hi." Rosemary smiles and squints into the sun off Jordy's shoulder. "Been a while."

"Yeah. I've been, I don't know."

"Trying to kick it." Jordy stretches his arms and arches his back. "That's a good thing. But I knew you'd be back."

Rosemary averts her eyes. "I guess." She takes a deep breath. "So, how have you been?"

Jordy sneers and shifts his weight as he bends down to the window. "What do you care?"

"I care. I do. You know that." She turns sideways to face him. "So? How are you doing?"

"I'm doing like shit, that's how I'm doing."

"What?" She notices his hands shaking.

"I've fucked up royally. Broke my rule."

"What do you mean?"

Jordy snorts for effect. "I've put all my profits in my nose."

She purses her lips and places a hand on Jordy's hand. "Oh, Jordy, I'm—"

Jordy jerks his hand away. "Don't 'Oh Jordy' me." He pulls a bottle from the side pocket of his backpack and tosses it into the car. "That should do you for a while." He turns and starts to walk away.

"Hey, wait." She rifles through her purse looking for her wallet.

He turns, holds both hands up and says, "It's on me. Think of it as a homecoming gift."

"Jordy, come on—"

"No need to thank me." He turns again, then stops and takes a few steps toward the car. "Look at you. You got everything. But here you are. What the fuck are you doing?" Jordy shakes his head, turns and leaves.

Rosemary closes her eyes and begins to weep. She looks up and Jordy has crossed the parking lot and is heading toward the school. There are no other cars in the lot. She wipes her eyes on her arm. The bottle is on the floor in front of the passenger seat. She unbuckles her belt and reaches for it. She sniffs and wipes her eyes a second time, then opens the bottle.

By the time she gets home, she is calm. She is no longer perspiring and her breathing is deep and steady. Pulling into the garage ahead of her is another car. She waits at the curb. Mr. Hillman and Christopher get out. She opens her window and waves to her husband and son.

CHAPTER 29
Jenna Goode

Jenna holds Ryan's hand as they stride across the hospital lobby to the green elevators. He pushes the up button and they wait. She stretches her back and considers whether to go to the lady's room before the ICU. She decides she can wait. Her eyelids are sagging from sleepless nights and napless days. She feels disappointed that when she got on the scale this morning she'd gained five more pounds. She got on and off three times and then changed the battery and tried again. Five pounds it was. "My God, Jenna, you look beautiful. It's all baby, don't worry about it." Easy for Ryan to say. He isn't popping veins in his butt or trying to put out a constant fire of indigestion in his chest. "Maybe try some Tums." A cup of water on a forest fire.

Nevertheless, Jenna looks happy, even calm, despite the lack of progress with the problem down below. "Still there," her midwife said brightly at her most recent visit. "But still plenty of time." She is getting better at compartmentalizing these things and focusing instead on the little life that is growing unfettered inside her. At times she feels waves of confidence, as if nothing could possibly go wrong because, well, just because.

Today is one of those days. On the way to the hospital, they stopped at Wegman's where she carefully examined the bin of cauliflowers before selecting the perfect one, its vibrant clusters of white florets looking like a bridal bouquet. "This is how big she is," Jenna said in a whisper to herself. So substantial now, so real. She cradled it on her lap the whole way to the hospital and then laid it gently on her seat, patting it affectionately before tramping down the parking ramp to the hospital entrance.

She smiles, thinking of it as they wait in a gaggle of visitors for the elevator light to reach G. *Ding!* They herd in and press their backs against the side wall in front of a poster about shingles. Ryan, his hair messy from the wind, heaves a sigh and looks at the floor. He fiddles with his hands and his chin shifts back and forth as he chews the inside of his cheeks. She squeezes his hand, but he doesn't seem to notice. These visits, now so routine, are still hard. He hopes and hopes and hopes, but his hope is seldom rewarded. Yes, there's the finger movement, which he and the nurse have witnessed, but it hasn't led to anything. In fact, he hasn't seen anything in a couple of weeks. He still talks about his father "waking up," as if he is asleep and only needs a desperately shrill alarm to return from his slumber.

Jenna doesn't challenge this. She presses both hands against her belly. She understands the foolhardiness of hope, the reverie at the heart of anticipation. It is her daily manna, appearing whether summoned or not, part of what it means to be "with child."

In recent weeks he's stopped talking about the mysterious 'C'. He still has his father's dog-eared journal on his nightstand but it has disappeared under *People* magazines and ice cream cookbooks. Maybe he doesn't want to know what it means. She's unsure. Could his father be a different person than Ryan has known all his life? Could he be more than a father, a complex person with all the secrets that shroud most people? Is there some darkness behind the light? Some imperfection inside the perfect picture? Jenna is relieved that Ryan has given up on 'C'. There are many more matters of consequence than whether his father may have done some something long ago.

Ryan extended the season for Curly's, but snow will arrive in the coming weeks and customers will head for cover until spring. For now, Ryan is ignoring this since business has remained steady. Jenna's medical leave from work has been extended. The bank president remains supportive although the last time she spoke with him, he seemed sour. Could the bottom fall out? What will they do when Curly's closes for the season, if her job is also at risk?

Though important, these are mere mosquito bites compared to the uncertain futures of her baby and her father-in-law. They share the same dilemma of being locked in, of not having a clear exit from their current situations. Jenna wants nothing more than to hear her daughter's piercing scream when she finally emerges into life's stark light. As for her father-in-law, she is unsure what to hope. All she knows is that one way or another his imprisonment must end. Someday. Who knows when?

She shudders when the elevator door opens to the sixth floor. Everything is white or pale green on the sixth floor, everything except the uniforms of the helpers, some light blue, others dark blue, still others combat green. And, of course, the white-coated ones, the carriers of secret knowledge.

Jenna is surprised when a familiar voice calls to them, "Good morning." It is Frankie sitting outside the unit in the family lounge, her travel mug in hand. She stands and straightens her back before crossing the floor and embracing them in turn. Even though strain is written on her face, her demeanor is gracious. "You look wonderful," she says to Jenna. "I love that bump." Frankie pats her belly, something Jenna usually resists from others, but not from her mother-in-law. Jenna beams. Frankie hugs Ryan. "Well, I guess we're all heading in the same direction. He's doing okay today, I mean, at least he's calmer than he usually is in the morning. Sometimes he can be pretty agitated, but not so much today. I know you've seen that, Ryan. They were giving him a bath so I decided he might need some privacy."

"Did you stay last night?" asks Ryan.

"Yes." Frankie grins and wobbles, her balance in flux.

"Mom—"

"I know. Sometimes it's just easier than going home. He's here, so why should I be there." Ryan shakes his head. "How are you feeling, honey," she says, eyebrows raised as she reaches for Jenna's hand.

Jenna thinks for a moment. "Good," she says definitively. "I'm doing good today."

Frankie massages Jenna's palm with her thumb, then squeezes her hand and let's go.

"That's wonderful, Jenna. It is. I'm glad that someone is feeling good today. Well, I guess we should head in." Ryan presses the silver button on the wall. The double doors open wide and in they go.

In the early visits, Jenna's eyes were glued to her father-in-law as soon as she entered his room. More recently she helps arrange the chairs into a semi-circle for ease of conversation and then decides whether to open the blinds. She puts her most recent copy of *Parent Magazine* on the plastic table top with her thermos of decaf coffee (yuck). Once everything and everyone is in place, she goes to Gavin's side, though he could easily be mistaken for a piece of furniture. She is alarmed by her blasé attitude, resulting from weeks of desensitization to the quotidian details of living while dying. Perhaps they will *always* do this. Perhaps when their baby teethes or starts school or loses her first tooth or plays her first soccer game or piano recital, perhaps they will stop by the hospital before or after, just to check in; they will pencil it into the calendar weeks in advance along with mowing the lawn and grocery shopping and planning birthday parties and holidays.

Ryan won't admit it, but she can see the same dreariness in his eyes when they come and when they go. In between he performs for his father, the same play over and over, encouraging him, reporting to him on the minutiae of daily life outside the hospital, cajoling him to "move that finger of yours, so everyone can see." Like every mania, it is followed by a free fall into the rest of his life, the worry about the baby, the uncertainty about Curly's, the struggle to maintain favor with his mother.

Frankie, her jaw tight, her eyes stolid, her back straight, appears to have an Amazonian indomitability. Is she fearless? Confident? Indifferent? Jenna watches closely as Frankie kisses Gavin's forehead, squeezes his hand and then takes a seat, all in a single practiced motion. Can a tragedy be so overwhelming that it quashes all emotion? Hollowing out even the most loving, the most sensitive person?

Despite their closeness in recent months, it is still hard for Jenna to read her mother-in-law. "I think that's the way she likes it," says Ryan. "It's like no matter how close she is, there is distance built in; I don't know. Maybe it's just me. Dad says I over think these things." Ryan has always borne the worrier's mantle, but Jenna now wonders if it was fostered by a mother who wasn't sure how to love him. He was the shy boy who was hesitant to join in, slow to take up any challenge, afraid of almost everything. A shadow image of the worst qualities in his father. He told Jenna that when he closes his eyes and thinks of his mother, he always sees disappointment in her eyes, no matter the expression on her face.

Jenna watches Frankie's profile as she chats with Ryan about the weather, the news, the list of items they cover when they meet. There is a faint smile on her face, a Mona Lisa smile that could turn into a broad grin or a deep frown. Which way will it go? That is always the question.

Not that she is ever overtly mean or confrontive or belittling; it's more that she disappears, becomes invisible right before your eyes. She goes away.

As she watches Frankie, Jenna's attention is drawn to her left cheek, just below and to the left of her eye. At first she is unsure she sees anything. But then there it is again. A faint quiver, a twitch just below the surface, easily missed. And then she coughs for a moment uncontrollably. She takes a cough drop from her purse, unwraps it and tucks it into her left cheek. The cough subsides, but the tic doesn't. It is animated, vigorous, overtaking the surface of her skin. She doubts that Ryan even sees it. Frankie presses one finger against the spot. It stops briefly, but begins again. She blinks, purses her lips and clears her throat.

"Can I get you some water?" says Jenna.

"No thank you."

There is grit in her face, but it is belied by the vulnerability Jenna sees in her eyes. Frankie coughs again, this time a hacking, gagging cough. Both Ryan and Jenna start to get up, but she waves at them with one hand and they stop. She swallows and gathers herself, then laughs.

"Just a tickle, really." She forces another huffy laugh, her throat and neck muscles clenched. The cough returns. Her face reddens with anger and embarrassment. "Maybe they need to pull another bed in here. Or Gavin and I could double up." The smile melts from her face, replaced by an apologetic gesture of one hand. "Don't know why I said that." Soon the cough is under control.

The twitch is more prominent now, quaking across her upper cheek to her nose, an emotional fault line. Jenna wants to reach out, but hesitates. Frankie clears her throat one last time.

"Frankie, I'm so sorry…"

"It's okay. I'll be fine."

"No I mean I'm sorry for all of this."

Gavin is moving now. His arms and legs flail and his head turns side to side, as if he too is on the fault line. Frankie is on her feet. She watches and then goes to her husband's side. She pulls up his cover and adjusts his pillow. Gavin relaxes. She rests both hands on the side rail.

"Ryan." Frankie's eyes are glued to Gavin's hand.

Ryan looks over her shoulder. He throws his head back and pumps his fists to the ceiling. "That's it! That's what I've been talking about. Look at that! I'm telling you, he's back."

Jenna cranes her neck and sees the pointer finger on her father-in-law's left hand standing up straight as a flag pole. She covers her mouth with her hands. Ryan's eyes well up. Frankie's jaw loosens and her mouth opens slightly. She reaches for Gavin's finger and nestles it in the palm of her hand. She startles when it begins to move again.

"Gavin?" There is a whispery rasp in her voice. "Gavin?" Her left eye closes by half as her cheek begins to pulse. "Is that you, honey?" She kisses the tip of his finger and squeezes it tightly. "I can feel it," she says, her voice full of discovery.

Ryan folds his hands on top of his head, his smile broad, his eyes glistening. "What did I tell you?" He takes Jenna into his arms.

Jenna's eyes are wide, still unsure what to think. Is her father-in-law responding to them? Is he consciously reaching out? Or is this just something that happens? A random act that to the hopeful eye seems miraculous?

She looks past Ryan to Frankie, whose face is transfixed. The lines have receded, the color has returned, her eyes have new depth.

"Honey, can you hear me?" Her hand wags with his finger. "If you can, I want you to know how truly sorry I am. Please know that I love you. Always. Please forgive me." She kisses his finger again and presses it against her cheek. "Please."

Jenna's eyes narrow with confusion. What is she talking about? Ryan seems not to have heard his mother, his head now on Jenna's shoulder. Jenna watches as Frankie's pink cheeks turn red again.

"Frankie?" she says pulling away from Ryan. "Frankie, are you okay?"

Frankie reaches for Jenna and takes her hand. She pulls Jenna near, takes Gavin's hand and places it on Jenna's belly. Jenna holds her breath as she feels Gavin's finger quickening. Then the kick, the baby's kick, firm and forceful. Again and again. A foot? An elbow? Then again. She laughs and cries and gasps and doesn't notice that Gavin's finger has stopped. That his hand is again at rest although his legs tremble and his head wobbles to and fro. She places her hand on his. She is surprised how warm it is, how alive. Her eyes meet Frankie's.

"Is everything okay?"

Frankie ignores this. "May I?" she asks while instinctively pressing her hand on Jenna's belly.

Ryan follows, rubbing Jenna and kissing her neck. "Wow. I've never...she's never done this...I mean, she has, but not like this...not so...I don't know..."

"Determined," says Frankie.

CHAPTER 30
GAVIN GOODE

In the murky timelessness of his current state Gavin puzzles less about where he is than why he is. What sense does it make for him to be in suspended animation, like a dormant seed or a hibernating animal that awaits a new day? He doubts that he will ever go from seed to seedling to full grown tree. He will never awaken and rise up through the earth to meet a new spring.

And yet. There remain restless molecules of hope inside him that hold onto the improbable, that entertain the nearly impossible. This miniscule, yet scrappy, hopefulness clamors for recognition. It wags its finger; it launches its signals, faint semaphores from a distant deck insistent on being seen by someone on the far shore.

In the early weeks, his attempts at signaling are a failure. His body is too busy for any one part to stand out, to rise above the chaos. But he persists until once, then twice, someone out there touches his finger, holds it and when they do, energy emanates from that touch. It surrounds Gavin, vibrates in and through him, awakening elements of who he once was and still may be. It feels like Ryan, the vibration, the sound. It feels like Ryan, who always has a trembling presence, a presence that has to be noted, has to be attended to. It feels like Ryan, that first time.

Ryan? Gavin listens. He lends all of his energy to the signs, the signals that his finger sends. Ryan, it has to be him. Why else would Gavin feel such familiarity, such at-homeness mixed with hesitancy? I miss you, he thinks. How are you? How is your mother? How is Jenna? Are you a father yet? His questions assume the passage of time; that life has progressed. But how long? How far? Why am I still here? What reason could there be?

He exiles these questions from his mind, realizing there are no answers. Instead he settles for the feeling of being connected, if only fleetingly. It is enough.

After that brief docking, that return to shore, he drifts again for what seems like an eternity. He waves his finger again and again and again, until there is little energy left. No one reaches out to him. Eventually, he stops. And he waits; for what, he no longer knows. Something inside him holds on. Something senses that his family is there, faithfully in his orbit. They have to be.

In the meantime, he tugs on memories to keep his family close. His recollections come to him, shards of his former life. He remembers that when they started dating, Frankie often wore a peasant blouse, white, with embroidery around a scoop neck. The short sleeves were puffy and they crinkled. She pulled her hair back on both sides with colorful barrettes, her bangs hanging uneven to her eyes. He remembers how her arms seemed like a young girl's arms; her hands were small, though her nails were long and red. When he held her, she fit perfectly into his chest. For a moment he would disappear, light as air, all of life's weight gone. Her hair smelled like rain, her skin like leaves in springtime. He lost himself in her. And found himself, as well. He grew more confident in her gaze, less afraid, more assertive and self-assured. He believed in himself when she looked at him, when she smiled at him and called his name. Before they met, he had been lost, he had been nothing. When he would tell her this, she would laugh and wave him off as if he were joking. He'd laugh, as well, not because she was right, but because she was wrong.

She was like a hummingbird, always on the move, sudden, but steady, floating, hovering, strong, but fleet. "Why do you love me?" he would ask. Her nose would wrinkle with thought, as if she couldn't find an answer, her eyes dancing with mischief. "I don't know. I just do. I don't have a list of reasons. I just feel it." He'd pull her close in those moments, not wanting her to fly away. Although he knew it was foolish, he wished she could say, one, two, three, four, these are the reasons I love you. Then he could write them down and make sure he always did whatever it was that made her love him.

Time helped him feel more assured of her love. Having a son. Living through life's ups and downs, losses, illnesses, challenges, like new jobs and business startups, all create a protective layer on a marriage, a sense that history is the validation of love. It is evidence-based support that resilience turns love into steadfastness. Such a marriage, like a great redwood, is immune to the savagery of fires that might level an average forest.

Immune even to infidelity. The whole thing with Conner. Her confession. He accepted it; he believed her. He could see regret in her eyes, the regret borne of recognizing that the rock had been lifted, revealing the worst in you. Even much later when he discovered that Frankie had started up again, even then he clung to the daily evidence of their commitment to one another, the coffees on the porch, the laughter while watching TV, the commiseration over Ryan, the joy of Jenna's pregnancy, the still tender love they made, the threads of a fabric sewn tightly. That was stronger than anything else.

"Who is perfect?" he wonders. He isn't. Far from it. He can't judge her. Doesn't everyone have some darkness into which they recede from time to time, a place where they are their worst selves, not their whole selves, but their worst selves? A place from which they hope to one day escape? Gavin understood what Frankie had done; perhaps better than she did. He was in no place to cast the first stone. Of that he was sure.

Does every secret have to be revealed? he wonders. Does every window have to be opened? Does everything have to be exposed? Doesn't the unseen define us as much as the seen? These questions confused him, which is what he wanted. The grey made it easier to go on, much easier than seeing things only in black or white, guilt or innocence, bad or good; terms that seemed quaint when it came to the long view of love.

He is happy to have the memory of his perfect day, the day he would go back to if he could. And despite the pain, he is happy to have this other meddlesome memory, as well. It is part of a life now ebbing. To retain any of that life, he would gladly embrace all of it.

Today he tries again. Today he musters the strength, the resolve to reach out once more. Today he moves his finger and waits, like a fisherman in a lazy pond. He expects nothing, but hopes for something. He knows there is movement in the room. He feels the presence of others. Not the medical 'others' who flit and flutter indifferently. But a sustaining presence, the presence of pilgrims or mourners or the determined few who still believe. "Will they notice?" he wonders. "Will they speak to me with nimble fingers?"

Mid-swipe of his restless pointer, something takes hold. He has a bite. He keeps moving and it stays attached. It clutches him; someone is near, someone is melding to him. It is a familiar feeling, this skin on skin. Warmth passes from his finger tip to his hand and up his arm and across his chest and belly and down his legs. Is that my heart beating? My lungs breathing? He hooks his finger in embrace. Frankie, he thinks. This is Frankie; it has to be; who else. His slug grey eyes hint blue again. Frankie, it's you. He moves his finger vigorously and she holds tight, seemingly satisfied to be caught on his line. He feels her hand enveloping his finger and then her other hand gently swaddling his.

He is not alone, after all. He is tethered. He is remembered. Someone sits with him. Someone loves him. Nothing else matters, neither pain nor suffering, neither life nor death, only this one thing.

Gavin's body feels a wave of calm wash over it. He settles, the tremulousness gone for the time being. He has come back to the surface, where the air is plentiful and deliciously sweet. Who cares how long it lasts?

His hand lies warm and limp in hers. He feels her raising it to her lips, then pressing it to someone else's flesh. This other skin feels taut, smooth, alive. It is as round as a globe, a planet at his finger tip. He presses his finger against it, like he is planting a foot onto the surface of a new world. He feels a perceptible push back, playful but sure. And again. And a forceful rolling motion, a somersaulting show-offy tumble that triggers a tingle in his hand. Then it is gone.

He is exhausted. His finger can stand no more. Though his hand shakes, his pointer rests and is motionless. He thinks Frankie is still holding his hand, but he can't be sure. His plug is half way into the socket now, wobbly, at best; the connection is weak and the light flickers and fades.

The darkness engulfs him again, but when he squints he can see that it is peppered with light. There is a smile somewhere in all of this. He searches until he finds it and then he rests.

CHAPTER 31
FRANKIE GOODE

Frankie studies her hands, the backs of them full of ridges and raised veins; dappled with brown spots. Her nails don't reach the tips of her fingers. Her knuckles are creased and the skin around her wedding band plumps. No longer supple, when she bends her wrist, the skin accordions tightly. The lines on her palms look like tributaries flowing from an unseen source. One is her life line, she is sure, but which one is unclear. There is a knot in one palm, the result of surgery, that remains puckered whether her palm is open or closed.

She feels older than her hands. She is surprised by this because age has never mattered to her. She has always felt years younger and looked that way, as well. But not now. Years are not the enemy, though. Years come and go and they aren't necessarily the measure of age. She feels weathered not by years but by what fills those years. And by how they are handled. Frankie has always been a good handler. She has always been able to stay ahead of the wave. Until now.

She looks up at the twenty-third Psalm, beautiful in rainbow tiles. The words, though, are wearying today. "The Lord is my shepherd, I shall not want…" She looks at her hands again, both palms open in her lap. She folds them together, much as she had done when she held Gavin's finger, when she felt his quickening inside them. She had looked at his face, expecting something, a smile, a glint of life, but the pasty mask she saw didn't match what she felt in her hand.

She regrets having doubted Ryan all those weeks. When he'd leave each day, he'd ask her to watch for "any movement at all," and she would promise. She would watch for several minutes and then stop, feeling it was foolish, feeling she was wasting hope when she should be preparing for what was coming next, for the decision she felt certain she would face — whether to continue keeping watch or to let Gavin go.

Both her thinking and her days are organized around this one thought. She goes to the Shop rarely and when she does, stays long enough to catch up on what is happening or to sign off on orders that have to be made. Otherwise she spends her days at the hospital. Some days she goes to the gift shop before ever going to the ICU. She wanders the halls other days, even discovering a Barnes and Noble in a distant corner of the complex. She eats at the cafeteria or one of two cafes. There are coffee carts everywhere and though the baristas don't know her name, they know her order, cappuccino with skim.

She sits with Gavin each and every day. Jenna and Frankie's employees urge her to stay home, even for just a day; "go somewhere, anywhere" just to "get your mind off" of what her life has become. "You have to take care of yourself." She appreciates everyone's concern, but doesn't listen. The thought of not being at the hospital when her husband is barely alive is too much. Adding her infidelity to the mix makes the vigil even more imperative. She can't say fifty, or a hundred Hail Marys for this, but she can sit with it every single day.

Has her faithful waiting paid off? She is still stunned by the contact she made with Gavin; how she felt him, how he was present in an inexplicable way. To hold his finger and his hand, to kiss them, to marvel at them, these were painful gifts. She became aware that the drip, drip, drip of daily surveillance had numbed her feelings of love and affection for Gavin. Feelings that she had bubble-wrapped to protect her from the anguish of loving someone who is present and absent at the same time.

All of this increased the heat of shame she feels over her affair with Conner, feelings that boil over again and again, leaving blisters and scars that no one else can see, that no one can tend to.

"Excuse me." Rev. Lorde enters the chapel from behind the altar, a stack of Bibles in his arms. He seems surprised to see Frankie. "Well, hi, how are you doing?" He smiles broadly as Frankie looks at him sheepishly and returns a half-smile from one corner of her mouth. Lorde places the Bibles on the floor and sits down, two chairs from Frankie. Then he is quiet. He sighs and looks up at the twenty-third Psalm. She looks at him from the corner of her eye as he appears to read it. She closes her eyes and retreats for a moment into the silence. He takes a deep breath, a preamble to speech she assumes, so she opens her eyes once more. He shifts his weight in the chair and scratches his jowly cheek. He turns sideways so he can face her directly, but instead of speaking, he waits for her to make eye contact and then grins faintly and raises his eyebrows.

"He moved."

"He what?" Lorde's voice rises in barely controlled elation.

Frankie tells him the whole tale and he chuckles with delight.

"Wow." He's shaking his head now, as if he's just heard the story of Lazarus. "What did you do? You must have been thrilled."

Frankie turns forward, looking at the stack of Bibles on the floor, all black covers and gold tipped pages. "I told him I was sorry. I asked him to forgive me. For what, I never said."

Lorde doesn't respond, at first. He seems to be considering what to say, perhaps how to tamp down his own enthusiasm about this mini-resurrection.

"What was that like for you?"

That's the question, isn't it? Does it matter if she asks for forgiveness from someone who can't respond, and if he could, wouldn't know what she was talking about?

"You know, he has been texting me. Conner, I mean. I may be sitting in the ICU with Gavin, listening to those droning monitors, and then there'll be a ding and it's him. So odd. Unsettling."

"Have you been answering?"

"No. But I've read the messages. Asking about Gavin. Hoping all is well. Telling me he misses me." Frankie places her bag on the seat beside her and looks at the altar. "You know, in the last fifteen, maybe eighteen years, I bet we've spent no more than thirty, maybe forty hours together." She shakes her head and looks down. "Had no real conversations. I mean, we talked, but…" Frankie shrugs. "At the fifth conference, I don't know, maybe three, four years after he had moved away, he told me how 'deeply' he missed me, that he might even love me. By then he had a new store, a men's boutique that was going well. He wished we could work together. Wanted me to leave Gavin and move west to be with him. It was all very exciting, head-spinning stuff. He felt magnetic. And I wanted to feel something…different. I wanted to escape, to be free from the tiresomeness of my life. But I didn't love him. I liked him. I enjoyed him. But I didn't love him." Frankie leans back in her chair and crosses her arms. "It was just that my life seemed set in cement. Like there'd never be another new thing, if you know what I mean. Even when it was good, it was always a version of the same thing. Don't get me wrong. Mostly I was happy, satisfied. But sometimes, satisfied didn't feel like enough." Frankie puts her chin in her hand and leans on one knee. "Saying this out loud, it sounds ridiculous, sophomoric. But it was true. And so when I was with Conner I could live this little fantasy, never thinking, seriously at least, of doing anything about it. Seems so foolish now. So wasteful."

Unsure if Rev. Lorde is still listening, she turns and looks at him for the first time. He is studying his thumbs which are twiddling. He takes his usual deep breath and lets it out, as if clearing the way for the words. "So. What was it like to ask for forgiveness?"

"Haven't you heard anything I've said?"

"Yes, but I can't get past the first thing you told me, that you apologized and asked for forgiveness. And I get that you didn't say what you were apologizing for. But you and I know that he, in all likelihood, knew; and has known for a long time. The journal entries about 'C'. It isn't your secret alone, but one that the two of you shared for years and didn't even know it. The real secret isn't what you did; the real secret is that it was never acknowledged; that nothing was ever said about it. It was this 'thing' that was there between you saying, 'Hey, here I am! Does anyone see me?'" When her face sags and she doesn't blink, he seems to back off, giving her an out. "I don't know. I could be all wrong. I often am."

Frankie's eyes whelm with tears. He hands her a tissue.

"I feel like I could apologize from now until forever...but there's no eraser. I don't know what to do."

"Who does?"

In the conversations they had had before, Frankie always appreciated Rev. Lorde's respect for her non-religiousness. He never pushed anything on her, never tried to convert her or convince her of anything. But today she wishes he would. She wishes he would give her an answer. She wishes he would raise his arms to the heavens and the sky would open to a white robed choir; and the light would shine down on her, a light that would shepherd her through this "valley of the shadow of death," as the Psalm says.

She looks fiercely at Rev. Lorde, her eyebrows wedged, her lips taut. "I don't mean any disrespect, but how do you do your job day in and day out when the best you can offer is 'Who does?'? Doesn't your religion, your God, whatever, tell you anything? Don't your beliefs or your faith, or whatever you want to call it, give you something more than that? When you go to bed at night, isn't there something more that helps you sleep and get up to face the next day?" Frankie stops mid-breath and lets out a sigh. She looks at her hands balled in her lap. "I'm sorry. I didn't mean to..."

Rev. Lorde shuffles and shifts and adjusts, resetting himself, maybe wanting to get more comfortable before speaking. He puts one hand to his mouth and clears his throat.

"Sometimes when I go to bed at night, I pray. Sometimes that is enough, not so much because I get answers, not because anything is revealed, but because before I'm done, I fall asleep and whatever was bothering me doesn't matter for another six hours or so. More often than not, though, when I lie in bed at night, I feel like I'm hanging by a thread; and the thread is stretching and I'm afraid it's going to break and I'm going to fall to the bottom, wherever that may be. But I keep holding on and the thread gets longer and longer until it's as thin as a filament. But it doesn't break." Lorde leans forward, elbows on his knees. "For me, holding on is faith; and the thread, well, the thread is grace."

CHAPTER 32
ROSEMARY

Rosemary sits on her bed, bottle in hand. She plays with the cap and looks over her shoulder to the open door of the bedroom. She listens, but no one is there. Her husband is at the dealership. And Christopher, where is Christopher? She assumes he has gone across the street to play with Magee. She holds the bottle up and shakes it; the pills collide, the bottle almost full, money in the bank. She has taken fewer than usual in the last week. The other day she went to the grocery store on her own and for the first time in a month or more, she didn't have to abandon a cart full of toilet paper and cereal and cleaning supplies and canned vegetables and ice cream and bread and pork chops in a random aisle. She waited in the check-out line, her perspiration less visible than usual. She smiled at the cashier and commented on the weather— "Spring can't be far behind." She pushed the cart to her car unaided, loaded the trunk, sat for a few minutes until someone beeped at her and then she went home. This was the best outing she had had since her disastrous trip to the hospital.

Rosemary starts counting the pills and stops, realizing that her neck is tightening and her shoulders are starting to ache. She doesn't need the pressure of knowing. Pretending that the supply is endless is better. She stands, lifts up the mattress and puts the bottle back.

As she leaves her room, she notices that the door to Christopher's bedroom at the far end of the hall is closed. Usually she can see all the Buffalo Bills and New York Yankees posters taped to the wall above his unmade bed. She can see a pile of clothes on the floor and super hero actions figures strewn here and there. They made an agreement that Christopher could be in charge of his room, no matter how awful it looked, just so he didn't let his mess overrun the house. But he does have to leave the door open to, well, freshen the air.

Christopher is her little compromise. Shortly after she started working at the dealership, she got involved with Ben Hillman, soon to be president and CEO of Hillman's World of Dealerships. He was older by ten years or more. He doted on her and helped her learn the ropes and she became enamored with him, especially when he let it slip that he was separating from his wife. Two months later, she was pregnant. Six weeks after that she tearfully agreed to an abortion, because "it would totally fuck up the divorce and we'd lose everything to that bitch." Eight months later, she was pregnant again and had her second abortion because everything was "still in process." That time he promised that it would all work out and soon they would be together, married and, yes, she could get pregnant again, no worries. A year later they married. It took another year for her to get pregnant.

The marriage went stale, but motherhood was a dream. She and Christopher went everywhere and did everything together. No need for play dates. They were their own play date. He was a cuddly, affection little boy with fleshy hands and sad eyes. She breast fed him until just before his fourth birthday. She was at Barnes and Noble for story time when Christopher unbuttoned her blouse, loosened the strap on her bra and began to nurse. She noticed the disapproving eyes of other moms and the lascivious looks of some fathers.

Christopher made the ensuing transition without trauma. Rosemary was depressed for weeks. When he started kindergarten, she came to a complete stop for several months. Her husband convinced her to come back to work. Three weeks later she slipped off the curb and hurt her back. And Christopher grew as some kids do, largely invisible, as his father grew the business empire and his mother grew a habit.

Rosemary taps lightly with one fingernail on Christopher's door. "Honey?" She waits but there's no answer. She steps away from the door, then decides to try again. Perhaps he is sacked out or not feeling well. She knocks this time and tries the door knob, which is locked. "Christopher, honey? Are you in there?" He doesn't answer, but she can hear his bed springs creaking. "Are you okay?" She hears his voice but can't make out what he's saying. There is a click and she tries the knob again. She pushes the door partially open and peeks around the jamb, a smile on her face. "Peek-a-boo." But Christopher doesn't reply. She opens the door wide and enters. "Christopher." Her tone has changed.

No longer trying to be playful or cute, her voice has the adult sound of worry.

Christopher is lying on his bed in a soft fetal position facing away from his mother. His Yankees cap is on the pillow. He still has his Nikes on, even though he has been warned about putting "those ratty things" on the furniture. His jeans are rumpled from several days of wear. He has sleep hair, his straight reddish brown mop in tangles and knots.

"Honey, I thought you were going to Magee's to play."

Christopher shifts but doesn't speak. She sits on the bed and places a hand on his shoulder. His deep brown eyes are open and Big Bear, threadbare legs and eyeless face, is in his arms. She grins and pats Big Bear. "Honey, where did you ever find this old friend?"

"The closet."

"Boy, there are a lot of good memories in this old guy, aren't there?"

Christopher shrugs and squeezes the bear more tightly.

"I don't even remember who bought him for you. I know you were tiny, just a peanut. You loved having him in your crib. I remember you babbled at him, like you were talking and he was talking back. So cute. Before long he was in your arms. And there he stayed."

Christopher rolls over on his back, his red, puffy eyes scanning the ceiling. She runs her fingers through his hair, moving it away from his face. She places a palm on his forehead. No fever. "Do you feel okay? Is there something wrong?" She feels frustrated when he doesn't answer and pulls her hand away. She tries to smile but he isn't looking at her.

"Christopher, really. Don't ignore your mother, please. It's rude." She starts to get up.

"How is that man, Mr. Goode, how's he doing? Is he, like, still alive and everything?"

Startled by his question, Rosemary stands up straight and then sits again, this time at the bottom of the bed. "What made you think of him, honey?"

"I met him, didn't I, like at that store with the lady, what's her name, his wife?"

"You mean, Frankie, Mrs. Goode, yes, I guess you did. I'm sure you went with me to visit her. I don't remember Gavin, Mr. Goode, ever being there when we were there."

"He joked and he asked me lots of questions about school and baseball and stuff. He was nice. He laughed a lot, even if no one was saying anything funny."

"Yes, a nice man."

"He got hurt bad, didn't he?"

"Yes, he got hurt very bad."

"Is he gonna make it?"

"They don't know."

A cloud seemed to cross Christopher's face.

"You visit his wife, don't you? I mean, you go to the hospital, right? Have you seen him? Is he talking or anything?"

"Yes, I've gone. Many times. He's just quiet. He doesn't talk, no. It's a terrible thing but not something for a little boy to be concerned about." She slides closer to him.

"How does he look?"

"Well, he looks…mostly like he's asleep."

"Asleep. Not dead."

"Christopher—"

"Do you think they'll catch him, the guy who did this? I mean, the police gotta know something; they just aren't tellin'."

"It doesn't appear that they're any closer to figuring this—"

"If he dies, the guy would get the electric chair, right?"

"Christopher, what—"

"I mean, isn't that what happens to people when they kill someone? If someone kills someone, they should be killed, too."

"Why are you talking about this? It's nothing for you to be concerned about, honey. Why don't you get up? I'm sure Magee is wondering—"

Christopher sits up and pushes himself back against the headboard, stuffed animal now in his lap. He pulls his knees to his chest. Rosemary notices for the first time that the baby fat around his jaw and along his neck is gone. His face is longer and the expression on it looks old.

"I mean, it's fair, right. He was alive and then he was dead, or almost dead, and someone has to pay, and, well, Magee said his dad told him that if they catch the guy, they should just take him out and shoot him. That's what he deserves."

"My God, Christopher, that's an awful thing for him to say. Don't listen to that. He's just upset that this happened, that Mr. Goode got hurt—"

"Shot, you mean shot, Mom."

"Well, yes, shot. But Christopher, you know, for one thing, Mr. Goode isn't dead; he may even make it. For another, it looks like this had to have been an accident; not like someone went into his office and shot him on purpose. Lastly, why are you worrying about this now? It's been months. Was it because of what Magee told you? I'll talk to his mother, if you'd like. I don't want you to be upset for no reason."

Rosemary places a hand on his foot, but he pulls it away.

"It's all jumbled up. I try not to think about stuff, but sometimes I can't help it. It just comes in my head and I can't make it go away. I try as hard as I can, but it doesn't work. It's stuck in there, you know what I mean? When I talk to Dad, he says 'get it out of your mind, it's over' but it doesn't feel over. It feels like it's gonna go on and on and on and I'm never gonna get rid of it."

Rosemary's stomach is knotted now. She pulls her hand back, but then moves closer to her son. She leans forward to get a better look at his face, now hidden in his hands. "Honey," she whispers. "It's okay." She takes one of his hands in hers. He looks ahead blankly. "What did Daddy mean when he said 'get it out of your mind, it's over'? Did he say what he meant?"

"Dad said don't say anything to anybody. Just talk to him. But when I talk to him, he gets upset and tells me to stop and then I don't know what to do."

Rosemary takes Christopher's face in her hands. "Honey, sweetheart, you can always talk to me."

"No, I can't."

"Yes, you can. Look, I was sick, but I'm getting better. I know I wasn't the best mom there for a while, but remember, I explained that I had a very bad—"

"I can't."

Rosemary sits back on the bed. She feels like she's lost the first round of a fight she didn't know she was in.

"Okay, honey. I'm sure Daddy didn't mean you couldn't talk to me about this. Whatever it is. When I was your age, I had lots of big worries, but when I told them to someone, they got very small very quickly. It's always better for things to come out."

"I'm not supposed to tell you."

"What?"

"Daddy said not to tell you anything about this. He said you wouldn't understand and that it would make things worse. He said it would upset you."

Rosemary breathes evenly, trying to cool her reddening face. She's glad her husband isn't there, because if he was she would smash his face in. She looks at her little boy and tries to forget her husband and herself.

"So today I told Magee that I had this secret thing, that I might have done something I shouldn't have, and he got all Catholic on me cause his brother's a priest and he was like asking me if it was a venial sin or a mortal sin, because venial isn't so bad, but mortal is like you end up going to hell forever and no one can get you out. But I didn't want to tell him what it was because I didn't want to know if it was, like, mortal. Then he kept saying I needed to confess it to a priest, whatever it was, and I told him we weren't Catholic, that we were Christian. And he said that made it even worse cause since I wasn't Catholic I didn't have any way to reach God and explain things and God really hates that and —"

"Christopher, Christopher." She reaches for him as he rocks side-to-side almost unaware that she is there. His wrist is damp and limp. She holds his hand to her face and kisses it. "Honey, you can tell me anything, you know that. I love you." Christopher looks at her, his face white as vanilla cake frosting. Rosemary reaches for him as he gulps and tries to smile but can't. "Honey, what happened? You can tell me."

His face crinkles and folds as tears stream down his cheeks. "Mommy, please don't hate me."

Rosemary holds back her tears and runs her fingers through his hair again. "I could never hate you. I love you too much."

He bows his head as if in prayer. "I'm the one; I'm the one that shot him."

PART 3

CHAPTER 33
IN THE NEWS

The big news hitting the area in the last few weeks has been the opening of the first ever Chick-fil-A in the five county region. It has definitely caused a stir. Chief Rockaway, anticipating a stampede, assigned police officers to the area surrounding the new establishment, hoping to control the tsunamic traffic jam that ensued. "Great chicken," said the Chief, as he wiped his mouth with a Chick-fil-A napkin. "But public safety is our top priority." Some area residents weren't happy about their new neighbor. Protestors carrying signs emblazoned with chickens covered by thick black Xs sat in front of the main entrance. "Hell no, we won't eat your chicken!" they cried. One gentleman who was sitting on his front porch said, "Craziness has taken over our community!" One nearby resident had this to say: "This is unbelievable! (pointing at the long line of cars) Don't these people have jobs or families or somewhere else to be? All this for some damn chicken!" When asked if he had tried Chick-fil-A, he said, "Yes, best chicken I've ever had in my life." The regional office of Chick-fil-A did not respond to requests for comments, but Bobby Applebee, the local manager, said, "God bless America! Release the fryers!"

In other news, a longtime local resident, Hector Rodriguez, will be deported back to Honduras, the result of an immigration hearing this week in Buffalo. Rodriguez and his fiancé, Shondra Williams, were leaving a movie theater in Henrietta when they were surrounded by ICE agents who handcuffed Rodriguez and remanded him to a detention center in Batavia awaiting transfer to Buffalo. ICE agents had been following Rodriguez's movements since his name appeared in a news report about a local shooting several months ago. Rodriguez and Williams had been cooperating with local police regarding the as yet unsolved shooting of Gavin Goode.

Rodriguez came to the US with his parents at the age of eight. He has no criminal record.

The entire Pittsfield community is mourning the death of Jordan "Jordy" Watson, a high school senior who was captain of both the lacrosse and basketball teams, as well as class president. Watson's mother called him to get up for school on Wednesday morning, but when he didn't respond, she went to his room and found him lying on the floor, drug paraphernalia nearby. Family members have refused to talk to the press, but Sergeant Devan Crawford, who runs the district's Dare Program, said "I mean, Jordy, what can I say, he was a great kid; I've known him since middle school; in fact he was planning to take over some of the grade school presentations as part of his senior project; I mean the kid was a straight arrow, if ever there was one; great family, great young man, great everything; a role model, I'm telling you; I hope my son grows up to be another Jordy; I mean that; something just went terribly wrong; someone must have goaded him into, I mean, Jordy just wasn't that kind of kid."

In area sports, the Buffalo Bills faced the New England Patriots at Buffalo's New Era Field in a much anticipated rematch on Monday Night Football. Unfortunately, the Bills got clobbered 52-9 extending their losing streak to six games and almost assuring that the team will miss the playoffs. When asked why the Bills were on such a skid, their head coach said, "The other teams are scoring more points than us."

CHaPTeR 34
LesTeR

Lester attends to Mr. Waverly who was admitted to the ICU after a stroke. Maureen, his wife, sits nearby, a smile on her face. She presents Lester with another in a long line of coffee cakes. "You have been a godsend to Benson and me." Lester demurs. "Don't be modest now, if it weren't for you and all the others, who knows what would have happened to him?" Mr. Conners labors to shake his head and strains to say, "Yeees." Lester bows and thanks them. He takes the coffee cake and places it near the door, saying (as always) that he will dig into it when he gets home. Instead, he will toss it into a trash barrel on the way to the parking garage.

There is no doubt, though, that he likes the Waverly's very much. They are the kind of patient and family that benefit the most from the ICU. They arrive in unspeakable distress; they work hard with the treatment team; they do what they're supposed to do, in Benson's case daily, sometimes twice daily, trips to PT and OT; they move on to another floor and eventually home to take up their life again, altered though it may be.

By every possible measure, this is success. Healthcare resources put to the best possible use for the best possible outcome. If only this was always the case.

In too many instances, patients are admitted to the ICU who should not be there. They are what Lester labels "lingerers," patients who come and stay long past any reasonable heal-by date. And once they are in the system, consuming vast amounts of healthcare resources, there is almost no way to gracefully get rid of them. Once they are on life supports, their bodies don't have to contribute anything to staying alive. They could live forever! Families are loathe to unplug a loved one, and providers hesitate pushing them for fear of lawsuits. So they dance around the subject, hoping the family will see the light; in the meantime, the patient turns into a potted plant. It's ridiculous.

Lester wonders if the hospital would benefit from the shockingly un-PC notion of "death panels," groups of qualified professionals who would make level-headed decisions about who should live and who should die whenever a family is unable to consider the matter rationally. Thumbs up or thumbs down. At a recent staff meeting, Lester floated this idea to his colleagues who, missing the earnestness of his proposal, giggled and snorted. His supervisor guffawed, as well, also taking Lester's suggestion as a welcome release of black humor. Lester joined in the levity, not wanting to put his judgment (and his job) in jeopardy.

But he never abandoned the idea. The Goodes are a perfect example. Don't get him wrong, he loves Frankie and Jenna; he has even started to like Ryan; he can't figure out why they allow a junkie into their circle, but who is he to judge. And, as far as he knows, Gavin was a decent man. Who stays and stays, making no progress apart from a finger movement that the family has transformed into a bizarre resurrection fantasy. During the same period of time, twenty patients have come and gone from Lester's other room. Every single one of them have made it home; granted they weren't exactly the persons they were before they were admitted, and granted six died within a few months of going home, but the point is they left the hospital alive. That is success, clear and simple.

There isn't going to be any success for Gavin Goode. Would Lester have to be the sane one? Would he have to be a one person "death panel," quietly making a decision in the shadows that should be made in the clear light of day?

Lester stands in the hall outside of 12 watching Frankie and Ryan who are checking the monitors and straightening pinched tubes and tucking exposed feet. Though their loved one remains inert, Lester notices changes in the mother-son relationship that he would not have anticipated. In the beginning they didn't look at each other, at least not simultaneously. They would alternate glances, checking out the opposition, though never making eye contact. When they did speak to each other, it was as if they had received a script in the morning that they hadn't had time to rehearse into a passable conversation—"Hello, how are you?" "I am fine, how are you?"

When Jenna was there, things flowed more smoothly. They both spoke to her which created the illusion that they were also talking to each other. But with her pregnancy hitting a rough patch, she comes to the hospital less often. In her absence, mother and son are finding that ignoring each other for hours at a time is intolerable. And now that they have both witnessed the magic finger in action, they have drawn even closer, like Scouts huddled around a flickering campfire.

Ryan seems less, well, Ryan-ish. He doesn't pout. He stands straighter. He doesn't trip over his words or leave the room every time his mother expresses doubt. For her part, Frankie looks at her son more often; she listens to him; she even smiles and says "Thanks" when he brings her fresh coffee.

Lester leans to one side so he can see better what mother and son are doing. Ryan's palm is on his mother's shoulder. He reaches for the back of her neck and caresses it. He is whispering something. She bends over her husband, her head nearly touching her son's. She takes Gavin's hand and looks at Ryan.

Lester worries that Frankie has crossed over to the other side, that she has drunk Ryan's Kool-Aid. For the first time he feels disappointed in her. Though they've never discussed Lester's views on the matter of mercy killing, he has always felt Frankie was an ally. When Ryan went nutty over the finger, she remained supportive but cool, never joining in the lunacy, though never chiding her son for his foolishness. She was steady, level-headed, immune to the distortions of emotion. As far as Lester was concerned, she had already moved on; she had already grieved her lost husband despite having to pretend otherwise. Sometimes when their eyes met, he saw in the lines curling around the corners of her mouth an expression of agreement, of consent.

All that changed after she saw his finger, too. She latched onto it and gobbled it up, like it was manna from heaven. She had been starving and now she was being fed. By lies.

"Good morning!" Lester walks briskly into the room. "And how are the Goode's doing this fine day?" He doesn't wait for an answer or hear what they say. "I don't believe I've ever seen two more faithful people in all my years working in the ICU. How long has it been now? You are remarkable!" He turns to his patient, checks his tracheotomy, peruses the heart monitor, adjusts the drip that balances Gavin Goode's electrolytes, pulls back the sheet to eyeball the catheter and empty the bag, then examines his feeding tube for any infection.

When he turns, there are four expectant eyes glued to him. They still hope that he will have news of some difference, a breakthrough or eureka moment. They don't understand that he is the just a maintenance man now.

"He seems to have more color," suggests Ryan, his puppy eyes eager for a bone.

Lester smiles. Gavin Goode's color hasn't changed since the day he arrived in this room.

"He looks more like himself." Ryan sighs. "At least to me."

Frankie takes up Ryan's cause. "We remember who he was, what he looked like. It must be hard for you, never seeing your patients when they were healthy. I'd think it's impossible to judge their improvement without that baseline." Her voice rises at the end, as if imploring Lester to agree.

"Yes, it would be nice."

Frankie's eyes don't blink.

"I mean, of course it would help if we knew more about our patients before they came here, but…" Lester raises his eyebrows in a shrug. "I guess we depend on family for that." His eyes and Frankie's eyes lock. "So…it's good that you're here, you know, otherwise I wouldn't know if his complexion was any better."

"Have you seen any finger movement this morning?" asks Ryan. "It's been several days. When we saw Dr. Azziz, he said he hadn't noticed. But he's in and out so briefly. You're the one who's here."

"It's been more like a week." Frankie's tone is factual.

"No, I'm afraid I haven't." For weeks when Ryan has asked him this question, Lester has always added a hopeful tagline, like "maybe we just aren't looking at the right time," but he's stopped doing that.

"Hmm. That's odd. I've kept a little chart and there for a while he was moving it every two or three days. Sometimes for a minute or more. Mostly a few seconds, but still." Ryan looks at his father's hand. "Well. We'll just keep waiting." He says this to his mother, who nods.

"It's very hard," she says to Lester. "By now you must have developed a healthy resistance to all this. Not that it doesn't affect you, but you must have figured out a way to…" She gestures with her left hand as if to say "I don't know." "We've never had to go through something like this. Ever. Not that there haven't been losses, but this, this isn't quite a loss, it's something else, something in between."

"Defintely not a loss." Ryan quickly adds this corrective. "I mean, I feel him with me all the time and when I come here, it's like I get recharged or something, like I feel him, his whatever you want to call it, life force or something. So, no, it's not a loss." Frankie taps his arm softly with her finger tips, but her face is grave. "Coming here keeps me going. I hope we keep him going, too. That's the idea anyway. At least until he comes back," says Ryan. Frankie's hand falls to her side. She takes a seat near her husband. "Hope is all we have, but I think it's enough."

"I remember a family, it must have been four, maybe five years ago, whose loved one, a woman in her forties, came in with head trauma after an automobile accident. She was here for the longest time. And the family, especially her daughter, came as often as they could, sometimes twice a day. The daughter, I don't know, maybe twenty-three, twenty-four, was an inspiration. She had hope. She talked to her mother; she caressed her; she washed her face and hands and rubbed her feet and talked to her. And believed. Much like you." Lester nods to Ryan. "Everyone, all the nursing staff on all the shifts were invigorated by her. Everyone pulled hard for her and her mother."

Lester pauses, considering his words, not wanting to sucker punch Ryan but also not wanting to coddle him. "When her mother died, the young woman was completely unprepared. She was shocked, in fact, and blamed the doctors and the nurses and more than anyone else, herself. She just never thought that death was even in the mix." Lester swallows hard and licks his lips. Frankie watches him closely and Ryan seems to be holding his breath. "I loved her hope. I did. But I knew early on that the chances her mother would survive were, like, zero. Once I asked her if she considered the possibility that her mother might not make it. She glared at me and didn't say a word. I would never have taken her hope away. But hope can't replace reality. Much as we'd like it to."

None of what Lester is telling them is factual. There wasn't a woman in her forties who had an automobile accident. No daughter so full of hope that she was blindsided by her mother's death. No outburst of blame and guilt. None of it had happened. At least not on Lester's watch. He is sure that something like this must have happened to someone somewhere, maybe even in this hospital. There are always automobile accidents and victims who end up in the ICU and families that hope for miracles, so while his story isn't technically factual, it is, in all likelihood, true. That's the point. The truth of this whole situation, as Lester sees it, is simple. But for it to get through to Ryan, it has to be wrapped in a package that is visual, that is attention grabbing, that is emotionally similar to what he is facing. That is how way to reach him. And, perhaps, Frankie, too, since he can no longer tell where she stands.

Ryan's face is white. His mouth is dry. He sits awkwardly in his chair and looks at his father. Frankie watches Lester, waiting to see what he will do next.

"I mean, don't get me wrong, there is still some brain activity. I think Dr. Azziz has kept you apprised of that. That's something to hold onto. He is alive, depending on how you think about being alive. It's not the 'alive' he used to be, I'm sure, but, yes, he's alive, it's just…what does that mean now?"

Ryan gets up from his chair and stands beside his father. He reaches for his hand and holds it open in his palm. He lifts it to his face and looks at the finger. "I know you're still in there," he says in a whisper. He kisses the finger and then lays his father's hand on his chest and leaves the room.

Lester's shoulders are taut. He feels perspiration forming in the small of his back.

"I don't understand," says Frankie.

"What do you mean?" Frankie doesn't answer. "I guess I felt that he needed to be aware of —"

"Of what?"

"Of what is coming. I mean, I've seen the damage of false hope. It can blind you to what's ahead. I've felt that damage myself. You hope that someone will do something they never do; or say something, even once, that they never say; or show feelings they never show; you hope that someone will be understanding, but they never are. And never will be. In my experience there's a point at which it isn't smart to hope. At least not too much. You can get hurt, sometimes badly, irreparably." Lester's eyes shift and he blinks rapidly. "Don't get me wrong. I'm not saying that you shouldn't hope at all. Especially when a loved one is ill or injured. I'm just saying be careful. It can turn out to be false. And when you find out it's false hope, you'll suffer. I don't want anyone to suffer."

"I know my son. I know that he's already suffered in his life." She looks away as if wanting to be invisible. "I'm sure of it. And I know he will suffer again. And again. That's the way it is. But if someone takes his hope away, the suffering will be intolerable." She turns her head sharply. "And I don't want anyone to do that to him."

Lester takes one step back, his body folding inadvertently into a slight bow. "I'm sure. I didn't mean—"

"As for what is coming, I know exactly what is coming. You'll be relieved to know that I have no hope. I guess I shouldn't be suffering, should I?"

CHAPTER 35
Ben Hillman

Ben Hillman squints at the spreadsheet on his computer screen as sales staff come and go pitching deals and discussing trade-ins. The last week of each month is always a killer. They are seventy-eight cars short of their quota with only a few days left, so he is accepting almost anything his staff brings to him. The "We Gotta Get Rid of 'Em" sales "extravaganza" is well under way and a slew of new commercials have hit local TV stations starring "Big Ben" smiling ear to ear and bellowing, "COME ON DOWN! BRING THE BIGGEST NET YOU GOT, CAUSE, I'M TELLIN' YOU, THEY'RE FLYING OFF THE LOT!"

Hillman opens his desk drawer and reaches for a pill bottle, half ibuprofen, half valium. He swallows a handful dry, then gulps vodka from the Poland Spring water bottle in his desk. The combination loosens his clenched fists and knotted neck. He looks at the 18X24 framed photo of his father on the wall. Bald head with grey plumes around the ears, boxer's nose, double chin covering the knot on his neck tie, hefty bags under his eyes. He would be dead six months after he sat for the portrait. For what? Cars?

Cars had never been Ben's passion. He worked summers washing cars and setting up the lot when he was a teenager and during college. His plan was to go into medicine until he took his MCATs. It was a long fall from being a physician to hawking cars. He never recovered.

He is determined not to end up like his old man. But how? He hasn't yet developed the ulcers, high cholesterol and hypertension that plagued his father, even though, by his own estimate, he has faced considerably more stress than his father ever did, what with a drug addict wife and a son who has killed someone.

As far as he is concerned, Rosemary is a lost cause. He should never have married her, but she kept getting pregnant and he thought he'd better do the right thing after he divorced his first wife.

But Christopher is a different story. He's just a kid, innocent, no matter what he did. It wasn't his fault. Of course, he shouldn't have had the gun; he shouldn't have shot the gun, but, come on, it wasn't his fault. It just kind of happened. Could have happened to anyone. But it happened to Christopher and, goddammit, he isn't going to let his son be permanently scarred because of something he didn't mean to do. Accidents are called accidents for a reason. Just like collateral damage is called collateral damage for a reason.

He is worried about Christopher who has hit the wall in the aftermath of the unfortunate incident. He's missed school, gotten into some trouble and he's gained a ton of weight, something Ben can't tolerate. "Eat less, Christopher! You know how fat kids get treated!" When he talks to Christopher about these issues, the conversation always comes back to the shooting. Christopher cries and wants to tell his mother and Ben has to cajole him or threaten him, whichever works, so he won't talk.

"Look Christopher, this isn't some little mistake like not doing your homework or dumping a kid's lunch on the floor in the lunch room. This is big. Bigger than anything you will ever do in your whole life. The only way to keep it from taking over and ruining everything is if you don't tell anyone, especially your mother. You know your mother's, how should I say this, she's not in the best of shape. This would break her heart. You don't want that, do you?"

By this time Christopher is usually in tears and shaking his head no. Ben comforts his son and explains that everything will be alright if he does what his father says. Eventually, Christopher nods passively and his father pats his back firmly, like he has just sold a new car to a customer who wanted a used one.

There is a knock on the door. Ben looks up expecting a salesperson to burst in, wanting to discuss another deal. But no one enters. Ben looks at his spreadsheet again. There is another knock.

"Jesus Christ, what is it?"

The door opens and in steps Rosemary, her jaw set, her eyes wide but steady.

"Oh, it's you, honey." Ben forces a smile and stands. "What's up?" He says this as he gestures to a chair in front of his desk. Rosemary doesn't speak. He notices that she has had her hair done, short again after so many years. Her face is also made up, skin smooth, lips red, lashes long. She is wearing a black pencil skirt and pink blouse, buttons open at the top. And heels, she is back to her four inch heels, patent leather, glistening. "Look at you," he says with a broad grin and raised eyebrows. "Too bad it's so early in the day, cause I could use—" She takes three quick steps forward and before he can finish his thought, her stiffened palm smashes the side of his face. His hand goes up for protection, but she is too quick and another blow reaches his reddening cheek.

"What the fuck!" Lips curled, he lurches toward his wife.

"Christopher told me. Everything."

Ben stops. He stands straight and adjusts his sport jacket and tie. He looks at her but doesn't say anything. He falls onto a nearby chair, rubbing his jaw.

Rosemary stands over him. "What in the world were you thinking?"

"I can explain everything." He pulls a tissue from his pocket and dabs blood from his nose. He looks at it and dabs again.

"There's no explaining this."

"It was a goddam accident."

"You know our rules about rifles."

"Our rules! Your rules. Never mine. He's eleven years old. When I was eleven I owned my own gun. I went hunting with my old man. I killed all kinds of things by then. It was the time of my life. And here's my son, like a little baby hiding under mommy's apron, afraid of everything. When I brought that rifle home, you should have seen the look in his eyes. He was a man all of a sudden. It's in his blood, just like it was in mine. A boy needs a gun. Simple as that. It's no crime—"

"Stop it! He shot someone with a gun that you bought and let him use."

"It was an accident."

"My best friend's husband has been in a coma for weeks because you let our son shoot a gun—"

"Wait a minute! You act like I put the rifle in his hands, took him to the window and said, 'Go ahead and pull the trigger; see if you can get someone'. I hid that rifle. I hid the ammo. I hid the magazine. How was I supposed to know there was still a bullet in the fucking chamber and that your son would tear the house apart looking for that rifle?"

Rosemary slumps into the chair opposite her husband, swollen hand in her lap. "Why did you ever marry me?"

"Oh Jesus, not this. I married you because every time I looked at you, you got pregnant. I married you because I didn't want you blabbing to everyone about what was going on between us. I married you, Rosemary, to shut you up."

Rosemary is expressionless as tears stream down her cheeks. Ben shakes his head. He goes to her and kneels on the floor. He reaches for one hand and kisses it. "Look, let's not do this. Not now." His voice is soft; his tone is silky smooth. "Look, Rosey." What to say. "I mean, the one thing we have in common, the one thing we love most is Christopher. Right? It doesn't matter how this happened. It happened. What matters is that we protect our son." He lifts her chin with his hand. "It doesn't matter what you think of me and it doesn't matter what I think of you. What matters is how much we love our son."

Rosemary sniffs. He gives her a tissue. Her shoulders relax. "I think that when we explain everything to the police—"

"What?" Ben stands up. "What police? There's not going to be any police."

"But we have to tell them—"

"No, we don't. We don't have to say anything to anybody ever."

Rosemary stares at him, her mouth open.

"Look, honey, do you know what they do to little boys in juvey, or whatever the fuck they call it? Do you know what big boys do to little boys? What guards do to little boys? Do you want to visit your son once a month; never be able to touch him? Do you want to wait until you're God knows how old, before you can hold your son again?"

Rosemary closes her mouth. She swallows hard. "That wouldn't happen, would it?"

"Who knows? It could. When it goes to a jury, no one can predict what those lunatics will decide. Do you want that for our son?"

"But—"

"There are absolutely no 'buts' here. I'm telling you." Hillman wipes his nose and looks at the tissue, then at Rosemary. She sits, limp as a dish rag.

"Look, this is the best thing we can do for Christopher. Keep our mouths shut. His mouth, too. In time, it will all go away." Rosemary turns her head to him, but her eyes are focused elsewhere. "It will, I'm telling you."

CHAPTER 36
Jenna Goode

On the kitchen table in front of Jenna are a zucchini, a ruler and her laptop. She measures the zucchini. Thirteen inches. She glances at the information on the computer screen and then extends the ruler another two and one half inches. That's how long her baby girl is this week. She leans back in her chair and holds her belly. She reads more. "Mommy's weight gain should be about 18 to 25 pounds." Jenna laughs. The baby is almost three pounds. The baby's skin is getting smoother and her brain is getting wrinkly. Her little girl is active. The occasional Braxton Hicks take Jenna's breath away. Most important, if the baby were born today, she would make it.

The bleeding that shocked Jenna in the early weeks and months seems normal now. It comes and goes and "is to be expected," her midwife explains. She will have yet another ultrasound this morning. Jenna tries to remain hopeful.

"Good morning, honey." Ryan enters the kitchen, opens the frig, grabs a half gallon of milk, then heads to the cupboard for some Honey Nut Cheerios. Pours the cereal, then the milk, takes his "Daddy" mug from the shelf, hits the Keurig and then sits at the table opposite Jenna.

"Well, are you ready for today?"

"Yeah." Jenna takes a sip of her decaf tea. The cup rattles as she places it back on the saucer.

"Look, I've got a feeling that today will be the day that it's moved back to where it's supposed to be. Don't you?"

"Well—"

"I mean, it's gotta get out of the way. Simple as that. Anyway, you said yourself that your midwife isn't that worried, right?"

"I don't know what she thinks. If she was worried, I doubt she'd tell me. It doesn't work that way."

"You gotta be more positive, Jenna."

By now Ryan is ready for another cup of coffee.

Jenna has learned that it is one thing to stay outwardly positive, but it is another thing entirely to know deep inside that your body has a mind of its own, that you are just along for the ride, that anything can happen. In the months since Ryan's father entered the hospital, she has gone from admiring Ryan's steadfast confidence, something that seemed like a strength, to being worried that it is merely willful blindness, plain and simple. Can't he see what's coming?

She worries that the same thing is happening with the baby; that his cheerleading has no relationship to what is transpiring in her uterus. That he is turning a blind eye to a gathering storm. Almost immediately, she feels guilty for her questioning, thinking that her own doubts could be as detrimental to the pregnancy as her husband's misguided expectations.

"Are you coming with me this morning?"

Ryan turns, his face looks incredulous. "Of course, I'm coming. Wouldn't miss it. My mother will be at the hospital and Josey is opening the parlor, so I'm free." The first frost hit earlier in the week and in its aftermath customers stopped coming in for cones and shakes. Ryan insists there will be a warming spell just around the corner, so he continues to open for a few hours each day.

Jenna joins him in a bowl of cereal and for a short time it is quiet.

The silence continues on the way to the hospital. Jenna clutches the arm rest and looks out the window at orange-leafed maples lining the street, then at bumper to bumper expressway traffic, at city houses huddled in tight rows, at airliners skimming the treetops, at the blocks-long collection of oddly shaped buildings that is the hospital, and finally at the parking garage with its seeming endless levels. She tries not to breathe the exhaust as she walks with Ryan to the elevator. He takes her hand and squeezes it. She is relieved to have him there; she needs his confidence. She squeezes back.

Jenna is buoyed by the secretary's warm reception at check-in. "You look great!" A nurse in the hallway waves and says, "Good to see you." As she slips carefully into a seat in the waiting room, Jenna feels calm again. There are so many people pulling for her; so many people who have gone down this road with other women, that she suddenly feels carefree.

This lasts ten minutes until a nurse comes to the waiting room door and calls, "Jenna Goode!" Ryan takes her hand and steadies her as she stands. Together they head for the first stop—weigh in. She's gained about thirty-five pounds, but today she doesn't care. In the exam room, the nurse takes her blood pressure and checks her heart and lungs. Today she has one question---Is there an opening for her baby?

They wait another ten minutes until a tech comes in to goo up her belly so she can conduct the ultrasound. She doesn't say anything when she's done. Ten minutes later, Mandy, her midwife, enters the room. This time, though, she has someone else with her.

"Hi guys, how are you doing today?" Mandy doesn't wait for their response. "This is Dr. Gordon. You may remember way back at the beginning that we have OB/GYN consultants who work with us, especially during a high risk pregnancy."

Jenna knew this term. She had read about high risk pregnancies on line. She had been moved by first person accounts of women who struggled valiantly with high risk pregnancies. She had wondered how they managed, how they kept going through that kind of dark fog. But she had never thought of her own pregnancy as high risk. And Mandy had never used that term before.

Jenna looks at Ryan who holds her hand tightly. He is listening intently to Dr. Gordon who has been speaking for a minute or more. Dr. Gordon is older; her brown hair is in a tight bun; her wire rim glasses are glistening; she is wearing a white lab coat, her name stitched on her chest pocket in blue. She is matter-of-fact but sober. She doesn't make eye contact. Mandy is trying to make up for this by scanning back and forth between Jenna and Ryan like an anxious and protective labrador.

Jenna tries to catch up to what Dr. Gordon is saying.

"...of course, our first concern is the baby. But we are also concerned for your welfare, Mrs. Goode. The mother's health is the baby's health after all." This sounds like the opening statement for a lawyer's closing argument. "Mandy has kept me apprised of your progress and the nature of your complications. Today's ultrasound doesn't show any change in the placenta previa, which is to say, it's still covering you cervix. Now, I should hasten to add that this could still change, but to avoid anything catastrophic…"

With this word— catastrophic— Jenna can listen no longer. She looks at the green walls and the charts and the happy mural on the opposite wall, a mother and father holding a newborn. She tries to take deep, even breaths, but her chest won't expand. Her face grows warm and then hot, perspiration gathering in sheets. She can feel nausea rising as the room begins to wobble.

"I don't feel well." She says this softly. Ryan turns to her, puts his arm around her. The doctor doesn't seem to notice.

"Are you okay, Jenna," says Mandy.

"I need to lie down." There is nothing more for her to do. Any control she might have had is relinquished. She closes her eyes and tries to breathe. She is limp. She closes her eyes and tries not to throw up. Her whole body, now fully immersed in perspiration, starts to cool. The nausea congeals into a fist, and then a knot, smaller and smaller. She takes her first deep breath; it feels intoxicating.

Everyone is moving fast. Dr. Gordon calls for a nurse to bring an EKG monitor. They attach the leads. Jenna is not worried, though. She knows there's nothing wrong with her heart. It's her soul that has lost oxygen.

"Have you had any breakfast this morning?" asks the nurse. Jenna looks at her and shakes her head. "Let's get you some juice. Orange? Apple?"

"Apple," says Jenna as she closes her eyes.

"What's happening?" Ryan is flushed as well. "Is she going to be okay? What's going on?"

"The EKG looks fine, but your BP crashed. The juice should help. This isn't unusual in pregnancy. Not to worry." Dr. Gordon's tone has changed. The medical edge is gone. She seems amiable, almost chummy, like they were sorority sisters commiserating. "How are you feeling? Your color is coming back little by little, that's good."

The nurse returns with the juice and everyone is smiling.

"Are you sure everything is okay?" asks Ryan.

■   ■   ■   ■   ■

It is quiet again in the car as Jenna and Ryan head for home. Jenna looks at Ryan's stone cold face. She remembers the doctor saying something about "activity restriction" and Ryan saying, "What's that?" and Mandy interjecting "Complete bed rest." She remembers words pouring from the doctor's mouth: "be cautious...prolonged inactivity...constipation...low birth-weight...minimal, but regular activity..." She can see Mandy's face moving close: "All it means is that you start mothering earlier than expected." There is a smile across her mouth, but her eyes look weary, sad. Jenna doesn't respond, still focused on breathing, still holding her belly.

Once home, Jenna lies on the front room sofa where the sun shines in the midday. Ryan brings her a glass of orange juice. He places it on the coffee table, then sits on the floor beside her. He asks how she is doing and at first she doesn't know how to answer. She wants to say "tired," but that doesn't capture it. "Worried" comes closer. "Afraid" comes closest.

"I don't know," she says.

"Yeah, I know."

Ryan explains how shocked he is about "the whole thing." He's angry at Mandy because she didn't warn them this could happen. But she did, thinks Jenna. She did warn them when she went over the list of things they needed to know about placenta previa. They never talked about it and without the reinforcement of discussion her warning evaporated. With Ryan's father being in the hospital, there wasn't any room for another big worry. There wasn't room for anything else. Everything was about her father-in-law. What did Dr. Azziz say? What did Lester think? Why isn't he more positive? Did Dad move his finger? I think he still has a chance, don't you? Of course the baby was important, but it was still a promise, something to look forward to, something that was waiting for them down the road. Gavin's situation had already arrived; it was here now, lingering and emergent all at the same time.

Jenna can feel the pulse in her neck. She takes another deep breath and closes her eyes. For a moment everything is still, everything is far away and she is alone. She can hear Ryan breathing but he doesn't speak. The clock strikes the hour. She feels the sun on her left hand, warm and soothing. The baby moves a little. Then more and soon she can feel an elbow crossing her belly and maybe a little bum. She pats her baby who is just inches below her hand. She is glad that her little girl is exploring, rolling, turning. Jenna is happy her little girl doesn't know anything about the outside world, that her innocence is protected. She wishes it could stay that way. If only the baby could stay in her warm, little world unaware of what is outside.

Jenna caresses her belly with both hands. She leans over so she can hug her baby. She understands that her wish is just that, a wish; not something that is possible. She knows that no world is completely safe, not even the tiny world which is home to her baby. At every turn her baby will face challenge upon challenge. Jenna kisses her hand and then massages the kiss into her tummy. Her baby doesn't know anything yet, not really; she doesn't know that her first and maybe most important challenge is already here. How will she get out; how will she leave her warm amniotic home and burst into the world itself, where her life awaits, so full of so much?

Jenna still feels afraid, but it is a smaller fear, a tiger cub rather than a tiger. She knows the fear won't go away, but it won't maul her either. She feels bigger than she was. She breathes deep.

"Feel this," she says.

"What?"

"Come here, feel this."

Ryan kneels beside her. She takes his hand and guides him to where his baby is playing. He smiles and kisses her belly and then her cheek.

"I love you," he says.

She weaves her fingers into his as together they trace movements here and movements there.

"You and I did this." For a brief moment, it all seems simple. "We're going to have this baby."

CHAPTER 37
FRANKIE GOODE

"I'm leaving now." Frankie whispers this to Gavin. She studies his face like a cartographer hopelessly trying to locate a place she once knew so well, looking for the months-ago Gavin who would smile back at her, who would wink and kiss her while patting her on the behind. She examines the lines, the folds, the creases that weren't there before, evidence of this new Gavin, this shell-of-Gavin. "I love you." His eyes dart; his arms shutter. She doesn't look at his finger anymore.

She stands and turns to leave as Lester enters the room.

"Leaving?"

"Yes. I have a few things to do."

"I understand."

She doesn't like the implication in his raised eyebrows and gently nodding head, the sympathy in his lowered voice suggesting that having "a few things to do" means "there's nothing to do here anymore."

"I'll be back."

"Of course. I'll take good care of him in the meantime."

Frankie stops at the door and turns back. Lester is standing over Gavin speaking, his voice lowered, one hand on Gavin's arm.

It has been two weeks since Jenna started bed rest. Frankie has spoken to her several times but hasn't visited. Today is the day. She heads home to pick up the cinnamon breakfast cake she made, Jenna's favorite, and some gossipy magazines. On the way, she stops at the grocery store to buy a bouquet of sunflowers.

She pulls into her driveway and turns her collar up when a gust of wind shuts her eyes and lifts her shoulders in defense. She frowns, thinking of Ryan and Curly's. The warm spell did not return. Cold wind has replaced the summer heat and humidity. Pumpkins adorn neighboring porches. The sun is gone by seven. Soon the leaves on her lawn will be replaced with snow. What will she do when snow fills the driveway and Gavin isn't there to blow it away? Gavin loves winter. He loves the snow and his boots and his parka and the motorcycle buzz of the snow blower. He loves Christmas, although in recent years she has convinced him they don't need to cut a live tree. The trees that the Boy Scouts sell are fine. He loves the crunchiness of January, the frigidness of February and the unpredictability of March. She hates everything about winter except Gavin's love of it.

Entering her house, knowing that no one will be there, that no one will come, has been the hardest part of her ordeal. Not that watching Gavin each day hasn't been its own kind of torture, but there is something about an empty house, with all its reminders of what used to be, that is its own special hell. For weeks after the accident she called, "I'm home!" each time she entered. Now she is hesitant as she stands in the foyer. She kicks off her shoes, no longer taking note of the bench where Gavin's black bomber jacket still lies in a pile. She doesn't go into the front room or the family room or any room other than the kitchen, the bedroom, and the bathroom. Sometimes she looks into those other rooms, wondering where their life has gone.

Frankie goes into the kitchen. She takes saran wrap from the drawer under the counter and carefully covers the cake to seal in its moisture. She closes her eyes and listens for Gavin's voice. If she was going to hear it anywhere, she would hear it here where they sat together over dinner each night, talking about the day, sometimes laughing, making plans, or just remembering; a ritual they protected against the busy-ness of their lives.

She thinks of Rev. Lorde, how sometimes you have the thinnest of filaments to hold onto; how holding on is faith and the filament, ever strong, is grace. She likes the sound of these words as they echo in her mind, despite not knowing exactly what they mean. Sometimes she feels like she is holding onto nothing at all; that the act of holding on itself is what matters even if there's nothing in your grip.

She stands at the top of the basement stairs, reaches for the switch and turns the lights on. She goes down to Gavin's office where the cool air is damp and a perfect sheen of grey dust covers everything. She sees evidence of Ryan having been there, hand prints and smears on the desktop and drawers. Frankie sits in her husband's swivel chair and leans back to rest her head. She needs to see for herself. She needs to hold in her hands the evidence of what he knew, what he kept as secret knowledge.

She rifles through the desk drawers, wondering if Ryan has returned the notebook or journals or whatever they are. At the bottom of his left hand drawer, underneath lose papers, boxes of bics and several rulers, she finds them, piled neatly. Ryan must have been so shaken by her anger that he returned them, buried them, in this vault where he must have assumed they would remain untouched.

She pulls out the notebooks and places them on the desk blotter. She turns on the desk lamp but then hesitates, unsure whether she wants to see what's in them. Should she respect what he obviously wanted to keep private? Is this fair? Before she can answer these questions, she is opening the first notebook, which is empty. She tosses it back into the drawer and opens the second one. Here she finds his craggy handwriting, jerky and almost indecipherable. She glides her fingers over the letters, feeling the faint spikes and curlicues, thinking of Gavin bent over his desk recording what seem to be tiresomely mundane details of everyday life. Weather, haircuts, illnesses, Ryan's activities, her own comings and goings, routines, routines, routines. Then she finds the first reference to 'C'. The page is dog-eared and numbered in pencil – 1. She flips through the notebook to identify the other folded pages.

There is a single fly buzzing ferociously at the block window opposite the desk, desperate to get out. It stops and then dashes against the glass again and again. Frankie takes one of the notebooks, stands and swats the fly which falls to the floor behind Gavin's desk. She sits back in the chair again, lapsing into moments of quiet, feeling nothing. She wonders what Gavin thought as he sat here writing. How did she not know that these notebooks existed? It wasn't as if they didn't talk, that they didn't share intimate parts of their lives with each other. Or did they? She closes her eyes and imagines them together on the porch or driving somewhere or shopping at the mall or lying in bed together after making love. Their faces are transparent, welcoming, honest. Was he thinking of 'C' all that time, hiding his real feelings, not wanting to confront her? Was he angry? Afraid? Ashamed? Did he keep loving her?

She looks up through the egress window at grey clouds rushing. She turns again to the eight entries. Something about them puzzles her. She looks at each one in turn. The first, the second, the third, and so on. She tears off a scrap of paper, grabs a pen and writes down the dates. Once she has recorded all eight, she closes the notebook and studies the list of months, days, years.

Her chest is throbbing now, her hands trembling. But she does not cry. There are no tears left.

She looks around the room, a map of the United States, one of the world, another of the solar system; gardening shoes in the corner; a sagging sofa dividing the space, a tilting reading lamp beside a platform rocker she had once used when Ryan was a baby. She looks at the list of dates in her hands.

She goes upstairs to her office adjacent to the sunroom. There are windows all around, a print of Monet's waterlilies, a poster on an easel from the grand opening of her dress shop, three lean but comfortable teal suede sitting chairs, wide plank floors and a fringed oriental rug with light blue accents. She sits at her glass top desk, turns on her computer and opens her calendar. She places the scrap of paper on the keyboard as she scrolls through the years. She stops at the first date, then the second and third. She leans forward, elbows on the table, bemused. Again she compares the dates with her calendar. Still perplexed; she reviews the dates yet again.

In the kitchen, Frankie chooses a pod of coffee and opens the Keurig. Then she changes her mind, replaces the pod and opens the wine refrigerator on the granite counter next to the toaster. She chooses a Finger Lakes Riesling. Uncorks it and pours a tall glass. She places the glass on the kitchen table and slides into her chair. She takes a sip and then another.

It would make most sense for Gavin's 'C' entries to match the dates when she had been away at a fashion show or conference, dates when she would have been with Conner. But they don't. None of the entries were written on days that she was out of town. In fact, they were often off by months. She pours another glass of wine and goes back to Gavin's office.

CHAPTER 38
Jenna Goode

Jenna reaches for her iPhone and checks the time. She tosses it back on the bed and looks out the window. Frankie should have arrived an hour ago. She is never late; in fact, she is usually early to everything by exactly five minutes. She reaches for her laptop and returns to the YouTube channel for pregnant women on bed rest. Who knew? It's called "Grounded but Grateful." There is this blonde woman, her hair straggly and her eyes weary, talking about being in bed for two months. She smiles, gestures constantly, and talks with manic enthusiasm about her situation, how she is happy to be "locked down" if it means her "little Jakey" will be "perfect." She exudes false confidence. "No doubts here!"

She goes on to explain that she is lying on her left side so her baby won't press on major blood vessels and explains that her husband checks her for bed sores and massages her twice a day. "Little Jakey" was not getting adequate blood supply so he wasn't "quite the size he's supposed to be." She smiles at this and looks at her bulging tummy. Then she looks at the camera, still smiling, her eyes filling with tears. Jenna closes the site.

She opens Facebook to "Bedresters Unite!" All the mothers-to-be seem resilient and resolved. And confused. "I lay in bed all night and most of the day, but I gotta pick up my daughter at preschool. Is that pushing it?" "Does this mean totally staying in bed all the damn time and only getting up to pee or take a shower???" Then there are the pros: "I've been on bed rest 4 months; as my doctor puts it, we're walking on eggshells until my baby arrives. He does want me to get up sometimes to avoid leg clots or bad back pains. My advice — listen to your body and talk to you doc. All will be well."

There are precious few who come off bed rest.

Jenna reaches for her water bottle and takes a long drink. She always has two bottles nearby. She gets up several times a day and walks around the bedroom. She has a resistance band that she loops around her feet and pulls with both arms. She eats many tiny meals a day, trying to avoid the crushing heartburn that plagued her in the beginning. Ryan bought her several colorful pillows to put under her legs and behind her back. She meditates. Talks to the baby. Washes her hair and, when possible, puts on makeup. Talks to her baby. Talks to her baby.

Her boss swings on a pendulum from quasi-empathy ("I'm sure this is not that easy.") to thinly veiled exasperation ("You know better than I do that the bank doesn't run itself.") "Are your doctors sure this is a real thing?" he asked most recently when they started talking about how much work she could do in her current state. She negotiated working several hours a day from home so the bank wouldn't dock her salary. Or fire her. She needs the insurance. She had the OB write a letter, and she contacted her lawyer just to feel safe.

The weather finally convinced Ryan to close Curly's so their finances are on thin ice. Even though she is in no shape to do battle with anyone, it falls to her to keep the wolves from the door.

"No change" is the report at each checkup since taking to her bed. "I am taking this as a positive," says her OB, who is much more involved now. "Anytime things don't get worse, we must think of it as progress." She reassures her and Ryan that their baby is doing well. Everyone praises them for "doing a fabulous job." Jenna leaves each appointment feeling uplifted. Until she rolls into bed again and reckons with the utter lack of normality surrounding her life.

Jenna eases out of bed and goes to the window. She pulls the curtain back and looks down the street but there are no cars in sight. She then goes into the bathroom and takes a seat. She places her elbows on her knees and cradles her face in her hands. She feels her little girl move.

"There's my little sweet pea." She smiles broadly and closes her eyes.

While she hasn't told Ryan, she has added prayer to the list of things she is doing for the baby's welfare. She is a little embarrassed by this because she has never been religious. Her parents weren't atheists; they just didn't think about such things. Same with Jenna. She had friends who went to church and Bible School and Youth Group. She went with a friend once. It was pleasant enough, but she didn't see the point. In adulthood, the only time she was aware of religion was when something terrible hit the headlines. Mostly, the whole idea of religious institutions made her shake her head.

But this is different. She isn't signing onto anything. She isn't taking vows or pledging allegiance. She is responding to something deep inside that wells up from time to time. Her prayers are unsophisticated at best. No "Our Father" or "Dear God," nothing like that. Not even an "Amen." Her favorite prayers are simple: "Help, help, help, help!" Or: "Why, why, why, why?" And sometimes: "I'm holding on as best I can! Really!" Other days during the long quiet of mid-afternoon, when she can hear birds at her window and watch trees bending in the wind, and her baby is moving like today, she says, "Oh my, oh my," softly but right out loud. And for a moment she feels confident; she feels that everything will be okay.

She hears the front door opening and then a voice calling. "Hello, it's me; I'm here!" Jenna tilts her head, confused by the loudness of Frankie's voice, so uncharacteristic. She hears her mother-in-law clomping up the steps and watches for the bedroom door to open.

Frankie blusters in, her hair a little disheveled, her face red, her smile crooked.

"How's my favorite daughter-in-law doing today?"

"Fine." Jenna looks at Frankie warily.

"And that little baby girl, how is she doing?" With that, Frankie lunges toward Jenna and sits awkwardly on the side of her bed. She reaches for Jenna's belly.

"It's me! It's Grandma!"

She leans in and gives Jenna a sloppy kiss on the cheek. When she sits back, the smell of wine remains. Jenna is unsure what to say or do.

"Are you okay?"

"Am I okay? Am I okay? That's a very good question, my dear. Hmm, am I okay?" She heaves a deep sigh and runs her fingers through her hair. She leans a little to one side and smiles again. She stands and waves her arm. "Who of us is ever okay? Who of us is ever doing well, you know what I mean? Everyone has a truck with their name on it, you know. A truck that's going to run them down sometime or other."

"Frankie?"

"It's true. It is." She tries to sit up straight. "Anyway, how are *you*? How are *you* doing cooped up here?" She laughs again. "You and me, we're both trapped, you know; we're both trapped waiting for the next thing to happen. Hoping it's no worse than what's happened already." Frankie stands and walks to the window, then tumbles into the rocker. Her face, always supple, is strained and hollow-cheeked.

Jenna swallows hard but remains still, both hands now over her belly.

"Frankie, please, something's wrong."

Frankie looks at Jenna through half-masked eyes.

"Your husband, the detective, the snoop. He was right."

Jenna shakes her head, both puzzled and frightened by Frankie's behavior.

"I don't understand what you're—"

"The Cs, the Cs. He was right about them. He was right about his father. He was. The Cs don't lie, do they?"

She pulls a yellowed envelope from her pocket and waves it in the air as she walks in a circle around the room. She heads for the bed and stumbles onto it. She takes Jenna's hand in hers and kisses it, then lets it go. She comes closer and squints into Jenna's eyes. "And here's the real surprise. What is true of Gavin is also true of me." Her eyes widen and her mouth makes an O. She snickers and then stops abruptly. "Neither of us was true. And neither of us knew. How 'bout that? The truth is that there were lies between us, it would seem. There were lies, things we did in secret; things that we were ashamed of but couldn't stop."

"Frankie, I think you're a little…I think you're not thinking clearly."

"Thinking is never clear. It is always muddled. But that's what we have."

Frankie drops the envelope on Jenna's pillow. "Look for yourself." Jenna takes the envelope in her hands, its seal long ago broken. She slides the folded paper out and opens it. "Dearest Gavin," it begins. She closes it.

"Her name was Connie. A colleague. His name was Conner. A colleague."

Jenna opens her mouth but nothing comes. Frankie lays her head on Jenna's lap. She closes her eyes: Help, help, help, help!

CHAPTER 39
Gavin Goode

There is no doubt that Gavin is still here. "Here" being in this room, in this body, in this bed, attached to his tubes. He is obviously still here. Who can question this? Who can doubt it? His face, his hair, his eyes, his nose, his thin dry mouth, his purple legs, his boney fingers, even his bodily organs are here. His chest moves up and down with the help of a relentlessly devoted ventilator. They bathe his body and massage his feet and turn him many times so his skin won't get sores.

If Gavin weren't here, why else would Lester come? Why would Frankie and Ryan and Jenna come? Why else would the insurance company keep paying (some of it, anyway).

Since he is here, they turn the lights on during the day. They turn them off at night (not all of them, of course). They never shut off the machines. God forbid. Doctor Azziz comes with his coterie of other doctors. He runs tests. Gavin's case is reviewed every day. Young doctors are learning from him. He is their teacher. Notes are entered electronically. Carts come and go.

Room 12. Gavin Goode's room. On the sixth floor of a major medical center. A room devoted entirely to him. Housekeepers clean his floor and remove his waste and put new plastic bags into his garbage cans. They, like everyone else, depend on him being here. He is a part of their job. He is definitely in the room.

While he may be in the room, there is no doubt that Gavin Goode has already left the building.

His brain hangs on. By a thread. The world outside is closed off now. There is no link. There is no reaching out, no finger wagging. There is no returning. There is also no shock or sadness or even awareness. His leaving comes as evening comes, with dusk and then darkness and soon, pitch.

Gavin is floating somewhere. He is adrift but not lost. He is wandering but not afraid. He is gone but feels no loneliness.

There is only his semblance lying there, so dear to those who love him.

And so, the machines machine on and the doctors check his reflexes and his eye movements and his response to pin pricks. The EEG has its ear to his brain, listening to life's echo.

CHAPTER 40
ROSEMARY

Rosemary didn't go to the funeral. She planned on going, but when the day came, she stayed in bed instead. She told her husband that she was coming down with something. He snorted and went to work. What was she supposed to say? A boy that I used to tutor in high school died unexpectedly of an overdose. And, by the way, he was my dealer.

When Rosemary heard that Jordy had died, her first thought was, What am I going to do? Her second thought was, Why did he do this to me? Her third thought was, I can't believe he's gone. It was this third thought that enabled her to go to the wake. To stand in line with tearful teenage girls and awkwardly stoic teenage boys, weepy teachers and stalwart administrators. Many shaking their heads in disbelief. The family lined against one wall, chairs for his mother and father whose exhaustion and despair shown on their numbed faces. There are pictures of Jordy as a baby, his first day of school, vacations with the family, Christmases. Nothing in them hints at what was to come.

Rosemary is surprised by what happened, but she isn't shocked. His hands were always near the fire. Her eyes well up as she looks at a picture of ninth grade Jordy, the year she met him. As she leans over, she feels someone beside her. She straightens and turns to the boy in the black suit, white shirt and rumpled black tie. He is taller, thicker than Jordy. His hair is curly brown and his face is pock marked.

He sticks out his hand, "You must be Rosemary." A smile creeps into one corner of his mouth as his eyes meet hers, unblinking.

"Yes, I am." She reaches for his hand, a quizzical look on her face. "Do I know you?"

"No, but you will." His eyes search hers.

"I don't understand. Were you a friend of Jordy's."

"More a business partner. But also a friend." He smiles broadly. "It's a tragedy, isn't it?"

Rosemary lets go of his hand and steps back. "Yes. His poor parents."

"For you, I mean."

"I beg your pardon."

"Look, I'm Jeff. You'll find a little something in your purse. If you need anything, call me."

She glares at him as he walks away, mourners piling up in line behind her. She turns back but doesn't look at the photos again. She reaches discretely into her purse and feels a bottle. She closes her purse and snaps it shut. She takes a breath and looks at those nearest her, none of whom seem to know she is even there. She turns around again, but Jeff is gone.

Two weeks later she meets Jeff again, this time in the same parking lot where she had met Jordy so often.

"Hey, pretty lady, that was quick." Jeff makes himself comfortable in the passenger seat as Rosemary leans away. "I didn't expect to see you for another couple of weeks. Jordy said you were a slow burner. But when you needed it, you needed it. I guess you need it."

Rosemary doesn't like Jeff. She is revolted by his arrogance. At least Jordy treated her with respect most of the time. And when he didn't, Rosemary thought he was showing off for her, trying to be a bigshot. This feels different. As far as she can tell, Jeff is the kind of kid who doesn't care about anyone or anything, the kind of kid, who in twenty years will either be a CEO or an inmate. Or both.

But there's no denying that he has what she wants. What she needs. The turmoil in her life requires some escape, no matter the cost. She tries to be polite, business-like.

"Thank you for giving me, you know, for being thoughtful at the funeral home. I needed, I needed to feel better. So thank you. I knew Jordy for a number of years, but I didn't know he had an associate, so —"

"An associate?" Jeff's head flies back dramatically as he forces a derisive laugh. "Look, we were, how would you put it, competitors, maybe rivals is better. When he got stupid and bankrupted his business by dying, I stepped in to meet the needs of his customers. We knew each other, but that was about it. So, no need to get all sentimental on me."

"Well…okay." Jeff is leaning toward her, inching across the divide. Rosemary's back tenses and her breathing shallows. She feels pinned against a wall. "Maybe we should go ahead — "

"No hurry." Jeff pats her on the knee. He takes a bottle from his hoodie pocket, balances it on his palm and them closes his fist around it.

Rosemary opens her purse and looks for the envelope.

"Wait a minute, wait a minute. Aren't we gonna take a little time to get to know each other. I mean this is our first date. But I doubt it'll be our last."

He opens his fist and shakes the bottle while sliding his hand up Rosemary's calf to her thigh. Rosemary grabs his wrist and forces his hand away.

"Don't do that." Rosemary grimaces as he twists her hand into his.

His eyes meet hers again. All the boy in Jeff's face is gone. "Don't ever try that again. Understood?"

Rosemary stops breathing as Jeff presses his hand between her legs. "Unzip your jacket. Please," he says, his eyes like knives.

Rosemary closes her eyes and turns her head as she pulls the zipper down a few inches. Jeff reaches in with one hand and grabs her left breast tight, then fondles it. "Wow, these are so much better than my girlfriend's." He laughs and then sits back again. "That's all for now. Like I said, it's just the first date. I want to be a gentleman."

Rosemary is frozen in her seat. She closes her jacket and holds one arm against her chest. She takes the envelope from her purse and throws it at Jeff. He smirks as he opens it and counts the contents. "Perfect." Then he puts his hand on her knee again. "I'm sure there are ways to discount this. Maybe even next time. Think about it. Dress more appropriately." He drops the bottle between her legs, opens the car door, slams it and is gone. Rosemary doesn't move for another five minutes. Her hands shake. She feels like she might throw up. She opens the door and leans out, trying to catch her breath.

She stares across the parking lot at the high school where she was once a student. She feels nothing. She looks in the mirror but doesn't recognize the woman gazing blankly back at her. She wants to cry. She wants to scream. She wants to kill someone. But she sits. She looks at herself, her body like a stranger; no longer a part of her.

Rosemary opens the car door again and throws up on the pavement.

"Are you sick again?" The next morning Rosemary's husband stands over her as she pulls the covers up, hiding her face. "Seriously, Rosemary, you should go to the doctor's." He says this in his I-know-you're-faking voice, something he always denies when she calls him on it. "What? Is it a crime for a husband to suggest that his wife see a doctor?" Today she doesn't bother to answer. "Ok, have it your way." Ben pulls a suit jacket from his closet and leaves the room.

Earlier Christopher had begged to stay home with her from school, insisting he could take care of her. He cried when she told him he had to go, he couldn't miss his math test, and anyway he'd missed so much work this year, he'd never catch up. He's seeing the school counselor, but she says he never talks. They draw pictures together, play board games and question/answer games; she even lets him reply with nods and shakes of his head. Nevertheless, nothing. Rosemary feels guilty about this, guilty that without being told, Christopher understands that he cannot talk about what happened.

By late morning, Rosemary is sitting up on the side of her bed. She pulls back the curtain and winces when the sun hits her eyes. She opens the drawer to her nightstand and removes the bottle of pills.

She doesn't have the energy to shower. She tries to hide her hair behind a wide hair band. She washes her face and examines it in the mirror. She can't find herself in the reflection. She opens her makeup drawer then closes it. She rubs her face with both hands.

Rosemary pulls a pair of velour sweats from the bottom drawer of her dresser and grabs a matching T. She puts on a pair of Bombas and then her Nikes. She adds a hooded sweatshirt. She is breathing hard now. She lies down again on the unmade bed, her heart and her thoughts racing. Nothing seems real anymore. She closes her eyes and pulls her knees up to her chest, her hands balled under her chin. How did she get here? How did all of this happen? She thinks again of Christopher and begins to weep.

The garage is cold. She thinks about getting a jacket but can't bring herself to go back in the house. She knows that if she does, she wouldn't be able to come out again. She would be stuck there unable to move in any direction. She opens the car door and gets in. Pushes the button and listens as the garage door lifts creakily into place above her, the afternoon light pouring in around her. Her hand trembles as she stabs the car key here and then there, trying unsuccessfully to find the ignition. She leans over, steadies her hand, puts the key in and turns it. The engine roars to life.

Rosemary passes Gateway Elementary School as she heads to the expressway. She slows down and looks at the children playing in the yard, but Christopher isn't among them. She hopes that when he goes out today, there will be someone for him to play with. A driver leans on his horn and Rosemary's attention swerves back to the road ahead. "Okay, okay," she says, as if to assure everyone around her that she is in control, that she knows what she's doing.

It is a twenty minute drive to the hospital made longer today by construction and speed traps. It doesn't matter to Rosemary. She enjoys the anonymity of being herded along with so many others. She is relieved to be invisible. At least for a short time.

She takes "Exit 20 Hospital" and soon enters the parking garage, ticket in hand, and circles to the top where a few empty spots remain. When Rosemary sees a half dozen or more people waiting at the elevator, she feels her breathing quicken. She decides to take the stairs, wrapping her arms around herself to protect against the chill.

She usually follows the red lines on the hospital floor until she reaches the red elevators which take her to the sixth floor where Frankie sits with Gavin day in and day out. When she reaches the elevator, she stops and watches as a dozen or more squeeze on. She hasn't seen Frankie since, well, since she made a fool of herself in front of the one person whose respect she ever wanted. She tried to go back several times. In the end she wrote a letter apologizing—"I don't know what came over me...I haven't been myself...I'm so sorry"—and offering her support, distant though it might be. "You and Gavin are in my thoughts always," she said, which, as far as she could tell, was true. A few weeks later she received a note. "Thank you, Rosemary. I hope you are well." It had the cold sincerity of a note that could have been written to anyone.

When the elevator door closes, Rosemary continues on, now following the blue line which parallels the red for another fifty feet until it makes a sharp turn left. She has walked down this corridor before, but she's always stopped before getting to the end. This time she doesn't stop.

She reaches the glass door into the waiting room and hesitates, but then opens it and enters. Three people are seated, each of them studying the floor or the wall, feet shuffling, hands wringing. Rosemary approaches the receptionist's window. No one is there. An icy chill runs through her, but then someone enters from an adjacent office. The young woman slides back the glass and smiles. "Can I help you?"

Rosemary wants to answer, but can't. She opens her mouth to try again but coughs and gags. She swallows and tears fill her eyes.

The young woman isn't smiling now. "I'm so sorry," she says. "Let me call someone." Another woman hurries into the waiting area. She is tall and thin and wiry with long arms and a narrow but friendly face.

"Hi, my name is Keisha. I'm one of the detox nurses. Can I help you?"

CHAPTER 41
RYAN GOODE

"What's wrong?" Ryan is frightened by his wife's tears. She has done so well on bed rest that he has accepted this unusual arrangement as normal. Not that he wants it to continue, but he is less anxious knowing she is in one place all the time and that, so far, things have been stable. But this, this breathless weeping. "Honey, are you okay?" He is surprised how calm his voice is. How much he sounds like his father who always kept a steady hand.

Jenna is sitting in the rocker by the bedroom window. Her face red. She looks more tired than usual. To be expected, the doctor had told them. Imagine what it's like, she said. Anyone would be tired every minute of every day.

Usually when Jenna is upset, she has both hands on her belly protecting the baby. This time her head is in her hands. She looks up.

"I'm so sorry…I didn't expect you…"

Even with the season over, Ryan goes to Curly's every day after he visits his father. The ice cream display containers have all been packed away. The red ice cream cone shaped napkin dispensers are empty. The Isaly's dippers are stashed in boxes. Chairs are neatly stacked on tables. There is nothing left to do. But he goes. And he waits, much as he had waited months ago for that call from his father to discuss the Buffalo Wing Ripple ice cream. At the time, the biggest problem he could imagine.

After visiting the hospital today, going to the parlor didn't seem to matter. It's obvious that his father is dying. Or dead. It's hard to tell. His chest rises and falls, his hair grows, his limbs move, though less and less; he is producing no waste any more. "Hi Dad, it's me," he says each day. "It's colder than cold outside. Hey, the Bills beat the Jets last night."

He doesn't talk about work. He doesn't ask for advice. He doesn't talk about Jenna's bed rest. He grins at his father, kisses he forehead. He rubs his feet. He looks out the window and describes what he sees. "Lots of ED traffic this morning." He fills time. It passes by inches. Tortuously. Yet he wishes it would pass even more slowly. That all of this would stop for a while so he could catch up to what is happening before it happens. "Hang in there, Dad," he says with a hope-filled tone as he squeezes his father's finger.

"I didn't go by the shop today." Ryan walks over to where Jenna is sitting. He places his hand on her head gently. "Did something change?"

Jenna takes Ryan's hand and kisses it. "No, nothing changed. Everything is…okay. I mean the baby, she's fine."

Ryan's relief is palpable. He kisses Jenna's head and kneels beside her so he can feel the baby. He pulls her shirt up and presses one hand on a bulge that is moving insistently across the left side of her belly. "Where are you going, little girl?" he says with a high squeaky voice. He looks at Jenna again. She puckers, then contracts her lips, failing a smile.

"Honey?" She looks out the window. "You're not telling me something. What's up?" He says this hoping that her broad grin will return; that she will tilt her head to one side, shaking it as if to say, "Don't be silly." When she does, his whole body will relax; the blood racing through his veins will slow down; the ache behind his eyes will dissipate. And he will feel okay again.

But the grin doesn't return. Instead she looks at him square, her face sober, her eyes deep, dark. Ryan stands, then sits back on the edge of the bed, his hands tucked between his legs.

"What? What is it?"

"Your mom stopped by earlier today."

■　　■　　■　　■　　■

It is pouring when Ryan pulls into traffic. He has put off replacing the driver side wiper and now it scrapes back and forth leaving the center untouched. Large droplets flow up the glass, like a river in reverse. Stop lights look like splatter art on his windshield, glistening in the darkness.

"Don't go." Jenna had grabbed Ryan's arm. "I saw her. You didn't. I've never seen her so, so agonized, so tortured."

"Wow, 'tortured'."

"Listen to me. Your mom was, I can't describe it, it was like she was lost, I mean, like a child or something, like she didn't know where to turn or who to turn to."

Ryan stopped at the bedroom door.

"Ryan, don't do this now. Give yourself time, please."

But for the baby, she would have followed him down the stairs; she would have reasoned with him; would have blocked the front door if necessary, to keep him from doing something he might regret. Ryan always counted on her to be the reasonable one, the one who could step back, who could look at things from every angle, and help him back away from whatever cliff he was charging towards. Today he wants to keep charging, no matter what lies ahead.

Ryan squints through the bottom of his windshield. And when that no longer works, he opens his window and sticks his head out, duck-like, the rain pelting his face. Car horns blare as he staggers along unable to find the center of the road. He pulls onto the berm and waits. The car rocks as traffic races by. He looks ahead, seeing nothing. He places his palms on either side of his head, bracing his temples as if to keep it from exploding.

He thinks of his mother, screaming at him when he hinted that his father might have had an affair. He was hurt by this initially, but then felt relieved; her rage was an apt antidote to his suspicion, driving it out of his system, cleansing, removing all symptoms of doubt, though never answering a direct question. He was glad to put it out of his mind, this ridiculous notion, this unfathomable indictment on the one person who had stood by him through everything.

And now this. Neither of them faithful. Neither of them what he had imagined or hoped for. Neither of them real. Falsehood upon falsehood. Was anything true? Were they just like every other couple? Every other statistic?

The rain stops. Ryan pulls a rag from the glove box, gets out of the car and wipes off his windshield. He tosses the rag onto the passenger side floor when he is done, puts the car in drive and pulls back into traffic.

When he reaches his parents' house, he parks on the street and sits for several minutes. The front of the house is dark but there is a faint glow coming from the back, probably the kitchen or his mother's office. Maybe she is cleaning up after supper, although she stopped cooking months ago. Or maybe she is at her desk going over orders for the spring. He gets out of the car and walks up the steps to the porch. He hesitates at the door, unsure whether to enter without announcing his arrival. He knocks and waits. Then he knocks again. When no one comes, he turns the knob and eases the door open.

The hallway is dark and the house is silent, not a creak, not even a settling groan. He sees his mother sitting at the kitchen table. Her back is rounded and her head is down, resting on one hand. He hears the murmur of her voice as she clicks her phone off and lays is on the table beside her.

"Mom."

His mother stands and turns. Her face is in shadows.

"Mom, I know. I know about you and Dad. Jenna told me everything."

She approaches Ryan. When she is a few feet from him, he can tell she has been crying. Her face is puffy and her eyes nearly closed. She knew I was coming, he thinks. His mother reaches out with both arms and places her hands on Ryan's shoulders. He braces himself for her explanations, her apologies, neither of which he feels ready to accept. She looks up into his eyes.

"Ryan, it's your father. He's gone."

CHAPTER 42
GAVIN GOODE

Lester stands in the middle of the room, stiff, unmoving, as the grating, nails-on-the-chalkboard alarm screams. Gavin is in full code. The heart monitor stopped beeping and slipped into a steady mind-numbing tone. Other members of the code team fly into the room, surround Gavin's bed and then stand as still as Lester, each watching but doing nothing.

"He's DNR," says one doctor.

"Yes," says Lester.

They huddle around him for another minute or so. The doctor sighs and looks at the clock. "I'm calling it. 3.26pm."

The team leaves. Lester stays. He takes the pillow from under his arm and drops it at the foot of the bed, no longer needing it. His hands shake as he closes Gavin's eyes.

"Goodbye, Gavin. I wish I had known you...before."

Gavin knows nothing of this. Not the squeaking of soft soled shoes scurrying across linoleum, not the cacophonous racket of monitors shrieking their failure, not the deafening silence when everything is turned off. It all goes on without him.

For Gavin, it is an October night and he is twelve. A full moon is rising in the eastern sky. It glows through chalk dust clouds. The air is brisk and smells of dried leaves. Gavin stands in the backyard of his childhood home watching his mother who is busy at the kitchen window. He calls his honey colored dog, Tammy, to his side. "Come here, girl." He scratches behind her basset ears. His father comes through the back door and down onto the cement patio. Tammy races toward him, tail wagging. "Come're, son," his father calls while balancing several waste paper bags in his arms. Gavin races to his side.

He takes two of the bags in his small arms and returns to the back of the yard. He stuffs them into the rusted wire barrel that sits in shadows on a burned out portion of ground.

"Thanks," his father says and then returns to the back door, disappearing for a few moments only to come back with his arms full again. Tammy is barking now, sensing a rabbit in the neighbor's yard. "Grab her," his father calls. Gavin takes her by the collar and holds her until her curiosity wanes.

"Settle," he says.

Gavin takes two more bags from his father's arms and waits for instructions. His father crushes several cardboard boxes and stuffs them into the barrel.

"More?" asks Gavin.

His father ponders the question. "Tell you what. Just one more for now." Gavin dumps one bag on top of the barrel and presses down so none will fly away in the breeze. "Good." Gavin smiles and steps back.

"I think your mom's ready."

Gavin runs to the back door, Tammy on his heels. He is met there by his mother who hands him a tray with hotdogs and buns on it. "Thanks," he says. Balancing carefully, he tight rope walks back to his father, not wanting to drop anything.

Gavin hands the tray to his father, much as an altar boy might present the elements to the priest. "Great," says his dad. His father then takes two long sticks from a nearby woodpile and pulls out his pocket knife, whittling the ends to sharp points. "There." He reaches for some shavings on the ground, takes out a pack of matches and lights their tips. "Ready?"

Gavin smiles and takes the glowing bits and pieces into his open palms.

"Careful now."

Gavin tip-toes toward the barrel, eyes locked on the hint of fire in his hands. He reaches and drops the shavings on top. For a moment nothing happens. Then there is a crackle and some paper flames. A box top follows and soon the barrel is engulfed. He watches from one side as his father watches from the other. Both tracking any pieces that might take flight. The packing is good, though, and everything stays in place as the fire reaches higher.

"C'mere, girl." Gavin kneels by Tammy who whimpers. "You're okay."

Gavin pulls his dog back a few feet as the heat hits his face, taking his breath away. There are popcorn crackles in the air and tiny paper embers shooting up the invisible chimney of heat, reds and golds disappearing in the darkness.

As the fire shrinks, his father adds more newspaper and chunks of a refrigerator box and shredded mail, and all the leftovers of family life.

Gavin takes one of the pointed sticks and looks expectantly at his father.

"Let's wait a little longer," his father says.

The sky is purple black, but clear now. The moon sits on the treetops. Stars arrive, some bold, some faint. His father opens a pack of hotdogs, breaks one into pieces and tosses them to the dog.

His father asks, "Ketchup or mustard?"

Gavin laughs low. "Nope. Just plain dogs."

"There you go. That's the best."

Gavin watches his father's chest rise and fall, a slight grin crossing his face. He looks at the fire and then raises his eyebrows at his dad.

"Yes, I think it's ready."

Gavin jumps to his feet, grabs a skewer, and sticks a dog on the tip like he's spearing a fish. He steps close to the fire. The wind stirs and the smoke burns his eyes. He waits, then steps closer, looking for the right coals. Near the bottom the ash glows hot, undulating, like waves on a miniature ocean. He reaches with his stick and the hotdog hovers over a hot spot. His father follows on the other side.

"I think you got the best spot this time," his father says. Gavin looks up and nods with satisfaction.

Soon the hotdog skin bubbles and cracks. Gavin turns it over and over as the charring nears completion.

He looks at his dad questioningly. "What do you think?"

"Looks ready to me."

Man and boy pull their hotdogs from the fire and cradle them into their waiting buns. His father tears a bun apart and tosses it to the dog. They sit cross-legged in the damp grass. Gavin blows on the end of his hotdog, then takes a bite. His father watches and then takes half his hotdog in one gobble.

Their faces are warm in the crackling heat while their backs are cooled by the encroaching night air. They lean back on their elbows. His father points at the sky. "Okay, what's that?"

Gavin studies the orange-ish dot. "Mars?"

"Yep." He points to a tiny dot just north and west of the planet. "And that?"

"Jupiter?"

"Try again."

"Okay. Saturn."

"Yep." He moves his finger across the sky to the west. "There's your Jupiter. And what's that one."

Gavin gazes confidently at a tight bright light on the western horizon. "Venus."

"Very good."

They lie back on the grass, looking at a dusty trail across the sky. His father points.

"The Milky Way."

His father reaches for his son and pats his stomach. "So many stars so far away that it almost looks like nothing at all."

"How long have they been there?"

"Since the beginning."

"How long *will* they be there?"

"Hard to say."

"Until the end?"

"Don't know if there is an end, Son."

When Gavin's father says this, Gavin's neck hair goes gooseflesh and chills shoot down his spine just from the shear enormity of what isn't known. Not even by his father. It frightens and comforts him all at once. To think that our forever is nothing compared to the forever out there.

"I like that it all started from the same place," says Gavin. His father turns on his side, propping his head in his hand. "I think it must mean something."

"I think you're right."

In his final moments, Gavin returns to this long ago evening in his backyard, when pondering beginnings and endings filled him with wonder. He longs for the damp grass and the flaming embers, the smell of hotdogs and the sound of Tammy panting, the steadfastness of his father and mother; he longs for all the moments, like pearls on a string, that came after; he longs for Frankie and Ryan and Jenna and life together. And yet he is also drawn toward the elemental stew from which he came and now returns like everyone and everything before and after him. It feels odd to have been separate, distinct, to have been caught up in the illusion of individuality, captured by the fantasy of importance, bedeviled by the tyranny of small matters. Now, like his father and mother and grandfather before him, and his uncles and all the others, he is returning to the shared stardust that he wondered at, though never completely understood.

He looks back, but there is no back; he looks forward but there is no forward. He is gone now. But never far away.

CHAPTER 43
LESTER

Lester stands on the sidewalk looking up at the spires that reach for the heavens. Miniature gargoyles, hunch-backed and contorted, perch in corners, spouting rain water. Stained glass windows climb up the sides of stone walls. A crucifix, Jesus head hanging, his face agonized, gazes down at all who enter there.

Lester's hair is plastered to his head. He has been standing on this spot, shifting his weight to and fro for almost an hour, trying to decide what step to take next. How does this work? he wonders. His parents were lapsed Catholics who had drifted away from the church long before its current controversies. Lester, though dutifully baptized to satisfy his grandparents, was born into a religious vacuum, where any devotion to creeds or doctrines or rituals had long since evaporated from family life. "Try to be a good person," was his father's advice. "You don't need religion for that."

Despite a vague curiosity about the church, being gay hadn't helped. It was obvious that the Catholic Church didn't exactly roll out a rainbow welcome mat to the gay community. Unless you were willing to admit it was a sin and swear you'd never do "it" with anyone, you were a cast out, left to live in the blemish filled world of the unclean. "Mostly, religious people are ignorant," his mother said. "And those who aren't ignorant are just plain stupid. Even cruel." She had told Lester this after some Catholic school kids had taunted him while he was walking home from public school. "Faggot publican!"

Nevertheless, after Gavin Goode dies, Lester finishes his shift and without giving it a thought, walks across town to St. Peter's Church with the robotic passivity of someone being drawn by a cosmic magnet.

While he has little or no understanding of Roman Catholicism, he understands guilt completely. He understands what it means to ignore the needs of others, to miss the opportunity for compassion, to behave in ways that are wide of the mark, off target, and, much worse than criminal, sinful. Can he find solace? Can he find forgiveness for what anyone with half a heart would consider unforgiveable?

Fifteen minutes earlier, a young priest accompanied by an old one walked past him and up the steps into the church. The old priest, black umbrella open, his grey wispy hair swirling in the wind, never looked up, never spoke. The young priest with longish hair and a smile on his face, completely unprotected from the rain, had said, "Hello, how are you?"

Lester inhales deeply and heads up the steps, hoping that the young priest will be in the confessional this afternoon. He stands at the back of the sanctuary, incense wafting from the front where the young priest is lighting candles on the altar. There is a single oaken box the size of a double wide phone booth in the back corner of the sanctuary. It is the grey wispy priest who is seated there, waiting to be pelted with today's laundry list of popcorn sins—someone lost their patience, another got angry at his wife, one may even have confessed to lusting after a neighbor. How often does he hear the real stuff, the major league stuff? The stuff that stamps your ticket to hell.

The woman in front of him dips her hand into the holy water and makes the sign of the cross, head bowed. Lester feels this is a good place to start, but he puts his whole hand in the water, then wipes it on his pants and, with what is left, tries to make the sign of the cross, which ends up looking more like the sign of the T-intersection. The pew creaks loudly as he sits. The woman doesn't flinch. She is already deep in prayer when the confessional door opens and her turn has come.

Lester closes his eyes but quickly opens them when he realizes he doesn't know what to pray. He watches the young priest move briskly about the altar as if he is getting everything ready for opening night. When the priest looks up, Lester waves, but the priest doesn't appear to see him. He goes to the back of the altar below the organ's pipes and disappears through a small door. Lester is alone now. He thinks of Gavin Goode, all those months, all the suffering his family has gone through, how much he wishes he had acted sooner. He shakes his head for the whole sorry mess.

The door to the confessional opens and the woman exits without taking notice of Lester. He stands, unsure whether to enter. Maybe he could slip out without anyone noticing. But he sees the shadow of the priest and feels that it would be rude now not to retreat. He pulls the door closed behind him and sits on the bench, then turns his attention to the screen, which looks like the wicker seat of an old rocker his grandmother once had, though much less worn.

The priest clears his throat.

"Oh…Father forgive me because, well…first of all I've never done this. I don't mean I've never done anything wrong, but I've never gone to someone like you to ask for forgiveness. So I'm new at this. The confessing part, not the sinning part."

Lester waits for a response but there is only a sigh.

"Okay. What I've got to tell you is not good. My bet is that this will be the worst thing you've heard today. Easily." Lester leans forward trying to read the expression on the priest's face but he can see nothing but darkness. "So, okay, well, I'll just start in. It all began when I killed someone."

With that there is shuffling on the other side as the priest leans forward and turns his head to look at Lester. "Are you serious, my son?"

There is alarm in the priest's voice. Gentle alarm, if that makes sense.

"Yes. Very."

The priest leans back, although Lester is certain that the priest's leg is pumping hard because he can feel the confessional shaking.

"Please, tell me more."

"This was many years ago—"

"How many exactly?"

"Uh, twelve; it was twelve years ago."

"I see. What happened?"

"I'm an ICU nurse now, but I was working in an extended care unit back in the early days and there was this woman, her name was, well, I guess her name doesn't matter now." Lester goes on to tell the story of Irma and her suffering and how he wanted to help her, to relieve her of the excruciating pain that had swallowed her entire life and the life of those who loved her. When she wouldn't die on her own, he decided to "move things along" by "adjusting the morphine drip" so that she might "sleep away" without anyone being the wiser. Lester paused several times during his tale to see if the priest would say something, anything, but he remained silent throughout.

When he is done, the priest coughs and shifts in his seat, then mumbles to himself and finally speaks.

"Well, my son...this is...have you ever heard of the Ten Commandments, especially number five?"

"What?"

"Thou shalt not kill."

"Of course, of course, but that's not why I'm here."

"But...there's nothing worse than this."

"Really? Then why is it number five instead of number one or even two."

Stone silence on the other side.

"I'm sorry. I'm not trying to be flip."

"This is very grave, what you have done. Do you understand the gravity of it?"

"Look, I was her angel of mercy. I don't have any trouble with...well, with how I helped her cross over. As far as I'm concerned it was an act of love, something that anyone with the guts to set social convention aside would have done. Wasn't Jesus all about compassion?"

"But...I'm telling you wrong is wrong!"

"Maybe behind that screen wrong is wrong, but where I live, well, let's just say it's messier than that by a factor of one thousand. Anyway, that's not why I came here. I just felt I needed to set the stage. The real problem happened today."

"My God, you didn't kill someone else, did you?"

"Exactly."

"What do you mean?"

"I didn't kill someone and I should have. Months ago."

"Oh my God...Hail Mary, full of Grace..."

"Instead, I hesitated. Don't get me wrong, I had the opportunity. Often."

"...Blessed art thou among women..."

"I'm not sure why I didn't do it. I mean, for a long time his wife held out hope, like anyone would. Which was fine. You know, you love someone, you don't want to believe they're going to die, no matter the evidence. I just loved her. So I held off. But eventually she understood what was going on. She understood the whole thing. But she still came each day and watched anyway. She watched and waited, knowing nothing would change; knowing her husband was long gone. I could see her dying with him, inch by inch, her face losing its color, its tone, its beauty." Lester shakes his head and his mouth falls open. "Then there was the son. I don't even know what to say about him. He was pathetic. I mean, he thought his father was trying to talk to him; with his finger, no less. He loved him that much, he loved him enough to go a little crazy just so he could maintain some hope, you know what I mean? But eventually he gave up, too."

"…And blessed is the fruit of thy womb, Jesus…"

"So it was left to me. I was with this gentleman more than anyone else. I washed him and changed his bed and made sure his drips were clear and I read his monitors and wrote endless notes and kept his doctor apprised of everything. We all knew what the deal was. We just didn't know when it would happen. So why not help out? Why not trim the clock a little? I could have easily taken a pillow and, well, I could have ended his suffering in a matter of minutes. I mean, I don't know how many times I stood there."

"Holy Mary, Mother of God…"

"But for some reason I always stepped back. Then I would think— 'This is ridiculous, what they're going through'. And I'd stand there again looking down at this man and then, without thinking, I'd step back again and again. I couldn't do it. I wanted to, but I couldn't. I didn't have the courage. I couldn't let him go. I just couldn't bring myself to send him off." Lester stops. He leans back, his eyes on the wall in front of him. "That's the 'sin', if you're looking for one. And I hate myself for it." Lester's voice cracks and he bends over, his head now in his hands. He tries to speak, but his voice has disappeared down his throat.

"…pray for us sinners now and at the hour of death."

CHAPTER 44
FRANKIE GOODE

Dr. Azziz and Rev. Lorde meet Frankie and Ryan in the hall. They usher them into a private room where families get bad news. There are Styrofoam cups and coffee rings and candy wrappers on the table. They pull up their chairs. Dr. Azziz leans forward and takes Frankie's hand. He looks at Ryan, a faint, waning smile in his eyes. He explains what happened, that Gavin coded, that they honored the DNR, that it was painful for everyone involved, that nevertheless it was "peaceful" at the end. He squeezes and shakes Frankie's hand as he says this. She nods and reaches out to Ryan who is staring at the floor.

"Ryan?" she says.

"Why did my father die?" Ryan's eyes are wide while his face is blank.

Dr. Azziz leans back in his chair, takes a deep breath and holds it. Rev. Lorde is about to speak, but Azziz steps in. He explains again the damage to his father's brain; how that had affected multiple organ systems, including his heart; how, in the end, his body had experienced a "catastrophic failure." Dr. Azziz's eyes flutter uncomfortably. "But it is important for you to know that your father never suffered during this. He didn't."

Frankie reaches for her son's hand again, understanding that he is asking an entirely different question; one that no one has been able to answer; one that has eluded the police and everyone associated with the shooting. "No one knows why your father died," she says.

Rev. Lorde stirs, shifts in his chair, coughs once and sniffs a long breath. He gestures broadly with one arm, but says nothing. His arm comes to rest in his lap. He scratches his head and then looks at Ryan. "We don't know why this happened. We don't know who did this. But we do know that your father's suffering is over and that his spirit is free now."

Ryan shakes his head and looks away.

Azziz stands. "We would be glad to go with you to the room."

Frankie stands, her coat folded over her arm. She is barely breathing, her chest unmoving, her heart fluttering, her hands chilled. "No, that's not necessary. Thank you, both of you, for everything you've done. We couldn't have...well, thank you so much." She shakes Dr. Azziz's hand and hugs Rev. Lorde. Ryan stands but doesn't speak.

They part company in the hall. Frankie watches as Azziz and Lorde disappear into the waiting elevator. She turns and steadies herself as she looks toward Gavin's room. Ryan is several steps ahead of her. He collapses in a chair before reaching the bedside, his chest heaving, his faced twisted.

Frankie enters and stands behind Ryan, placing both hands on his shoulders. The blinds are pulled, casting the whole room in shadows. The silence is startling, as if the room itself has died. The monitors are gone. Lester is gone. Nothing but stillness. The bed is raised so that Gavin looks like he could be resting his eyes. His arms are folded on his chest. The sheet is tucked firmly under his feet.

"Come with me," she says to Ryan, nudging him with both hands. "Let's do this together. That's the way your father would have wanted it."

Ryan gets up hesitantly. She guides him to his father's side and then stands opposite him. "Take your father's hand, Ryan." Then she takes his other hand.

There is still a hint of warmth. His hands are soft, his fingers pliable. It feels odd to Frankie, not seeing them move. She pets his hand and rubs his arm, skin patchy and rough, hair bristly. She puts her hand behind his neck and leans down to give him a kiss. Tears fill her eyes when his lips don't respond.

She remembers the day. She and Rosemary, like young girls. She wishes she could still feel the wind in her hair, so freeing. Since that phone call, she hasn't felt the wind again; she hasn't felt young. She knew it was her fault; that her infidelity had rearranged the universe somehow and made it inevitable that Gavin would be made vulnerable. For a time, she thought, she hoped, that her guilt, so visceral, so molecular, would be enough to pull him through. That she could redeem his innocence with her shame.

But as hospital-time took over, it became apparent that she had little influence; that she was small, that her powers were local, not universal; that her shortcomings and faults, her defects and limitations, all-consuming and relentless, were, nevertheless, incidentals in this unfolding drama; all she could do was wait, be present, be a loving witness, and hold onto the thin thread even when she couldn't see it. Of course, discovering that Gavin knew cut her deeply; learning that he was also unfaithful cut her again. The blood loss left her reeling, made her dizzy, but taught her how to live in life's vertigo.

Still, sometimes at night when she can't sleep or when she thoughtlessly lets herself relax, fear grips her; the fear that she was right, that she was the one, that she brought it all on. At first she'd resist this, but often she would give into its smothering warmth.

Frankie studies Gavin's face. Someone has closed his eyes and mouth and combed his hair straight back. She re-combs it with her fingers, parting it where it had been parted all his life.

Ryan presses his father's hand to his cheek. Then he lies across his father's chest. "I'm sorry, I'm sorry, I'm sorry, I'm sorry…"

When he doesn't stop, Frankie takes him in her arms and helps him stand.

"Shhh, Ryan, there's no need for you to apologize for anything." She steps back from her son, her hands gripping his arms. "Your father loved you unconditionally."

"Someone has to apologize."

"What are you talking about?"

"Everything. What you did. What Dad did. All the secrets and the lies. It's like we were never what we seemed to be, the two of you, our family." Ryan backs away from his mother, shaking his head. He raises both arms. "Everything is lost."

Frankie doesn't move. She takes one hand in the other and lets them rest at her waist. She watches Ryan and then looks at Gavin. Is Ryan right? Has everything been a lie? Ryan, now huddled by the window wiping his eyes, looks like the littlest of little boys. There were mistakes. There were failures. Trust was broken. By Gavin, as well. They were both good people who sometimes did bad things, who sometimes kept secrets to avoid pain, who sometimes regretted what couldn't be undone; they were good people, though, who tried to love as best they could, who kept at it because it was the most important thing to do in life, to love, to reach for, to hold, to challenge, to protect, to comfort, to lift up. Had they done the very best? No. Had they done the best they could? Yes. Had they loved each other better than they could have ever loved anyone else? Yes.

Ryan collects himself and goes back to his father. He looks at his face and places a hand on his chest, as if checking for a heartbeat. He's lost, thinks Frankie. His rock has been reduced to rubble. He no longer has a guide to lead him down the path.

Frankie goes to her son's side and puts an arm around him as they both stand over Gavin.

"You know, it wasn't until our third date that your father kissed me. We had gone to a movie and then came back to campus for a pizza. He walked me to my dorm and then took me in his arms and kissed me. Softly. He smiled and said, 'I think I love you'. He kissed me again and then said, 'I think I always will'. Then he paused and blushed and said, 'I hope that's okay with you'. We both laughed. That is the moment I fell in love with him. I said, 'That would be fine with me'."

Eyes still on his father, Ryan says, "So when did it fall apart?"

"Your father and I never fell apart. We never stopped loving each other. Never. Were there periods of restlessness, of boredom? Yes. They come and they go in every marriage. And sometimes you do things, and you convince yourself they're okay, even though you know they're wrong. Impulsive things, embarrassing things, secret things. Things that make you feel ashamed."

Ryan looks up from his father, his eyes meeting his mother's.

"And sometimes it takes a while before you find your way back. Sometimes it takes a long time before you come to your senses, before you remember who you really love. Some couples don't make it through these times. Some do. You father and I did. All love has cracks, Ryan. All love bends in the wind, sometimes so far that you think it might break. But then it doesn't."

"You and Dad never talked about any of this. Why?"

Frankie steps back. Her eyes begin to well again. Why didn't we? What would have happened? She tries to imagine telling Gavin what she had done or Gavin telling her. What held them back? What kept them from being that honest with each other?

"Yes, why didn't we? Knowing your dad, in all likelihood he thought, what's done is done. He was probably relieved to put it behind him. As for me, it's harder to say. I didn't want to hurt your father. So I kept it a secret until I worked it through." Frankie lets her arms fall to her side. "Maybe the bigger reason was that I didn't want him to hate me. It was hard enough hating myself. I don't know how I would have gone on if your father hated me, too. I was afraid I would lose him."

"I thought you loved each other enough."

Frankie places her hand on her cheek trying to cool her face. She inhales deeply, a wan smile crossing her lips as she looks at her son.

"I don't think that was the problem. The problem was I didn't love myself enough. I didn't love myself enough to believe your father would forgive me."

As Ryan raises his head, she looks away, not ready to meet his eyes. She bends over Gavin, her lips next to his ear. She whispers, "Know that I will love you forever. And I forgive you." She feels Ryan's hand on her back as she stands. When she turns, he takes her in his arms and says, "It's okay."

CHAPTER 45
Jenna Goode
TWO MONTHS LATER

Jenna watches Ryan from her bed. He takes a flannel shirt from the closet and holds it in front of him, deciding. He puts it on, buttoning it deliberately. He pulls on a pair of jeans, loops the belt, buckles it and stretches his arms into the air, loosening his shirt at the waist. Ryan is expressionless until he looks at her and parts his lips as if to smile. His face, once so innocent, looks smooth and hard as a stone tumbled by the sea.

"How are you feeling this morning? How's the baby?" He asks these questions several times a day, often a few minutes apart, as if he is suddenly frightened and needs reassured. Jenna always answers, "Fine. Everything is fine, honey."

There are several magazines spread across her lap, a newspaper folded at her side, a tray with coffee nearby. She has two pillows at her back and one under the crook of her legs. Her hair feels stringy. Today she will wash it. She will get up, go to the bathroom and shower. Heaven.

She presses both hands on her mounting belly. "Emma is on the move." Her eyes gleam. Ryan sits at her side and places a hand on her stomach. He exhales a laugh. "Amazing," he says. They settled on Emma as the baby's name shortly after his father died. It was her idea. She doesn't know where the name came from. It appeared out of the blue. "Emma," she said to Ryan. He looked at her with crinkled cheeks. "Yes, Emma."

She had resisted naming the baby since so much was still uncertain. But when the name came, she didn't feel she had a choice. Since then she has felt closer to her than she could ever have imagined.

She can tell that Ryan is trying hard to attach to the baby, now that his father has died. He is home more, no longer needing to go to the hospital. He goes to Buy Buy Baby regularly to get whatever they think they'll need for the nursery. Crib, cradle, mobiles, stuffed toys, wall hangings of happy jungle animals, diapers, wipes, onesies, sleepers, pink things.

In recent days Jenna has caught herself thinking about what will come after the delivery, about bringing the baby home, the color of Emma's hair, her eyes, what her cry will sound like, all the things parents think about, the normal things that come after a normal, uncomplicated delivery. Until now she has avoided thinking about the future, about making plans. She couldn't see beyond the delivery, sometimes not even the delivery itself, fearful that hope would doom her, would doom her little girl.

Her OB/GYN and midwife explained that a decision about a C-section would be made closer to her due date. She had never imagined a C-section. She had never imagined cutting. At times she wishes she could keep Emma in her womb forever, protected from the outside, safe on the inside.

But with each passing day, she feels a growing desire, a longing, an unbridled eagerness for Emma's birth and everything it will bring. She is just as nervous as ever, but these other feelings keep crowding in, pressing her to hope again. She understands that Ryan, even if he feels the same, cannot show it, cannot allow himself to be happy. It would be disrespectful. In the first few weeks, he went every day to talk to his father where his ashes lay. But when the first snow storm of the season came, he couldn't, and thereafter he missed a day here and there and now hasn't returned in a week. She sees the difference. He smiles from time to time.

Frankie has come by every day since the funeral, shifting her attention from dying to birthing. She rubs Jenna's back and gets her tea and shops for her and sits with her even when there is nothing to do. They haven't talked about Gavin, though Jenna has tried. "How are you doing?" she asks. But Frankie is elusive. "I am how I should be, I suppose." In the silence that always follows these queries, Jenna assumes that her mother-in-law is addressing her grief elsewhere, where no one can reach. She hugs Frankie, who holds on an extra beat, letting Jenna know something, though she is unsure what. If asked,

Jenna would say, "Yes, we are closer than ever before," something she feels though she finds hard to quantify.

The more important closeness is between Frankie and Ryan. Whatever happened in the room the day Gavin died, the aftermath has been peaceful, like a long awaited armistice had been signed. Jenna is happy to no longer be in the middle, straddling the boundary between two proud nations.

"Are you okay?" Ryan comes to her side.

"Braxton Hicks again." She breathes deeply three times and her wincing face begins to relax. "It feels as real as can be, though, like she's coming any minute. Like she's going to shoot out right here in this bed."

"Soon enough." Ryan leans over and kisses Jenna on the forehead and then the lips.

"Sometimes I think this will never be over, like I will always be pregnant; I'll always be in this bed; she'll always be kicking and I'll always be waiting."

"The waiting will end. It always does." Ryan turns his head and gets up. "I'm taking orders for breakfast, little mommy. Pancakes, French toast, eggs, bacon, what's your pleasure?"

Jenna pulls herself up, raises her arms, as if to make a pronouncement, then lets them drop to the bed. "I am too tired to decide. Surprise me."

"Surprise you I will." He bends over for one more kiss then leaves the room.

"Don't forget another cup of that nasty decaf!"

"I'm on it!"

"Half 'n half and two Splenda!" But he's gone.

Jenna wraps the comforter tight across her abdomen and rests her head on the pillow. She breathes deep, calming her neck and shoulders, her back and chest, her arms and legs, her belly. She tenses and releases each set of muscles in sequence, pretending she will deliver naturally. She closes her eyes and imagines her happiest place, her favorite park. She is standing in front of an old inn and is walking toward the gorge where steep walls of shale, sandstone and limestone are framed by oak and tulip and fir. The waterfall below roars and foams. Beyond it, upriver a quarter mile, is another falls with what looks like a tinker toy train trestle high above it.

Overhead are swallows diving and a single red-shouldered hawk, wing tips flared, soaring. She sees herself stepping closer to the gorge where the mist fills the air like a gentle fog. It caresses her face, the damp, the cool, tranquilizing her head to toe. She rests her arms at her side as the Braxton Hicks begin again. The calming mist envelopes her.

But this time the contractions don't pass; in fact the pain surges, like knives piercing her. Her back spasms and throbs. What's going on? She struggles to breathe evenly. She feels wet all over as if she has fallen into the pool below the falls and is drowning. Her hands grip the sheets around her. Her eyes burst open as she loses her breath. Her legs are swimming in the bed covers. The water has broken! she thinks, excited and scared. Jenna throws back the sheets to look and then screams, "Ryan!" Everything is crimson, a slow moving river of red.

"My God, no!" Jenna struggles to get up from the bed. She stumbles into the bathroom and sits on the toilet horrified by the trail left behind her. She rests her head in her hands and tries to breathe. "Ryan!" She hears him running up the stairs.

"Honey! What is it?"

She tries to answer but can't. The toilet bowl is impenetrably dark. Ryan stands at the door, his mouth agape, his face drained.

"I'm bleeding," she whispers. "I can't stop."

Ryan pulls his cell from his pocket and dials 911. He clicks off the call and grabs several towels from the closet. He wipes the blood from the floor, leaving broad pink strokes across the tile. Jenna looks up at her husband and sees fear looking back at her. "I don't know what's happening," she says. "Something is wrong."

"Jenna, honey, you have to get up. We have to leave. Right now. We can't wait."

She struggles to stand, bracing herself against Ryan. He grabs more towels and she tucks one between her legs. Ryan picks her up and carries her to the staircase in the hall.

Together they look down the steps. "I think I can make it." Jenna stands but her legs fold under her. Ryan picks her up again and gingerly descends the stairs. He places her on the couch, races for the car keys, puts on his shoes, runs back upstairs for hers, grabs two coats from the hall closet. Jenna is lying on her side, her face white, her eyes like tiny holes in the snow.

"Jenna, Jenna! Stay awake, you've got to stay awake." She doesn't answer.

He picks her up and feels blood seeping onto his pant leg. Once in the car, Jenna tilts over against the door. Ryan presses more towels beneath her. She feels sleepy, but calm. Everything seems to be moving slowly, except Ryan, who is breathing hard and talking fast and screaming at other drivers and blaring his horn at anything and everything. She wants to say stop, but then she doesn't care. She is too tired to care. She closes her eyes but he shakes her; he shakes her again, and again until she startles awake, confused, frightened by Ryan and his erratic behavior. What is wrong with him? Her breathing is shallow; in fact she feels no need to breathe; there is no reason for it, no necessity; she can stop if she wants, it will be alright.

But Ryan is so loud, so frantic and the car is heaving this way and that. She opens her eyes and wants to tell him to stop right this very minute, to stop making everything so hard, when all she wants to do is rest, to slumber. He yanks her arm; he slaps her hand and then her face. She cries out wordlessly. He's shaking her and won't stop. She can't fight him, no matter how much she wants to.

Finally, thank God, the car stops. Ryan gets out. Everything is still for a moment. Then she is in his arms again and there is nothing but light, blazing light, scorching light, and people yelling and everyone running. Caps and gowns, caps and gowns. "Get her to surgery! Get her to surgery!" Someone is having surgery, she thinks, someone is in trouble and they are going to make it all go away. She opens her eyes again and it is Ryan's grim face looking down at her. She can't believe how much he looks like his father, but older. "Everything's going to be okay," he says.

Of course, everything will be okay, she thinks. Why wouldn't it? Ryan's voice fades as if he is drifting away. She is gliding; someone is pushing her and others are running beside her and they won't stop. She wants to say goodbye to Ryan, but it doesn't matter; she is floating, hovering; she doesn't feel a thing; all around her, it is quiet; everything grows dark just as they rush her onto the elevator.

CHAPTER 46
Ten Years Later

Jenna Goode is hunched over the computer studying a spreadsheet.

"Will you be staying long?"

Jenna checks the time.

"No, no, I have to get going, too."

"Do you want me to close up?"

Jenna looks at her cell again. "That would be great. Do you mind?"

"No, happy to."

Jenna smiles and turns back to the spreadsheet. Red month, black month, red month, red month, black month, black, black, black, black, black. She takes a deep breath, holds it, and lets her shoulders follow the exhale down, down. She closes her laptop and pushes back from the desk. She stretches and tips side to side.

Jenna goes to the powder room. Standing in front of the mirror, she sees a professional woman with a high bun and slightly puffy top. Her lips are rich Bordeaux and her eyes shimmer with copper shadow, light blush on her cheeks. Her gold pleated sheer blouse, open at the neck, hangs loosely to her skin tight high-waisted jeans, which are finished off with a pair of gold Christian Louboutin's. She knows that she's in there somewhere under all the fashionable camo.

"My God, I've never met a banker before that looks like that!" said Ryan the first time she came downstairs in her new look. Of course, he was right. But she wasn't a banker anymore. She takes cotton pads from her Sephora kit, squirts on makeup remover and wipes firmly across her eyelids. She drops the pad in the wastebasket. Squirts another and wipes her forehead and both cheeks. Drops another. Applies more remover to yet another pad and the red disappears from her lips. She smiles at what she sees in the mirror. "There." She unpins her hair, shakes her head, her hair cascading to her shoulders. Then she pulls her silk blouse over her head and drops it in her lululemon bag. Out comes a peach cashmere sweater. On it goes. She bends over, then flips her head back. She dumps her heels and digs through the bag for her Nikes. Ready to go.

On the way home, she stops for chips, dips, various cheeses, crackers, sparkling water, drink boxes, ice cream, toppings, decorative sprinkles and then dashes next door for wine, a Malbec and a Chardonnay-Riesling. Out of breath when she arrives home, Ryan takes her bundles, kisses her cheek and sets them on the kitchen table while she takes off her coat.

"Have you talked to her?"

"Yep," says Ryan.

"And?"

"And, she's excited. Very. All her friends are coming."

"That's great."

"Does she need any help?"

"Nope. She's got everything under control. As usual."

Jenna exhales a laugh. "That sounds about right."

"We've got about a half hour. I'm going to get some stuff done."

"Forms and reports, or reports and forms."

"Yes." They kiss and Ryan retreats to his basement office where he boots his computer, takes a few files from the cabinet beside his desk and dives into some insurance claims. Monotonous though the work may be, he finds comfort in the repetition, the predictability of his routine. The ice cream shop lasted one more year after his father died. The pity-patrons faded. His flavor choices worsened. By fall, Curly's was up for sale. Next came a food truck, but it was a money pit. He hated driving for Uber and his reviews showed it— "Why the hell is this guy driving anyone anywhere?" Rather than jump into something else, Jenna urged him to take a breath. So he didn't work for six months and they eked by on Jenna's salary, giving up cable and other luxuries, like eating out...ever. He recalled that his father had stayed home with him for a period, he couldn't remember how long, when Ryan was a boy. He wished he could ask him how he did it.

Around month five he saw an ad in the Suburban News—"Do you have people skills? Want to help others? Don't mind putting in a full day's work? Terrific training program leading to excellent pay and benefits." It was a local number. Why not? he thought. After he talked to the rep, he was convinced this would be the right move. Six weeks later he was working for Farmers Insurance. The offices were downtown now. After his father's shooting, the company decided a change of venue would be good for the workers.

Over the years he picked up a few of his dad's old clients. Usually they were sheepish about mentioning the connection, not wanting to awaken old hurts. Ryan, though, made a point of talking about it. He loved hearing stories about his father, things he never knew. "You know your dad came by one Christmas Eve with a turkey and all the fixings. We'd just had a house fire and we were living in a trailer. That was your dad." "He drove me to my doctor's appointment the day after my car got smashed." He this, he that, he was always there for people. Ryan's dad was still that figure on the road ahead guiding him.

He brought his dad's old desk to the house, refinished it, burned all the notebooks and other papers that were in the drawers and bought a new matching swivel chair. He added pictures of his dad, a pencil holder that Ryan had made him when Ryan was in the third grade, and his dad's old gooseneck lamp. Some Saturday mornings he sat at the desk with his cup of coffee and did nothing.

Ryan opens the desk drawer and takes a hospital identification bracelet from the tray. He holds it with two fingers and studies the name. He closes his eyes and hears the voices — "Go! Go! Go!" — as they raced down the hall to the elevator, like a bobsled team screaming off the blocks. Then they were gone and he was alone. And the emergency room went back to other things. For a moment he had wondered whether anything had happened at all. Had he been the one flying through traffic, blindly barreling through intersections, ignoring red lights, his forearm on the horn, emergency lights blinking, other drivers cursing his erratic behavior, as he sped frantically toward the hospital, wondering if he'd make it in time? Were Jenna's eyes really locking, going blank, as he furiously shook her, hit her (for God's sake!), trying to keep her awake as color faded from her face. "Jenna!" He winced thinking about the sound of his own voice, shrill, desperate.

He opens his eyes, his shoulders like a vice at his neck, his head ducking, his breathing shallow and quick. Later when the doctor found him, he said, "Fifteen minutes; if you had been fifteen minute later, there's nothing we could have done. We would have lost them both."

Ryan folds his arms and leans back from the desk, breathing evenly now, the memory receding.

■   ■   ■   ■   ■

Frankie pulls at the lapels of her coat as the frigid air turns her head. She squints into the sunlight as it shimmers on the virgin snow. She takes a slow, deep breath, puts on her sunglasses and smiles at the delicately contoured drifts pressing against the side fence. First snow, is there anything better? She grabs the railing with her gloved hand and steps cautiously onto the first step, then the second. She feels a little foolish, like she is an elder before her time, but since she broke her ankle a few winters ago, Ryan always warns her to "Be careful" every time it snows, sometimes adding "I mean it," as if that will convince her to listen. Truth be told, ever since she crossed the border between her fifties and her sixties she has become more cautious, more likely to listen without admitting it, more reticent about barging out into the snow or freezing rain or anything that might cause her to land on her face. She stops and looks at her neighbor's house, its Tudor tower snow-covered like a fir tree. Another step and then another, both feet square on the snow covered walkway that leads from her porch to the sidewalk.

She shakes her head at four inches of cushiony snow. There is no way Ryan will get here early enough to shovel it. And what would her company think, a snow covered sidewalk just lying there untouched, as if she couldn't be bothered and didn't care. Since there is no one to tell her "Please don't do that," she removes her gloves, tucks them into her pockets and grabs the snow shovel that is balanced against the railing. She pushes the shovel across the walk, its gravelly sound echoing down the street. "Push, don't lift," more of Ryan's advice. She then lifts the shovel and dumps the snow in the yard. She smiles. Again and again, as she works her way to the sidewalk. Once there, she studies the front walk and decides it's no big deal. She can do it easily. Push, lift; push, lift; push, lift; shit. She feels a familiar twinge in her lower back. She stands straight and twists this way and that, hoping it will click back into place. It doesn't. Push, don't lift; push, don't lift; push, don't lift; and the job is done.

Frankie looks back at the house, admiring its sloping porch roof, like a gentle ski run; the beveled glass in the two grand front windows. Gavin was right to push back when she had suggested replacing them with a picture window. The deep porch with its wide plank oak ceiling and floor, its rugged fieldstone front and stocky pillars, warm looking in the frigid air. On the side of the house, the mountainous stone chimney rises majestically up the side of the house; it was caged at the top a few years earlier to prevent birds, intoxicated by the rising heat, from falling dreamlessly into the fireplace below. Though dull in the midafternoon light, the slender stained glass window vaulting up the staircase inside, throws blue and orange and yellow ribbons across the living room floor when the sun hits four o'clock.

She is glad she didn't sell it, although it seemed like the right thing to do when she talked to a realtor in the year after Gavin died. But the thought of apartment or condo living, with the sounds of other people, the smell of their food invading her space convinced her to stay, to wait out the pain.

The wind whips Frankie but she lingers a moment longer, smiling. Looking at the house, her home, makes her feel settled, like she is in place. She takes a step and then stops, noticing a lose tile on the roof. It will have to wait until spring.

Again in her kitchen, she takes the cellophane off the angel food cake and removes the toothpicks that are protecting the drizzled pistachio frosting. She touches it lightly with one finger. Satisfied, she grabs a package from the top of the refrigerator, cuts along the dotted line and takes out the rainbow colored paper table cloth. She flaps it open and lets it drift and settle across the dining room table. She smooths it with both hands, goes to the front closet and, one by one, unfolds ten chairs and places them carefully around the table.

From the hutch she takes paper plates, each covered with an explosion of colorful balloons, as well matching cups and napkins, and arranges them on the table. She points and counts, then adds plastic ware.

Frankie takes a step back, places her hands on her hips and looks appreciatively at the table, imagining the excitement that will follow.

■　　■　　■　　■　　■

"Come on, honey, we've got to go!"

Ryan ascends the basement steps and picks up several plastic bags full of goodies from the kitchen floor. "I'll take these out. I'm good to go." He heads to the car.

"Be there in a minute."

Jenna walks up the stairs, trying to avoid any creaking floorboards. She hears singing and stops to listen. Unable to make out the words, she enjoys the squeaky melody nonetheless. She stands in the hallway. "Emma, honey, we should get going. Grandma's waiting and your friends will be there pretty soon." The singing continues unabated.

"Emma?" Jenna opens her daughter's bedroom door and peeks in. Her wisp of a child is talking to her cat, Jingle, who is staring at her from atop a pillow. "Now Jingle, you have to be a good boy while I'm gone." Jingle stares. "Oh, you are such a little honey." She kisses her cat who stares some more.

"Honey," whispers Jenna, and Emma whirls around, arms outstretched.

"Ta da! How do I look?"

Emma's ginger hair is pulled back with a green kitten-eared hair band. Her hazel eyes are framed by a pair of blue glasses that make her look almost pre-teen. She has on a pink 'Girls are the Best' shirt with green leggings and glittery black and white Sketchers.

Emma dances in a circle, "I'm double digits today!"

"Yes, you are, my sweet girl."

Jenna remembers almost nothing of the day Emma was born. She recalls being in the car and Ryan screaming. Nothing beyond that. She saw Emma only for breastfeeding during the week after delivery while Jenna recovered from a hurried C-section and excessive blood loss. When she was discharged, Emma stayed behind. Jenna remembers standing in this very bedroom crying because of its emptiness. Three weeks later it was full for the first time. And every day since.

"Do I look ten, Mom?"

Jenna leans back to get a better look. "My goodness, you do. You look exactly ten."

"Yeah!" says Emma, whirling and twirling.

■　　　■　　　■　　　■　　　■

"Grandma!" Emma runs, arms open, into Frankie's embrace. She holds her long and tight and when she lets go, looks at Emma and says, "You can't be my granddaughter, Emma. She is only nine years old and you are definitely not nine. You must be at least…ten."

"It's me, Grandma, it's me!"

"My goodness it is!" Frankie hugs her again, but not for long as Emma runs eagerly into the house where friends are waiting.

"Hi honey." She kisses Ryan and squeezes his hands.

"Hi Mom, thanks so much for doing this. She is…well, you can see she's just a little excited." Ryan heads into the house with arms full.

Jenna and Frankie exchange hugs. Frankie holds her out at arm's length to take a closer look. "How is everything going," she asks with raised eyebrows.

Jenna grins. "The shop is in good shape. Better shape than it's been in for months. Maybe years."

Frankie takes her in her arms again. "I knew I did the right think, putting you in charge."

Jenna blushes. "Thank you for trusting me with your baby."

Ten young girls screamed for the next two hours while having their nails done, diving into a free karate lesson, bouncing on foam mats in the basement, gobbling pizza, then cake and ice cream, then some more pizza, cake and ice cream. Then gifts, gifts, gifts, wrapping paper everywhere. Then since she is totally buzzed from the hoopla and nearly hysterical from the sugar, Jenna and Ryan cart a happily exhausted Emma home.

Bundled in her puffy winter coat, Frankie drags the first of several bags of wrapping paper and other debris to the sidewalk for pick up. The air is still; the temperature has plummeted, the snow squeaky under her feet.

She makes a second trip and then a third. She stops and sits on the top porch step. A full moon beams through the lattice of bare tree limbs posing against the sky. She inhales sweet, pungent smoke wafting from a neighbor's chimney. Gavin would have loved this, she thinks.

The neighborhood is empty except for a lone figure walking down the adjacent block. He pauses at the corner, then crosses the street and continues up Frankie's block. To her surprise, he stops in front of her house and looks up at the moon.

"Something, isn't it." His face, still in shadows, is difficult for her to discern.

"Yes, it is," she says. He looks up at the sky again. He is heavy set, his back broad, his gait, she notices, is more a lumber than a stride. And yet, there is something in his eager observation of the night sky that convinces her he's young. He turns back to her, a cautious smile on his face. "Nothing like the sky in winter."

"Yes, I love it dearly. Although I have to admit I'm not a big fan of this white stuff. It can all go away on December 26."

"I hear you," he says, chuckling. "Wish I'd learned how to ski. Maybe that would've helped."

"Exactly!"

He looks again at the sky, so long this time that Frankie wonders if he is unsure what to do next. Finally, he looks her way once more.

"Do you live around here?" Frankie says, brightly.

"No. I'm afraid not. I live out of state. Used to, though."

"Oh." As the young man steps forward, Frankie stands, unsure of his purpose. She reaches for the snow shovel.

"Yeah, lived here until I was about twelve or so."

"Do you come back to visit very often?"

"No, actually, this is my first time back since I left."

Frankie waves an arm in formal greeting. "Well then, welcome back."

"Thank you." The young man bows at the waist and they both laugh.

"Do you still have family here?"

"No, not so much."

"Friends?"

He smiles through what seem like saddened eyes.

"I wish I could say I had friends when I lived here."

"I'm sorry."

"I made a few friends later when I was at community college for a semester."

Frankie curls her toes, defending against the cold. They both watch a car pass by, its tires crunching the snow. At the corner, it turns and they are alone again.

"So, what brings you back?"

"Well." He coughs into his jacket sleeve and shrugs. "I guess I came to see you."

Frankie steps back making sure she is near the steps, although she realizes that escape would be nearly impossible.

"To see me? Why would you want to see me?"

"You don't remember me, do you, Mrs. Goode?"

"You know my name." Frankie seems only able to breathe in. She tilts her head as she examines him. His face hangs, his cheeks drag, his eyes droop, his shoulders slump; it is as if every part of him is bearing weight. "No, I'm afraid…"

"It's Christopher."

"Christopher?"

"Rosemary's son."

Frankie's hands go to her face. "Oh my, Christopher, of course, you were just a boy, just a little boy, and now you're all—"

"Mrs. Goode, I've come—"

"My goodness, how's your mom? It's been such a long time. She had so many…so many struggles."

"She's clean now. It took a long time, but she's clean. It's been thirteen months. She's in Colorado. Living in a halfway house. But the important thing is, she's doing good. She's happier than I can remember."

"I'm so glad. I'm so glad you came to tell me this. I've wondered for so long. Please let her know I miss her and that I'm so happy for her."

"I will." His jaws clench and he shuffles back and forth on the slippery cement, scraping ice with his boots. "But, Mrs. Goode, that's not the main reason I came here."

Frankie opens her mouth, but seeing Christopher's pained expression, hesitates before speaking. She places a hand on his arm. "What is it, Christopher?"

He lets his arm drop, as if not wanting her comfort.

"I've got this secret. I've had it since I was a kid. Keeping it has been the most important thing in my life. And I've been very good at it. But it's gotten too hard. It doesn't feel like *I'm* keeping *it* any longer; it feels like *it's* keeping *me*. You know what I mean? After a while, it just feels impossible. It's like all of a sudden you look at the whole situation that caused the secret in the first place, you look at it different, and you know something's gotta give."

He's breathing hard now; he looks at Frankie, his eyes searching. "How can I explain this? It's like when you get your first pair of glasses. And all of a sudden you see things clear, like you've never seen them before. It could be something you've looked at a million times, like a car across the street, or the moon, or a thing that happened long ago, a secret thing. And it's like you're seeing it all for the very first time. And when that happens, everything changes, even the secret. And you know somewhere deep that you can't go back to the way you used to look at things; you've gotta go forward, no matter where it leads." Christopher heaves a misty sigh into the night air. "When my mom got clean, that's sort of what happened to me. That's when I knew I couldn't keep this secret any longer. I had to tell somebody."

Frankie looks away, puzzled. She turns back to Christopher. "That's good, Christopher…I'm sure there's someone you can tell."

"No, not just 'someone'."

Frankie licks her chapped lips and shifts her weight from one leg to the other.

"What do you mean?"

"I can't just tell anyone. I have to tell you."

"You have to tell me?" Frankie's grip on the snow shovel loosens.

Christopher falters. He bends and places his hands on his thighs.

"Christopher? Are you okay?" She takes a step towards him, but then he straightens up, arms falling to his side.

"It's about the shooting."

Frankie's back stiffens. She folds both hands around the handle of the shovel again, trying to steady herself.

"I've had this secret since the day your husband got shot."

"Since Gavin got…" Frankie drops the shovel and her hands reach instinctively to her chest. "Christopher, what are you talking about?"

Christopher bows his head, his lips quivering. "That's when it all began."

Frankie steps forward, heart racing, and looks up into Christopher's empty eyes. "What began? Tell me. Whatever it is, I have to know."

Christopher begins to cry and then begins to talk.

About the Author

This is David B. Seaburn's seventh novel. He was a Finalist for the National Indie Excellence Award (2011), a second place winner of the TAZ Awards for Fiction (2017) and he was short-listed for the Somerset Award (2018). Seaburn writes a blog for Psychology Today magazine and has published numerous creative nonfiction essays. He is also a retired marriage and family therapist, psychologist and minister. Seaburn teaches writing at Writers and Books in Rochester, NY.

NOTE FROM THE AUTHOR

Word-of-mouth is crucial for any author to succeed. If you enjoyed the book, please leave a review online — anywhere you are able. Even if it's just a sentence or two. It would make all the difference and would be very much appreciated.

Thanks!
David

Thank you so much for reading one of our **Crime Fiction** novels.
If you enjoyed the experience, please check out our recommended
title for your next great read!

Caught in a Web by Joseph Lewis

"This important, nail-biting crime thriller about MS-13 sets the
bar very high. One of the year's best thrillers."
–BEST THRILLERS

Made in the USA
Coppell, TX
14 April 2021